URBAN LEGENDS
GHOST STORIES
AND
FOLKLORE

Urban Legends, Ghost Stories, and Folklore

This is a work of creative nonfiction. While the stories are true, they are delivered and embellished in a satirical, fictional way.

Some parts have been fictionalized for various purposes.

Every effort has been made to properly quote or cite all copyright holders. The publishers will be pleased to make good any omissions or rectify any mistakes brought to their attention at the earliest opportunity.

Copyright © 2022 by Micah Campbell

All rights reserved. No part of this book may be reproduced or used in any manner without written permission of the copyright owner except for the use of quotations in a book review. For more information email micahcampbellwrites@gmail.com.

First paperback edition January 2022

eBook ISBN: 979-8-9856387-0-7
Paperback ISBN: 979-8-9856387-1-4
Hardcover ISBN: 979-8-9856387-2-1

www.micahcampbell.com

DEDICATION

This book is dedicated to Luca. You were the truest and bestest friend a guy could have.

And if I ever find that jerk who dumped the deer carcass on our land that you just HAD to eat... I'll bite him really hard right in the face just for you.

R.I.P.

INTRODUCTION

Allow me to set the stage.

Before venturing any further, you must understand that this book - though written with much wit, humor, and sarcasm - is very much a book of secrets revealed. You hold in your hand an epitaph of historical proportions. Centuries of stories rest in your hand. I say "hand" because I truly hope that the other is occupied by a nice glass of bourbon or wine – or Kool-Aid for any of the youngsters. This tome of timeless tales is meant to be enjoyed. It's meant to be set out on the coffee table, borrowed by friends and family, highlighted, and marked in. This book is meant to be celebrated. Not for my writing - magnificent as it may be - but for the history, the mythology, the sagas, and the fables within.

Every story, far-fetched and fun as they may seem, was wrought from some truth passed down throughout the ages.

During the 18 months that it took me to research and investigate these tales I developed such a vast respect for the cultures and peoples that brought them to life. I laughed, I drank, I wept (I probably wept *because* I drank) ... and in the end I was changed completely.

I truly hope that these stories will touch you in much the same manner.

A little bit about me –

I trained under some of the most legendary martial arts masters of all times throughout the late 80s and 90s. I learned to kill, to maim, and to incapacitate my enemy with the help of VHS cassette tapes, DVDs and even some Blu-ray discs – though, I usually stayed away from the syndicated versions shown on television, as those were heavily edited and censored. It's like I always say, "You need to see hard and hear hard, if you're going to be hard."

In addition to my mastery of predatory lethality, I am also efficient in subterfuge and espionage. I'm a spy. I am a killing machine, but I am also quiet about it. I hunt the hunters. I stalk the stalkers. I kill the killers... pretty much anything bad that bad people do, I do to them. You get it, right?

I have used all these disciplines and skills - plus many, many more - to keep you, the reader, safe. I am a hunter. I bring to light that which would remain in the dark. I walk the shadows and bump into the things that go bump in the night.

I'll not bore you (or perhaps more appropriately, *frighten* you) with the details of my experience with all things creepy and crawly, but suffice it to say that I have seen some stuff, man. Monsters, demons, criminals, keyboard warriors, bullies, judgmental family members, etc. You name it. I've seen it. And I've slayed it.

What you are about to read is my personal diary written during my times - both local and abroad - hunting some of the biggest, and baddest baddies ever to have walked this mortal coil and beyond! These are the memoirs of my felonious frolics with the freakish fiends of faerie-tale and fable.

The stories are true…ish.

Go forth… if you dare!

"Pay heed to the tales of old wives. It may well be that they alone keep in memory what it was once needful for the wise to know."
— J.R.R. Tolkien, The Lord of the Rings

"I'll tell you a secret. Old storytellers never die. They disappear into their own story." - Vera Nazarian

"A restroom unsullied is an opportunity squandered." - Sensei Mallett, aka Rico Blade

"You can't parry death." – Chadwick VonApplejack

PICK YOUR POISON

Chapters

Wendigo..1

Hicks Road..14

Satanic Panic..26

The Lizard Man..46

El Duende...56

The Alaska Triangle...70

Deadly Valentine's Day..79

Vampires...85

The Pope Lick Monster...102

Bloody Mary...115

The Abominable Yeti..130

The Jersey Devil...145

Area-51..159

Boy Scout Lane...172

Pyramid Lake..184

Leprechaun	194
The Fouke Monster	204
The Lady in White	215
The Dogman	227
Friday the 13th	239
Hellmouth in the Heartlands	246
The White Thang	262
Krampus	274
The Ozark Howler	284
Werewolves	298
Hell's Gate Bridge	306
El Chupacabra	318

URBAN LEGENDS

GHOST STORIES
AND
FOLKLORE

MICAH CAMPBELL

CHAPTER 1

Wendigo

The wendigo was gaunt to the point of emaciation, its desiccated skin pulled tightly over its bones. With its bones pushing out against its skin, its complexion the ash-gray of death, and its eyes pushed back deep into their sockets, the wendigo looked like a skeleton recently disinterred from the grave. What lips it had were tattered and bloody ... Unclean and suffering from suppuration of the flesh, the wendigo gave off a strange and eerie odor of decay and decomposition, of death and corruption.

This is a well-known description provided by Basil H. Johnston, an Ojibwe teacher and scholar from Ontario, and one that expertly and aptly captures the physical characteristics that are most commonly associated with the famed wendigo.

There are numerous origins, societies, peoples, and names all related to or connected to the wendigo in one way or another. From ancient tribal peoples to modern cinema and culture, the wendigo holds a special place in folklore. The name itself, wendigo, or its many variations - Witiko, Wee-Tee-Go etc. - means "the evil spirit that devours mankind".

Common among all accounts is that the wendigo is purely evil, supernatural, and cannibalistic (having once been human, after all). Famine, starvation, greed, gluttony, fear, and cold are its most closely regarded allies.

Some legends focus more on the speed and cunning of this man-hunter, saying that it can traverse any terrain at great speeds and is at its most dangerous in the bitter colds of the northern biomes. Others focus more on its ferocity and brute strength. It is able to rip a man's limbs from his torso with nary but a thought. Some versions of this monster's genesis describe it as akin to bigfoot, yet others place it in the were-family.

While these tales meet a certain need within the niche of folklore and urban legend, they seem to stray from the very *real* and very *monstrous* origins from which this legend truly came. Unlike many fiendish cryptids of this ilk, the wendigo is set apart not only by its cunning as a hunter - despite its decrepit and emaciated form - but also in its skill to lure unsuspecting victims and infiltrate their minds in such a way as to turn them into wendigo themselves.

The Legend

The legend is widely known to have begun in the forests of Nova Scotia and The Great Lakes region in Canada and the US (specifically Wisconsin, though a few sightings and some stories have been reported from Minnesota and Michigan, as well) and is credited to the Ojibwe, Eastern Cree, Mushkego, Naskapi, and Innu tribes with its inception. The wendigo is a murderous human-like beast or spirit who is often corrupted by greed or gluttony. It was once human though could never be mistaken for one now.

The wendigo comes from Algonquian Native American folklore and says that long ago near the great lakes area in the dead of winter certain few men of a hunting party, unable to find food, succumbed to their hunger and began to prey on their fellow huntsmen. It is said that as expert hunters, they lured their companions into elaborate traps with a false claim of food and warmth, a fleeting respite from the brutal cold and fell winds of the unforgiving north. Those unrelenting winds and the near-constant snow provided the perfect opportunity for ambush as the cries and subsequent noises of the butchering and devouring of their friends would be muffled and carried off unheard, borne away forevermore by the frigid gale. The sin, however, would remain. A dark stain on their tormented souls.

This unforgivable act of murdering and consuming their fellow man condemned their souls to eternally wander, never to be accepted by the ancient spirits. It is told that this eternal damnation was too much for the lost souls and that they became twisted and deformed, demented, and grotesque, and obsessed with devouring the flesh of man. They searched and searched until they found and inhabited once again their old bodies, now decayed and rotting. The unnatural transformation that their souls had experienced bled over to their bodies and distorted them as well. Bones elongated - stretching and tearing the skin. Horns and claws formed as the creatures took up the mantle of HUNTER.

Legend says that so evil is the wendigo that the very ground it walks upon is cursed. It withers and dies immediately upon being trodden on by the beast.

So cursed is this creature that to even happen upon it by chance, even to see it and live, one's spirit would forever be stained, the mind would shatter and would never be the same.

The Cases

One of the most returned to stories in wendigo lore is that of a Cree trapper called Swift Runner. Swift Runner was a guide for the northwest Mounted Police and traded his furs with the Hudson's Bay Company. He was a tall, strong man and very good at his job. He was well-liked and well-educated. He was married with 6 children and he adored them all dearly. In 1878 Swift Runner and his family, under extreme duress due to freezing, blizzard-like conditions, and lack of food - which was quickly leading to starvation - faced tragedy when their oldest boy succumbed to the toll that the cold and lack of food was having on him and he died. Swift Runner then, just 25 miles from the Hudson's Bay Company trading post, slaughtered his wife and remaining 5 children, butchering them, and consuming their flesh in a stew that he kept throughout the winter.

   Post thaw, Swift Runner arrived at the trading post without his family. Suspicions were immediate and made all the more substantial when he did not offer any explanation as to their whereabouts. Worried for their daughter and grandchildren, Swift Runners in-laws pleaded with the northwest Mounted Police to investigate. Reluctantly, Swift Runner led officials back to his winter cabin and to a shallow grave where his oldest son was buried. He explained that his son had died of starvation and the Mounted Police were satisfied enough with that explanation to move on, that is until a sergeant stumbled upon a human skull.

   Swift Runner tried to belay guilt and say that he hadn't any idea of whose skull it was, but the gruesome discovery of human bones, innards, and skins strewn about the area soon had him confessing to the murders and to cannibalism. The detail with which he described the crimes was far too vivid for a book like this but suffice it to say that he had very intimate knowledge of what happened. He stated that throughout the winter and snowstorm his dreams had become tormented by a wendigo. It would call to him while he slept and give him visions of the deaths of his family. Soon, the visions haunted him even during the daytime hours and eventually he surrendered to his madness and became wendigo, killing first his wife, then forcing his 2nd oldest to kill the infant, as he was busy with the middle children. He murdered the 2nd oldest last, as it had taken the boy some time to kill the baby. Swift Runner then skinned and butchered the bodies and lived off their flesh until the thaw.

A disgusted and appalled group of soldiers escorted Swift Runner to Fort Saskatchewan where he was tried and hanged for his crimes but not before he was able to escape long enough to murder and consume his mother-in-law, who he said at his hanging was "rather tougher than the others".

Another oft-visited story of wendigo is that of Jack Fiddler, an Oji-Cree medicine man and chief. Fiddler was best known for being a wendigo hunter, having 14 wendigo kills under his belt during the course of his life.

These wendigo were either evil spirits sent by a rival enemy shaman or members of his own tribe who had given in to some base desire for human flesh. In either case, it was Fiddler's duty to react quickly and without mercy, killing the creatures before they could harm others. He was even forced to kill his own brother, Peter Flett, after he had turned wendigo during a particularly difficult season of famine. The legend of wendigo was well known throughout the tribes, missionaries, and traders of the area, and dealing swiftly with them was a necessity. There are numerous reports of people turning wendigo and eating human flesh within the Hudson's Bay Company records.

In 1907 after a successful wendigo hunt, Jack and Joseph, another of his brothers, were arrested for murder. It was later discovered that they had ingested the flesh of their victims after turning wendigo. Jack committed suicide before his trial, but Joseph was tried, convicted, and sentenced to life in prison.

Throughout the 1800s and into the 1920s wendigo cases were almost commonplace across the northern states and southeastern areas of Canada, but these became more and more likely to be cases of Wendigo Psychosis rather than actual Wendigo activity.

Wendigo Psychosis

Now, these cases might sound more like possession or mental breakdown or insanity… and that's because, more than likely, that's exactly what they were. As these cases were studied and because of the lore of wendigo so prevalent in the area, it was widely accepted that this, indeed, was wendigo possession. The wendigo is known to be able to sicken the mind and draw it into a weakened and fragile state until it is no longer able to ward off possession. From there it is a simple matter of the soul being twisted and warped by the pure evil of the creature and the victim would become wendigo themselves.

As more and more cases began to emerge and less and less actual physical sightings of wendigo were reported. However, a new more *medical* train of thought was developed.

Wendigo Psychosis

Wendigo Psychosis is the undeniable urge to consume human flesh even when alternate food sources are available.

The Jesuit Relations (a journal that French missionaries kept and later published) reported this, upon being asked to investigate a possible Wendigo possession:

> "What caused us greater concern was the news that met us upon entering the Lake, namely, that the men deputed by our Conductor for the purpose of summoning the Nations to the North Sea and assigning them a rendezvous, where they were to await our coming, had met their death the previous Winter in a very strange manner. Those poor men (according to the report given us) were seized with an ailment unknown to us, but not very unusual among the people we were seeking. They are afflicted with neither lunacy, hypochondria, nor frenzy; but have a

combination of all these species of disease, which affects their imaginations and causes them a more than canine hunger. This makes them so ravenous for human flesh that they pounce upon women, children, and even upon men, like veritable werewolves, and devour them voraciously, without being able to appease or glut their appetite—ever seeking fresh prey, and the more greedily the more they eat. This ailment attacked our deputies; and, as death is the sole remedy among those simple people for checking such acts of murder, they were slain in order to stay the course of their madness."

The International Statistical Classification of Diseases and Related Health Problems (ICD) details Wendigo Psychosis this way:

"Rare, historic accounts of cannibalistic obsession… Symptoms included depression, homicidal or suicidal thoughts, and a delusional, compulsive wish to eat human flesh… Some controversial new studies question the syndrome's legitimacy, claiming cases were actually a product of hostile accusations invented to justify the victim's ostracism or execution."

Another entry in the Jesuit Relations details what is widely believed to be the first written account of wendigo activity. It reads:

> "This devilish woman...added that [the windigo] had eaten some Attikamegoukin — these are the tribes that live north of the river that is called Three Rivers — and that he would eat a great many more of them if he were not called elsewhere. But that Atchen (a sort of a werewolf) would come in his place to devour them... even up to the French Fort; that he would slaughter the French themselves."

Notice the spelling of wendigo here - windigo. Some archaeologist and even some cryptozoologists (those who study cryptids) take this alternate spelling to indicate that the English language is very confusing and should be simplified. I mean, really... wendigo, windigo, their, they're, there, read, read, lead, lead, to, two, too, etc. I could go on! But I won't... this is not the place for a discussion on homophones.

Wendigo Psychosis eventually eclipsed the actual legend of the wendigo. It even became a valid defense in court, staying the execution of numerous criminals who would claim such a disorder, though it is not much of a defense today.

Conclusion

So where does this leave us?

Is one of the most well-known Urban Legends ever nothing more than a cannibalistic mental illness? No.

But our understanding of the wendigo is a bit warped by modern media's take on the creature and the natural order of things being lost and forgotten.

Much like the werewolf or the vampire, the wendigo of legend is an *Alpha*. There only ever were a handful of actual wendigo beasts. Those wayward hunters that we discussed earlier committed the ultimate sin - murdering and devouring their fellow tribesmen. It is not known how many men turned that fateful winter, but according to legend it was "a certain few". These "certain few" are the *Wendigo Alphas*. The true beasts of legend. The physical incarnation of pure evil. 15 feet tall. Skin stretched and torn. Horned and clawed.

Emaciated and forever hungry, this ravenous hunter of men still haunts the northern forests of the US and the Southeastern borders of Canada. It is cursed to do so for all eternity, as neither heaven nor hell will have it.

Damned to devour human flesh, its insatiable desire drives it ever onward, killing and eating. From these creatures came the murderous and cannibalistic stories that we are most familiar with and that are most closely associated with the term wendigo. "Turning wendigo" refers to Wendigo Psychosis and is, as we know now, a mental illness where the "victim" obsesses on consuming human flesh.

These *Alpha-Wendigo* have extremely long hibernation habits and rarely emerge from the depths of their caves except to feed. The likelihood of you ever encountering a true wendigo is so remote and your *survival* is even MORE remote... or would be if it weren't for the fact that you happened to be reading this book!

I would NEVER send my readers away unequipped and ill-prepared to face such a creature. Now, let me preface this by saying that if you ever encounter a person... eating another person... walk away, no... run away. Just leave, man... call the police. DO NOT GET EATEN. That's some messed up ish right there that you are *not* equipped to deal with... so just don't.

That being said, if you happen to come across a wendigo of legend, an Alpha-Wendigo, you need to know how to kill it.

Here's what we know:

They are intelligent. They are incredible hunters. Hard to kill during the day and nearly impossible to kill at night. So, if you're hunting one, do it during the day. They have supernatural and superhuman powers including the ability to mimic voices and sounds, super speed, strength, agility, senses, and stamina. They are immortal and invulnerable to normal human weapons.

As Dean Winchester, chief demon slayer and one of my personal research assistants, once so eloquently put it, "guns are useless -- and so are knives. Basically... we gotta torch this sucker."

Right you are, Dean!

Fire is one of only 2 ways to kill a wendigo. The other is Silver. A silver blade or stake. Iron, steel, and even some protective circles can slow the Wendigo down but **will not kill it**.

Native hunters would often use sheer numbers to overwhelm the beasts. Armed with silver daggers and axes, they would set traps and lay in wait for the creature. The wail of a lone baby in the middle of the forest would be unignorable to a creature such as this. So, it would come. The hunters would strike quickly and ruthlessly. Often 10-20 men at a time, but even in those numbers, the ambushes would end in disaster as the wendigo could easily go toe-to-toe with 20 men.

It wasn't until the hunters learned, through trial and error and much loss, to deploy pitch and fiery arrows when they launched their attacks. Then they began turning the tide!

But, as we discussed previously, the mighty wendigo is immortal. To truly vanquish the beast, its heart must be cut from its body and burned to ash. Then and only then will you know that the beast will not return.

CHAPTER 2

Hicks Road

Blood-Hungry Beasts or
Insane Asylum Tragedy

Alabaster, near translucent figures in dark and ratty, often dated clothing appear seemingly out of nowhere. Not a sound betrays their stealth as they stalk their prey, save for a blood-curdling, shrill shriek right before they strike. This is not like any scream that you've ever heard before or would likely ever hear again. There has yet to be a witness to this high-pitched caterwaul that hasn't turned tail and run, driven mad from fear. It's not a single lonely wail, but a cacophony of piercing screeches that come from all around, from all sides. A blood-cry, a come-hither promise of killing and feasting!

Tactile hunters and merciless killers, these beings seem to be well organized and convey a surprising level of community and order, but who… or what are they? Why do they stalk, hunt, and protect this desolate stretch of Hicks Road in San Jose, California? Where did they come from? What is their goal? Are they more human or beast? Let's find out as we explore the legend of The Blood Albinos of Hicks Road.

 Now I want to make a small disclaimer here - From what I've read on the term "albino", it can be a somewhat harsh and jarring word to use when describing a person with albinism. I don't know if that would be considered offensive or not, and it may be to some and not to others, but as far as I am able, I would prefer not to offend anyone or any group of people. I know that's not always possible and it's almost popular now to get offended over just about anything, so I'm not talking about that or anything political here... I'm just doing my best to respect others as much as I can.

 There are multiple sources that refer to these creatures as The Blood Demons of Hicks Road - instead of Albino Demons - and they are just as well-known for their ear-piercing scream as they are for their pale skin so I will be using this terminology henceforth

The Legend

 The first thing I found right off the bat as I started researching this one was that there is not a ton of HARD evidence supporting the legend... and if you know anything about me - hard evidence and solid facts is what I'm all about! I almost hung it up because it was starting to look like I'd have to fill in some pieces myself, you know... take liberties and try to fill in the gaps with my own narrative and I would *NEVER* do that in a hard-hitting investigative book like this. But, as I dug deeper, unwilling to be discouraged by the obvious cover-up that was afoot, I was led down a completely different path than where I thought this was going to go.

I **did** find that in 1999, Larry Lavell was released from San Quentin Prison after spending 30 months for undisclosed violent crimes and was a Megan's law registrant - so the guy was an absolute creep, scum of the earth type jabroni… right? Well, after his release he killed his ex-wife in a home on Hicks Road and fled to the Almaden hills where he was considered armed, dangerous and on the run… he was never found and is presumed dead. We can only hope that if this colony of blood-thirsty killers is real, that they ran into this piece of trash and had a good meal on his behalf

Ok, let's go…

The legend in its most simple form is this: There is a community or clan of pale, ghostly humanoid creatures that haunt and hunt a stretch of Hicks Road that leads into the mountains. If your car stalls or breaks down, DO NOT get out. If you ask for directions and what you're given takes you down Hicks Road, find an alternate route. If you don't you will fall victim to the cannibalistic cult known as the Blood Demons of Hicks Road.

There is quite a bit of contention as to the relationship of this brood. Are they some sort of demented family unit ah-la The Texas Chainsaw Massacre, something a bit more "man-made" like the mutant cannibal monsters in The Hills Have Eyes or something much more sinister and supernatural altogether... something more ghostly or demonic like the name "Blood Demon" implies?

Whatever they are, if you are unlucky enough to be found along this stretch of road when they are hunting, the jarring dissonance of their blood-thirsty cry may be the last thing you ever hear, as it is reported that hundreds of dark, red eyes can be seen stalking along the road just inside the tree line and that they communicate through animalistic screeches that get louder and louder right before they strike.

Like I was saying before, it was hard to find any real evidence to support any of this outside of a random report here or there of hearing things that sound like animal screeching but coming from a human throat or the red eyes that seems to track movement along the roadside... or the pale humanoid figures that "chase" hikers and trespassers who wander too close, but where did these stories come from?

The legend is said to have been started by a couple of teenagers back in the '70s who were hiking along one of the mountain trails and came across a very thin old man who was none too pleased with them trespassing and let them know it... shotgun in hand he chased them down the mountain and all the kids could describe him as was very skinny and very, very pale.

If that is the case and that is really all there is here - just a cranky old man chasing away some kids, and from that, the stories have passed generations and cultures like a game of telephone, turning the legend of Hicks Road into what it is today - then that'd be pretty much all she wrote. I wouldn't have much to give you here and I would have had to shelf this one... which is what I thought I was going to have to do.

But having come across a road so notorious, so infamous for all the wrong things that people will downright refuse to give OR take directions that involve it, I had to know more...

Alternate routes are apparently a necessity here, as most folks actively and intentionally avoid it. I'm not really sure what parts of Hicks Road are off-limits and to whom, but every article or story I could find gave the same grave warning: "Don't turn right at the fork. Whatever you do, don't turn right"

Hicks Road runs alongside Almaden Quicksilver County Park in San Jose, California and is surrounded by mountains - most notably, Mt. Umunhum which boasts the second most difficult climb in Santa Clara/Santa Cruz Counties and may be *the* most difficult mountain to pronounce.

Now as physically fit as I am and as avid an outdoorsman, climber and all around bad-butt as I am, I don't know how hard of a climb that is, but I assume having a colony of territorial, blood-thirsty, half-man, half-beast killers chasing me might make for a hard climb!

I had to dig deeper.

The road is said to turn from paved and well-lit to dirt, gravel, and dark pretty quickly and is notorious also for its hills and lack of cell coverage. There are abandoned, rusting cars along the way and a slew of old-huts and broken-down trailer homes strewn about as well. There are multiple stories of transmissions going out and stalled cars on the hills forcing travelers, hikers and climbers to abandon their vehicles and hike back down to the more inhabited areas. Many report hearing screams and seeing shifting red eyes following them the entire way, and with steep inclines on one side and even steeper drop-offs on the other, there are not many options on some parts of the road.

One unlucky traveler, or I guess we'll say *lucky* traveler was heading up Hicks Road to Mt. Umunhum for a climb when nature called. Being in a remote, thickly wooded area, he thought nothing of jumping out and taking care of business... but he is reported to have said that halfway through relieving himself he noticed a few pairs of red eyes out in the distance. Chalking it up to his headlights catching the reflection of some deer eyes or something like that he didn't really give it another thought... that is until that first few pairs blinked into hundreds and they seemed to be getting closer.

Not wanting to feel foolish or give into his imagination, he forced himself not to freak out, quickly finished and zipped up, and made his way back to the driver's side door. He had left his door open and engine running, and he credits that with saving his life, because as he headed back to his car the eyes began to dart about frantically and chaotically - and to move closer - at an alarming pace.

He jumped into his vehicle and slammed the door shut just as he heard what he called a "demonic howl" and the first of a few hundred thin pale humanoid creatures erupted from the tree line. Mouths agape, hungry and salivating they rushed his car - arms flailing, red eyes intent. He punched the gas and realized that he was in a bit of gravel as the car began to fishtail, the tires fighting desperately to find purchase with the dirt road below.

The last thing he remembers before getting out of there was one of the creatures slamming against his driver's side window and clawing at the glass. He is reported to have said that just for a moment their eyes connected and all he saw there was pure evil as his body went cold with fear.

Whew... Right?

Now I did not make that up. I found that report online. But it was 1 of only 2 that I could find. And that is just not enough to convince me...

Still just a lot of legend, no fact... right?

I hope you can see that up until this point I really didn't have a lot to go on except stories... and as fun as those are, I needed more... something about this area... this mountain range... intrigued me.

The Twist

Aside from Mt Umunhum, the Almaden area is - or was - also home to Cinnabar Hills, where the Cinnabar and New Almaden mines are located. The New Almaden quicksilver mine is believed to have been established well before the 1820s when it was discovered by a Mexican settler. It was a pivotal supply mine for the California gold rush. Cinnabar is a red mineral made out of mercury sulfide and quicksilver is another name for Mercury. These were mercury mines.

Both of these mines produced mercury and it is said that many of the people on the hills surrounding those mines went crazy from mercury poisoning. Mercury was used in shaping hats and this is where the term "mad as a hatter" came from. This is where the inspiration for The

Mad Hatter in Alice in Wonderland came from. The stuff is bad news. In fact, the inhalation of mercury vapors can produce side effects in the lungs and kidneys, also, in the nervous, digestive and immune systems. Some of the side effects of mercury poisoning are mental disturbances, skin rashes, twitching, tremors, neuromuscular and mood changes.

So, in these same hills where we supposedly have a community of crazed blood-thirsty lunatics, we have mines that produced minerals that are **known** to make people go crazy and mess with the mind and body in all kinds of strange ways.

Along with the mines - or maybe because of them - there was also The Agnew's Insane Asylum or Cinnabar Hills Asylum, as it was known to the locals, resting high on the hills overlooking the mines and the old dirt road that leads to it. Known today as Sun Microsystems/Agnew's Developmental Center, this gothic stone building with its giant clock-tower was once an insane asylum opened in 1889 to treat the mentally ill, that before that time, were housed with criminals aboard a ship named The Prison Ship Euphemia. The asylum was shut down just 21 years later as the greatest victim of the 1906 earthquakes. Masonry and stone broke apart and fell away amidst the quake, killing over 100 patients.

Many of the patient's bodies were never claimed.

The building was known as "The Great Asylum for the Insane" and was erected to house those who were deemed "mad" or "demented" ... a favorite term used for the patients there was "lunatic".

After the earthquake, it is said that hundreds of the "surviving mad" escaped and fled into the hills. They were never found. There is also said to be a mass grave where the unclaimed bodies were buried along with many other patients that died while in care there.

And let's not forget The Prison Ship 'Euphemia'

During the era of the gold rush, it was often easier and more effective to purchase boats and convert them into buildings than to actually *build* buildings. This was a common practice for churches, warehouses, hotels and... prisons.

San Francisco and her surrounding areas were growing quicker than civilization could keep up with. For every law-abiding family heading west and landing here in search of making their fortune, you had a criminal eager to steal, murder, assault and take anything that they wanted. Crime was outgrowing and overrunning the law and the streets. And the flimsy log building used as a makeshift jail that had been built to house these criminals was quickly overfilled and easily escaped from.

Enter The Prison Ship 'Euphemia' - a giant freighter ship that belonged to City Council member William Heath Davis and was purchased by the special committee established to contend with the roughians and crime taking over the streets of San Francisco in 1849 for 3,500 dollars. The boiling point that led to this was when a gang called The Hounds carried out a mass assault on the San Francisco Chilean community.

The Euphemia - meaning auspicious speech or good repute - began holding prisoners in 1850 and quickly became more of a deterrent than hanging, as the conditions of this monstrosity were horrendous and there was no accounting for life within her walls. She also became home to those who were deemed "insane" or "poorly unfortunate" and those poor souls were left to rot in squalor among criminals until their death either aboard the Euphemia or within the confines of the Great Asylum for the Insane - which fell in the quake of 1906.

One more thing I found and quite possibly the last piece to the puzzle is the still standing Hanging Tree of Cinnabar Mines - a mulberry tree that *still* stands to this day and can be seen below the old mine entrance.

A young boy was said to have stopped his father at the sight of the tree, holding his hand tightly and telling him that he did not like the tree. When his father asked why, the boy said that it had "perfect limbs for hangin' men"

And apparently it did.

From 1846 on - and even as late as 1933 when 2 men were hung for the kidnapping and murder of Brook Hart, a department store Heiress – executions, whether sanctioned or not, were carried out by hanging at this location, directly below Hicks Road and the Cinnabar Mines. It is a mystery as to *how* this tree is still standing, as it is reported that miners burned 700 cords of firewood a month that they harvested right there outside of the mine.

It's quite obvious here that the "poorly unfortunate" were those driven mad by mercury poisoning. It is just as obvious that those survivors of the asylum collapse escaped to the hills where – you guessed it – they were driven beyond the point of insanity and into the realm of lunacy.

These lunatics bred and multiplied year after year until, decades - and even centuries later – they had an entire army of insane, blood-hungry murder-hobos!

I'm not sure which way you're leaning - Crazed, lunatic, mercury-monsters or pale, animalistic demon people - but I hope that either way the story was fun and maybe even a bit frightening.

CHAPTER 3

Satanic Panic

Dungeons & Dragons

Ghostly wisps of mist meander across the marshy fields before you. With every step forward you sink a little further into the bog. The slurp and suck of each footfall betray your attempts at stealth and subterfuge. The sun must have risen by now, though you see no evidence of its brilliance in this dark place. Just ahead, beyond the swamp, it waits… beyond the gurgling and belching black waters of The Dying Moor… it beckons. Its shadow, cast by some fell sorcery, reaches out to you across the expanse, skeletal fingers crawling ever toward you… The towering spires of Mal-Grave Keep are barely visible against the gloom of the morning backdrop, yet the phantom shadows pursue.

A spine-chilling wail erupts from within the Keep's walls, a sinister reminder as to your reason for being here. You have not tarried throughout the night, battled behemoths, and buried friends, only to be cowed as you stand upon the precipice of your glory. The Beast has led you here, to its keep, in its land... on its terms. It is convinced that it has you now. The hellish howl has awoken the swamp. Animated corpses begin to gather from beneath the waters. Putrid flesh, bloated and stuck to the weeds and reeds of the quagmire, peels from their bones, and is left clinging to the vegetation as they rise.

Soon the cries of the beast turn into a cackling laughter. An army of distended and morose undead stand before you. Bolstering your resolve, you glance to your right and then to your left. Your friends are there and they are ready. Whether you forward to your glory or your doom, you forward to your destiny! The undead army charges. The beast bellows in glee. You and your friends are tired. You're cold and wet. You're out numbered and out gunned. But you are warriors. You are all from different races and backgrounds. You may have started this quest as strangers, but now you are family. You harness the powers - both arcane and of faith. Your prowess in combat, both martial and ranged, has been honed and hardened by victory and defeat. You are heroes... Please roll initiative.

What we just went through is your typical "you're about to fight a big-baddie - hope you're ready" moment in the Table-Top Role-Playing Game, Dungeons and Dragons. I guess your mileage may vary there, as not all DMs are created equal, but you get the idea.

I am probably the best DM (Dungeon Master) ever to live in history, ever – historically. So, don't be disappointed if your games are not as awesome as mine. Your DM is just not as good as me. It's just the way it is. Deal with it.

Before you turn away from this one, thinking that this is going to be some kind of "nerd-fan-service" chapter or something like that, hear me out. I think you're really, *really* going to enjoy this one. I'm going to do a couple things a bit differently here.

First of all, as always, I am going to take a deep dive into the legends and lore of this infamous 40-year-old pen and paper game that is usually played around the kitchen table or a fold-out card table… and that in itself will be a lot of fun. But we are also going to explore the real-world impact of this game that caused an all-out panic across not only the country, but the entire world. Dungeons and Dragons changed the landscape of, not only table-top games, but role-playing games, video games, and movies as well.

D&D gave a voice to the timid, a sanctuary to the abandoned, a family for the lonely, and an outlet to the oppressed. It allowed the weak to be strong, the cowardly to be brave and the victim to be the hero. It also became the scapegoat for parents, schools, and authority figures who failed to see or heed the warning signs of a generation before it was too late.

A Brief History

I was just talking to one of my friends the other day, whose mother had strictly forbidden *Harry Potter* from being read in their house. Yes, I said being **read**... this was waaay back in 1997 when Harry Potter wasn't an international sensation and didn't have a million different properties, from major motion pictures to Broadway shows to The Wizarding World of Harry Potter in Universal Orlando... or any kind of toys or collectibles in between. Before all that, Harry Potter was just an 11-year-old boy who found out that he was a wizard. But it didn't take long for Harry, or really J.K. Rowling, to be accused of all kinds of devilry and witchcraft. Books were burned. Protests and Boycotts raged.

Satanic Panic is nothing new. We've seen it time and time again.

Oh, by the way: My friend? Ya, years later, around the time that Goblet of Fire was in theaters, he literally walked in on his mom reading Prisoner of Azkaban and his younger brothers and sisters watching Sorcerer's Stone. As it turned out... Harry Potter, and J.K. Rowling for that matter, is **NOT** satanic.

So, like I was saying: Satanic Panic is nothing new. If you play Led Zepplin backward, you'll be possessed. The West Memphis Three committed heinous acts of murder because they listened to Heavy Metal, obviously the devil made them do it - by the way they spent 18 years in prison based SOLEY on that fact until they were exonerated in 2011 when DNA cleared them off all charges. According to *Identification, Investigation, and Understanding of Ritualistic Criminal Activity*, a distribution by the Chicago Police Department in the 80s, "Creative and curious kids from upper/middle-class families, punk rockers, intelligent kids, kids with low self-esteem, and kids that listen to Heavy Metal" were all prime suspects for satanism.

Of course, we can go back *way* before this and take a look at the Salem Witch Trials where over 150 men, women, and children were accused of witchcraft and 18 of those were killed by hanging, drowning, or burning. Only a few short years later, the Massachusetts General Court overturned all convictions and ordered a day of fasting for the travesty and tragedy of the trials and justice Samuel Sewall, a staunch supporter and pivotal character in the trials publicly apologized. Oops, JK… right?

Satanic panic has gripped the hearts and minds of people before, but never so much so as in the 1980s when a young child prodigy named James Dallas Egbert III killed himself with a firearm, and a washed-up detective who was hired to find him saw an opportunity to make a name for himself.

Dungeons and Dragons is a table-top adventure game that is focused primarily on story-telling and role-playing. It was developed in 1974 by Gary Gygax and Dave Arneson and was influenced by old tactical wargames such as 1971's *Chainmail*. It is credited as the grandfather of role-playing games and the most important influence of modern RPGs (role playing games) or any board game or video game that relies on role-playing or RNG (random number generation) to progress.

What is role playing? It is simply where you take on the identity (the role) of another person or character and play out your part as that character would. I know this immediately brings to mind some theatrical imagery of "nerdy" kids dressed up like wizards running around the backyard casting fake spells at each other... and while you wouldn't necessarily be wrong, that is a very short sighted and uneducated understanding of role-playing, especially in the context of video and board games.

In *Super Mario* you are taking on the role of Mario... or his brother Luigi (and of course the more modern we get the more characters we have to choose from). We take on that character and interact in that world *just as* that character would. In *Minecraft* you create a character and interact in that world *as* that character. In *Settlers of Catan* you are a *settler,* and you acquire and trade resources while building and developing trade routes. In *Battleship* you are a captain attempting to destroy your enemy's fleet. In *Risk* you are play a diplomat or commander who must capture territories while keeping in mind the politics and stratagem of your enemies, always staying 1 move ahead. I could go on and on… and on, but the bottom line is, from the classics to modern video and board games, you're usually taking on the *role* of someone or something else and striving to reach the goal of that character… you're role-playing.

OK, so we understand what role-playing is, what is RNG? RNG or Random Number Generation is an algorithm that determines numbers randomly. These numbers are then checked against a table of possibilities or results. This is used in almost any modern video and board game. Have you ever wondered why in, let's use *Mario Kart* here, you get a green shell instead of a blue one? Or why in *Tetris* you get a square piece when you desperately need a straight piece? This is RNG. It is the randomness generator that progresses the game. Of course, not everyone is a fan of RNG because oftentimes it replaces skill for chance, but regardless, it is a mechanic that a vast majority of games use. And while D&D wasn't necessarily the first to use it, it was the first to *perfect* it, and evolve it into its full potential.

Gygax and Arneson took these two ingredients (RP and RNG), sprinkled in story-telling elements and imagination, a deep and very mechanical set of rules and requirements (all of which or none of which you have to abide by or follow), and crafted a game so immersive, so enthralling, and so entertaining, that over 20 million people have or currently *are* playing it. Noted players include Stephen Colbert, Chris Hardwick, Moby, Vin Diesel, Matthew Lillard, Joe Manganiello, Mike Myers,

Patton Oswalt, Wil Wheaton, Robin Williams, Jon Favreau, Greg Grunberg, Felicia Day, Gerard Way, Dan Harmon, David Benioff, DB Weiss, Andersen Cooper, Martin Starr, Joseph Gordon-Levitt, Patrick Rothfuss, Deborah Ann Woll, um... Me, and many, many more.

D&D can be seen all over popular culture in songs by Weezer, Stephen Lynch and Jumpsteady, and on Television in Community, The Simpsons, Freaks and Geeks, NewsRadio, Buffy the Vampire Slayer, and most notably Stranger Things... even in Popular films like ET and Futurama. D&D is everywhere.

Although the game - and for some, the lifestyle - is more popular now than ever, that doesn't mean that it doesn't come with a bit of stigma... and I'm not talking about the "nerd" or "boys only" stigma. I think we can safely say by now that if someone is still harboring those kinds of feelings, then it says more about *them* than it does about the game and who plays it. I'm talking about the darker, more menacing, more threatening stigma... that of devil worship and witchcraft, of demonic possession and mythic portals, of cults and the occult, of magic and murder... I'm talking about *Satanic Panic*.

The Beginning

On August 15 of 1979, a young boy went missing from his dormitory room in Case Hall at Michigan State University. He had written a suicide note and simply disappeared. He had been missing for a month, when on

September 13th he reached out to a private detective that his parents had hired to find him. The boy's name was James Dallas Egbert III. I have chosen to leave out the name of the PI because while I have my own opinions as to why and how he decided to release the information of this case, I don't know him and I don't know his heart, so I don't want to besmirch his name if I've got it all wrong… But really, come on guys, I don't get things wrong.

It was because of this investigator's initial, extremely **ignorant** report that a most unsuspecting, inconsequential fringe fantasy game was blamed… and kicked off one of the most rampant cases of Satanic Panic that we have seen in modern culture - and remember, this was in the 80s! - We didn't have Twitter or Facebook. We didn't have a million brainwashed influencers or observers brainwashing everyone *else* through a blue-lit carnival mirror at a press of a button or screen. There was radio, newspaper, and television.

James Dallas Egbert III was a prodigy. At the age of 16 he was accepted into the computer science program at Michigan State University. Egbert was struggling with depression, pressure over his school performance, drug use, and perhaps even his sexuality, but we wouldn't learn that until years later. In fact, we wouldn't learn anything about the true nature of Egbert's disappearance until 1984 when the investigator-who-will-not-be-named released a book entitled *The Dungeon Master: The Disappearance of James Dallas Egbert III* - can you see why I have my doubts about this dude's sincerity? If you can't, you will soon.

The most obvious route in the investigation soon turned into a dead end, but with little else to go on, became one of conjecture, blame and apathy. In the infancy of his investigation, the PI (I'll refer to him as Thomas - fans of the 80s will get that reference) found a corkboard with a series of pushpins connected by ties of yarn. It didn't take long for him to establish a crude outline of the college campus, including the adjacent power plant. More specifically this was a map of the steam tunnels that led from the power plant and sprawled out beneath the college.

Thomas received permission from the school to interview some of Egbert's friends and classmates, as well as to enter the steam tunnels. After speaking with those peers, *Thomas* concluded that James was a good kid, a quiet kid - intelligent, introverted, and kind. He was also introduced to the game that James would play with a few of the other students and was told that they would sometimes go into the steam tunnels to play, for more of an ambient, immersive experience. The game was Dungeons and Dragons. A game involving alternate realities and role-playing.

Next, *Thomas* went into the tunnels, and there found evidence that Egbert had, indeed, been there. He found personal items belonging to him, including quaaludes and items that indicated that Egbert had come here alone to take his life. But he did not find Egbert. Now, instead of being responsible and taking this information to James' parents and continuing on with the investigation, *Thomas* went to the press. He concocted such a farcical theory involving satanism and the occult that today it would be laughable, at best… or maybe it wouldn't… we seem to be fantastically gullible when it comes to things that frighten or threaten us. He regaled the media with these theories, though coming from a place of counterfeit authority, these absurd stories struck a chord and the media ate it up. They ate it up and they ran with it.

Thomas reported that while he had not found Egbert yet, he had found evidence of a game involving demonic and ritual magic, complete with its own worlds, languages and alphabets. In these worlds nature did not follow the rules. There were elves and ogres and dragons, oh my! And not only that, but young James had been *involved* in this game, so much so that he and his friends would traverse the tunnels in some twisted form of live-action role playing called LARPing.

Thomas surmised that some players of this hypnotic and wicked game could actually become so entranced, so obsessed with the fantasies within that they would start believing that they were not themselves anymore, but instead were the actual characters that they were playing. He erroneously and irresponsibly told the media that he believed young Egbert was in such a state and was wandering the steam tunnels no longer as James

Dallas Egbert III, but as his Dungeons and Dragons character.

He believed that James had ceased to exist and that he was, body and soul, the character of his D&D campaign. *Thomas*, of course, did not mention *anything* about James' issues with drugs, depression, pressure, or his relationship with his parents... these things are real and they are devastating, but they don't make headlines. You know what *does* make headlines, though? The occult. Demons. Witchcraft... Satanic Panic.

Thomas' investigation took him across multiple states. After a month of dead ends, including a convention that celebrates such games as Dungeons and Dragons, comic books and computer games, Egbert reached out to the PI. He told *Thomas* that he was in New Orleans and that if he would come get him, he would return to his uncle, but not his parents. *Thomas* drove to New Orleans to pick Egbert up and deliver him to his uncle back in Michigan.

During the car ride back, Egbert told *Thomas* that he had indeed gone into the tunnels that day a month before. He had taken a bunch of quaaludes and attempted to kill himself. He said that the pressures placed on him by his parents and the school, along with his depression, was too much and that he had just wanted to end it. He then told the investigator that he had attempted to kill himself a couple more times since then while he had stayed with friends and made his way to New Orleans - most recently by consuming a cyanide compound - but continued to fail. He stated that he didn't really want to die, but could not handle the pressure anymore. He told *Thomas* that his games of D&D played no part in his depression or suicide attempts and were *not* responsible, in any way, for his disappearance. If anything, they helped him forget. He just had to get away. He said that he had wanted to return home but the media attention frightened him and he was afraid of how his parents would receive him.

Egbert succeeded in taking his own life on August 11 of the next year, though we would not hear anything about his conversation with the PI until 4 years later when *Thomas* would go on to publish his best seller, *The Dungeon Master: The Disappearance of James Dallas Egbert III,* in which he would divulge his conversations with Egbert on their way back from New Orleans. He says in his book that he was misrepresented by the media and that the reason he kept the true reason for James' disappearance quiet for 4 years was because he was asked to by Egbert, himself, and that it was a condition of James coming home. Like I said… there are some things here that I don't buy… But I'll let you draw your own conclusions. Rumors are as stupid as the people who start them and as false as the people who help spread them.

So, for 4 years, rumors and conjecture and the imagination of those who knew no better swam in the cesspool of the lies of a washed-up private detective. But in that writhing, squirming filthy can of worms that he kicked open with nary a concern of the consequences, the ideas and rumors mutated and grew. Like a parasite it fed and fed. It sickened and perverted. Again, this isn't the first time this type of satanic panic had gripped a people, but as Terry Ann Knopf said, "Old rumors never die; nor do they fade away. They simply lay dormant for a while until the next appropriate time appears."

Such is the nature of these things.

Thomas was not the only person to capitalize on Egberts real-life tragedy. In 1981, a novelist and writer for Cosmopolitan named Rona Jaffe, wrote a novel inspired by the case. It is rather telling of the state of things here, as it took Jaffe only 3 days to write the novel which centered around a group of college kids that played role-playing games in the caverns near the school.

One of the players suffers from mental illness so obviously he begins to believe that he *is* his character. The tale mirrors Egbert's story (the manufactured, false one) almost *too* closely. The book, *Mazes and Monsters* was quickly picked up by CBS and a young Tom Hanks was cast as the lead mentally-ill character. This happened to be Hanks' first dramatic leading role.

The Panic

Chick Publications released a pamphlet in 1984 called *Dark Dungeons*. In it the author, Jack T. Chick, a reclusive fundamentalist cartoonist who would suppose his wayward beliefs via morality plays in tract form, vehemently warns his readers of the dangers of Dungeons and Dragons. Of course, this is also the same idiot who warned us of the dangers of J.R.R. Tolkien and C.S. Lewis and if he were still alive would have warned us of Harry Potter. I'm not saying Chick was necessarily a bad guy, but he is a prime example of ignorant passion, which is a very dangerous thing. But what was this danger that he so ardently cautioned against?

Well, in the tract *Dark Dungeons*, Marcie, who from the looks of it is playing some sort of paladin or cleric, makes some bad rolls (remember RNG?) and her character is killed. She is distraught and pleads with the DM (the person facilitating the game) to save her character. The DM (a very menacing and angry woman) tells Marcie that she's sorry, her character is dead and that she does not exist anymore. Marcie begins to cry and leaves. Later the DM tells another player, Debbie, that there is a way for her to have *real* powers. The next slide shows a comically poor rendition of what a witches coven looked like in Chick's mind and reads: "The intense occult training through D&D prepared Debbie to accept the invitation to enter a witches coven", in **ALL-CAPS-BOLD-FONT**. The DM and Debbie are there and are performing initiation rituals.

We later learn - while Debbie is casting D&D spells on her father to make him give her money - that Marcie has hung herself. She left behind a note that admits it was her fault that her character had died and that she can't go on anymore. Debbie is seen lamenting the loss of her friend, but then the DM (who I have discovered is named Ms. Frost) berates her and tells her that she doesn't have time to feel sorry for that loser and instead must practice her darks arts.

This sounds ridiculous, but it is 100% true and it was everywhere.

I actually *remember* this tract! It was circulated around our church at the time. I was young… like really young and I remember my mom took us to a seminar specifically based on the tract and even at that young age I just saw right through it. I distinctly remember saying to myself "this is just utter nonsense" but people bit - hook, line, and sinker. It was such a blatant form of propaganda and control through fear that you look back and say "how could anyone believe this crap", but as evidenced time and time throughout history, with enough propaganda and enough fear, people will completely give themselves over to the lies and deceit.

Dark Dungeons was printed and translated all over the world and was even turned into a film, further spreading the fear and lies. It's important to note here that the term D&D or Dungeons and Dragons was a catch all for role-playing games at the time. Again, the average person didn't know any better (well, neither did the people spreading the fear and lies) and just took what they were told by those in supposed authority as truth.

BAD (D)

Let's talk about bad - B.A.D.D. In 1983 Patricia Pulling founded an anti-D&D advocacy group named BADD (Bothered About Dungeons and Dragons) after her son, Irving, committed suicide. Irving shot himself in the chest on June 9th of 1982. Patricia filed a wrongful death lawsuit against Irving's high-school principal, claiming that he was responsible for putting a "D&D curse" on her son, as it was at school that Irving had learned of the game. The lawsuit was dismissed, obviously, but that didn't stop Patricia from going public with her accusations. She told the media that D&D encouraged suicide and satanism. She stated that D&D was "a fantasy role-playing game which uses demonology, witchcraft, voodoo, murder, rape, blasphemy, suicide, assassination, insanity, sex perversion, homosexuality, prostitution, satanic type rituals, gambling, barbarism, cannibalism, sadism, desecration, demon summoning, necromantics, divination and other teachings."

Pulling went on to be a consultant for the police, encouraging police to interrogate youths suspected of ties to the occult by questioning their reading material and games that they played. She became an international ambassador against violence on TV and co-wrote the book, *The Devil's Web: Who Is Stalking Your Children for Satan?* In the 90s it was discovered that Pulling had misrepresented *all* her credentials and *all* her statistics and claims concerning percentages of suicides and violence connected to D&D. It had all been fabricated and disproven. After this, Patricia left BADD and shrank from the public eye.

I don't mean to disparage Mrs. Pulling. I know her grief was real. I can't imagine the sorrow of losing a child, but (and such is the case with our PI, *Thomas* and our cartoonist friend) there has to be some responsibility here. We can't just place the blame on a convenient target and then concoct lies and stories and create a narrative that pushes and supports our agenda at the cost of the truth.

Gygax is quoted as saying, "This is make-believe. No one is martyred, there is no violence there. To use an analogy with another game, who is bankrupted by a game of *Monopoly*? Nobody is. The money isn't real. There is no link, except perhaps in the mind of those people who are looking desperately for any other cause than their own failures as a parent". Ouch.

The American Association of Suicidology, after an extensive study, reported that there is no link between fantasy or role-playing games and suicide. Of course, it doesn't help that this was all taking place at the same time a similar panic was being stoked. Moral wars were being waged against heavy metal and horror movies.

In 85, two young men killed themselves days before Christmas. There was no connection between the suicides and the band Judas Priest - other than the fact that the 2 men listened to them - but that didn't stop the parents, and subsequently the media, from blaming the British heavy metal band for the deaths. The lawsuit was eventually thrown out, and one of the band members is even recorded as saying in court, when asked about subliminal or back-masked messages, that he didn't even know what a subliminal message was. Ozzy Osbourne and Metallica were also singled out as being responsible for the suicides of young men and women back in the 80s and early 90s, but again these were just witch hunts by those who would not or *could* not take responsibility for themselves.

Conclusion

In the late-80s/early-90s William Schnoebelen published a series of writings through - you guessed it - Chick Publications that not only stated that Dungeons and Dragons was written by real-life sorcerers, but that the spells within the game would and *could* conjure real-life effects.

These writings, and those by Chick, himself, also warned and promised that anyone and EVERYONE who played Dungeons and Dragons was automatically going to hell. Do not pass GO, do not collect 200 dollars. The articles stated that D&D was "a feeding program for occultism and witchcraft". Now, I have played D&D for years. I DM. I have read all the manuals and rules and books… and I can tell you that none of the things that D&D has been accused of are even *in* the books. But that didn't stop the vast majority of parents and adults in the 80s and 90s to become frantic with fear.

From Egbert to Irving, from our PI to Patricia Pulling, from Chick and Schnoebelen to the media and news outlets… the fear of demonic activity, witchcraft, possession, suicide, the occult, murder, etc. - the Satanic Panic surrounding Dungeons and Dragons was a prime example of what happens when people in authority, often self-appointed, make irresponsible and irrational assumptions about things that they have no concept or understanding of and are too lazy to actually put in the work to find out. It is a prime example of what happens when people, well-intentioned as they may or may not be, point fingers and blame and refuse to look at themselves. It is an example of how lies and deceit and propaganda can derail an entire people and cause hysteria, the effects of which can last decades.

Though research has shown that D&D is not only *not* harmful, but in fact very beneficial in a number of cognitive and social growth and developmental aspects - and is just a lot of fun to play - it is still banned from most prisons and schools because of the stigma started over 40 years ago.

CHAPTER 4

The Lizard Man
of Scape Ore Swamp

The fog rolling off of the murky, reptile-infested water seemed especially menacing this strange night in Bishopville, South Carolina. The dead and withered Cypress and Tupelo trees, black with moss and decay, seemed to lean and loom at more of an angle, showing an unsettling interest in the quiet and lonely stretch of Royer Road that happens to border Scape Ore Swamp. The rancid odor of decaying meat wafted about from within the gaping maws of alligators on the hunt. Bullfrogs bellowed, locusts buzzed, and grasshoppers sang - the crepitation a cacophony of nerve-wracking warnings. The Barred Owl hooted its cryptic questions and the Heron replied in a haunting call. The entire landscape was alert and ready, but ready for what... and why?

Perhaps it was because on this night, Christopher Davis - a 17-year-old heading home from work alone at 2 in the morning - would encounter the swamp's most tightly held secret and would barely escape with his life, kicking off a massive manhunt, newspaper and television reports, and a 1-million-dollar reward.

The Legend

On June 29th, 1988 Christopher Davis was driving home late at night after another exhausting shift at a fast-food restaurant. His commute had taken him on this route numerous times and most likely would have numerous more. There was nothing out of the ordinary, nothing suspicious or out of place as far as he could tell from within the safety of his vehicle, and so he drove on. He just as easily could have taken the more traveled and much more well-lit Sumter Highway, circumventing the swamps altogether, but where's the fun in that?

Just after 2am, Davis' tire blew and he came skidding to a stop on Royer Road. It was dark and it was desolate, and it was the 80s - there were no such thing as cell phones back in the dark ages and most 17-year-olds knew how to change a tire, so that's what he did.

Duracell powered artificial light gave him a narrow beam with which to work and work he did. Davis did not want to spend any more time there than was absolutely necessary. The swamp was one thing when you have 2 thousand pounds of steel between you and the whatever-the-hecks that are out there, but a completely different thing altogether when you have your butt turned to it and you're on your knees in the near perfect dark, every unnatural sound under the moon at your back!

It's safe to say that this was the quickest Christopher had ever changed a flat tire.

Christopher states that almost immediately after tossing the flat in the trunk and slamming it shut, he heard a "thumping" sound from somewhere behind him. A dizzying 180 brought him around to see a large bi-pedal creature lumbering towards him! One news article quoted Davis as saying, "its searing eyes, three-clawed fingers, and snake-like scales made him initially believe he was under siege by the devil himself".

Davis states that he ran and leaped into the car moments before the creature slammed against the side of the vehicle. The collision was so forceful that the entire car shook as metal bent and glass shattered. Davis says that the creature clawed and grabbed at the drivers-side door and then leaped atop the roof as he peeled off. It clung to the vehicle tightly as he swerved and skidded away. He says that he was eventually able to throw the creature off by zigzagging erratically at high speeds.

Safe at home later that morning, Davis found that the side of the car had been badly damaged and that there were deep lacerations or scratch marks all around the door handle and on the roof. Upon further inspection, there were also found teeth marks, hair, and muddy footprints. He decided not to report the incident, as he feared that he would look insane and would not be taken seriously. Weeks passed, but instead of forgetting about his encounter with the scaly humanoid creature, Davis was reminded again and again of that night as more and more reports came across the local evening news of a large lizard-like man being spotted in and around Scape Ore Swamp. Though the locations and interactions differed, the description of the creature remained - for the most part - the same: green skin, snake-like eyes (glowing red), scales, bi-pedal, and wet".

Bolstered by these reports, he made a police report that same day and stated that, "I looked back and saw something running across the field towards me. It was about 25 yards away and I saw red eyes glowing. I ran into the car and as I locked it, the thing grabbed the door handle. I could see him from the neck down – the three big fingers, long black nails and green rough skin. It was strong and angry. I looked in my mirror and saw a blur of green running. I could see his toes and then he jumped on the roof of my car. I thought I heard a grunt and then I could see his fingers through the front windshield, where they curled around on the roof. I sped up and swerved to shake the creature off."

After Christopher's report and the first bit of physical "proof" of an encounter by way of his damaged vehicle, news and media outlets became obsessed… and so did the public. The attention and coverage given to the areas surrounding Scape Ore Swamp and even to Christopher, himself, exploded. Local businesses and entrepreneurs began selling "Lizard Man" shirts and stickers. The Lizard Man of Scape Ore Swamp tours began and incited almost daily battles for the best locations to hopefully catch a glimpse of this burgeoning celebrity. Even the chamber of commerce got in on it, encouraging the rumors, reports, and media attention, saying that it was "good for the community".

The rise in notoriety, the media attention, and the almost daily sightings triggered mass hysteria. Fans captivated by the fantasy - the idea of the unknown becoming known - began to flock to Lee County. Bishopville became one of the hottest spots in the states, drawing both tourists and hunters in droves. A local radio station even offered a 1-million-dollar reward for anyone who could capture the cryptid alive.

The Aftermath

For weeks after Christopher had come forward and told his tale, Bishopville was a mecca for all things cryptid and paranormal - and rightly so. I mean how exciting to have this kind of thing happen right here in our own backyard! With so many sightings and with the media and news outlets hyping it up… it brought a unity, a commonality to the people. It was something that they could get behind and support, even if you didn't necessarily believe it, it was still fun to be a part of something that EVERYONE could get behind. Honestly, I wish we had something like this going on right now!

Reports came flooding in claiming that a large lizard-like creature was up to all sorts of mischief. For miles around it seemed that everyone knew someone who had had an encounter with the creature. From striking it with their vehicles, to seeing it steal their fresh-out-of-the-oven apple pies that were cooling on the windowsill, to narrowly escaping its razor-sharp claws as it attacked vehicles that happened to venture too close to the swamps, often leaving scratch marks and dents. The stories were endless.

One story - that I found quite amusing, was a woman who had reported that she had drawn a bath late one evening and went to fetch her towels and when she came back, the Lizard-Man was waiting for her in the tub. This one might be false, but the images that I am able to conjure from such a scenario are awesome!

The local law took all of this with a combination of unease and disbelief. Though they were quick to dismiss the frenzy and hysteria, they were concerned with the number of sightings and encounters that were being reported by trustworthy and reputable members of the county and beyond. The circumstantial evidence was piling up, but they had nothing reliable, nothing tangible. Nothing that is, until the sheriff's office was called to a remote area of the woods and served their first helping of hard, irrefutable evidence - tracks.

These were not human footprints, though they were definitely made by a creature or thing that walked upright on 2 legs. The gait was massive at approximately 40 inches and the prints deep, suggesting a sizable being. The prints were also 3-toed and claw-shaped. The sheriff had no choice but to begin an investigation and had plaster casts made. They were sent to a local biologist for inspection.

What the biologist at the South Carolina Marine Resources Department had to say was most definitely *not* what the sheriff wanted to hear. The biologist reported that these prints were unclassifiable and were not from any known animal or species recorded to date. These prints were not from any creature known to man.

Faced with this new and frightening information, the sheriff quickly began a clandestine cover-up. The plaster prints were buried and there was no report made to the FBI, as would have been protocol *if* there were anything to report. New reports were either ignored. Lost, or unheeded and the hype over the Lizard-Man of Scape Ore Swamp slowly began to fizzle out as summer began to wane. Days became cooler, vacations ended and reality slowly started to settle things. Things began returning to normal.

Late that summer, an airman stationed at Shaw Air Force Base by the name of Kenneth Orr reignited the fervor. Orr reported to officials that he'd had an encounter with the Lizard-Man near highway 15. He was so frightened by this encounter that he had fired at the creature and wounded it. Orr produced a number of large, bloodied scales as evidence of his experience and described the beast as a 7-foot-tall man-looking creature with claws and webbed hands, red eyes and a large stride. Orr took the mantle of local hero and go-to for the cryptid lore, but his celebrity was short lived as he was forced to recant his tale when the investigation concluded, and he was charged with unlawfully carrying and discharging a pistol and filing a false police report. Orr was reported as saying that he had made the entire encounter up as a way to keep the legend alive.

Sounds like a cover-up to me.

Officials pushed the narrative that these sightings - the scratches and dents in the vehicles, the encounters, etc. - were, indeed a dangerous and large bi-pedal creature. That creature just happened to be a bear. Life returned to normal and the Lizard-Man was forgotten, lost to the annals of legend and lore, only spoken of around the campfire.

The story took on many forms and strayed so far from the original source material that it was hardly recognizable as the years passed. Some maintain that the creature had scales, while others argue that it was covered in fur - more akin to a sasquatch - or that it was caked in mud and moss like the Swamp-Thing. Officials and skeptics mercilessly poked holes in Davis' telling: How far away Davis was from the creature that night. How was he able to see it in the pitch black of night with just a small flashlight and make out all those details.

According to officials, Davis' story changed multiple times when he was asked to make official statements. According to the Fortean Times, one official is quoted as saying that Davis' encounter "is quite literally incredible, riddled with both implausibility and impossibility. It may be sincere or it may be a hoax, but in either event no hard evidence of the creature has been found".

Though Davis *did* pass a lie detector administered by Southern Marketing, Inc. officials discount this as merely a publicity stunt and an attempt at celebrity.

The original story circulated through over 100 newspapers and media outlets.

Conclusion

Nowadays, the Lizard-Man is more Folk Hero than dangerous beast. Bishopville even started a new tradition surrounding the locally loved cryptid: The Lizard Man Festival, where cryptozoologists, paranormal investigators and even biologists gather to celebrate the creature. Speakers and vendors are lined up for the 3-day event and it draws quite the crowd. Even the COVID-19 pandemic couldn't slow down the Lizard-man's momentum, as this the festival's 3rd year (2020), was held completely online and STILL sold out!

Panels are held where experts and novices alike discuss the Lizard Man and other paranormal topics.

Guided tours are held over the weekend, visiting all the important areas and locations of various sightings and encounters, especially those in or around Scape Ore Swamp.

According to the South Carolina Public Radio Website, John Stamey, the festival's planner is 100% on board with Davis and believes the stories are completely true. "To be honest with you," he says, "there's something in Scape Ore Swamp. We will one day find out what is causing all this if we keep looking."

Lyle Blackburn, leading Lizard Man authority and cryptozoologist has spent countless hours investigating this legend and has even spent time in the files of sheriff Liston Truesdale, who led the investigations at the time. Blackburn has written a book entitled *Lizard Man: The True Story of the Bishopville Monster*, which is available on Amazon - so what he has to say about the matter you can take to the bank! He says that while he personally thinks that whatever was here during that summer in 1988 has most likely moved on, he agrees that if we were to ever catch a glimpse of it again, it would be right here in Scape Ore Swamp.

What do you think? Crazy teenage kid just looking for some attention? A legit cryptid case? A cover-up?

CHAPTER 5

El Duende

Reader Discretion is Advised

In a small home in Los Angeles County, California, where the peculiar and macabre are standard, where bizarre events are par for the course, and where your grandparents are healers and practitioners of the old arts, you'd think that steering clear of the more creepy-crawly places of the house - the darker, more sinister recesses of the home - such as the attic or basement would be a common practice. But for the child in our first story (now a man, of course) that was just not the case. Certain aspects of this narrative have been changed to preserve anonymity at the request of the gentleman who provided us this story.

> We were kids, just 5 or 6 years old at the time. We (myself and my cousins) would run around playing hide and seek. There was an added tension to our games, as certain members of my family would often be in the main rooms of the house performing healings and rituals. It was a

hard rule that we were not to be seen or heard during "business hours", so this really upped the ante when the chase was on! Even the slightest giggle or shout of "I found you!" would find *us* in hot water. One day, I had accidentally knocked over a lamp while trying to rush to a hiding spot and was frightened that someone downstairs had heard. I was hiding under the bed in the room I shared with my cousin and having a hard time holding in coughs and sneezes from the dust and dirt that I had stirred up as I flung myself under! So, I was immediately taken aback and worried for my cousins, when during a particularly riveting game, I heard loud bumps and bangs and scratching coming from the attic. It was so loud and repetitive… it didn't make sense why someone would be purposefully making that kind of noise. I slithered out from under the bed as slowly and stealthily as I could - remember, we were playing hide and seek after all, and no matter my concern for my cousin, I still didn't want to lose, and I didn't want to get caught. Our grandmother had told us on many occasions that if we were bad, a devil would come and "get us".

So, as I made my way down the hall and to the stairs leading to the attic, the noises seemed to get louder and synchronized, almost like a rhythmic cadence, a meter and measure of bumps, scratches, bumps, and bangs. I made my way up the stairs, slowly, praying that the weathered wood under my feet would not protest too loudly to my weight. I was willing myself to be lighter, gripping the rough, old railing too tightly as I rose. I felt a worn and splintered piece of the railing pierce my palm as a sliver of wood peeled off and into my hand. I stifled a yelp - remember, I was quite young - and continued on, now sucking warm blood from the wound, the salty, metallic tinge almost overwhelming my already heightened senses. I got to the top of the stairs and there, almost as if waiting for me was a little… person. From what I can recall it was a little under a foot tall and a little thicker than a Barbie or GI Joe. It had long hair and was wearing what looked like sandpaper colored clothing. It was wearing a wide-brimmed hat like an old farmer would wear. Its eyes were tiny slits, dark with no whites. The mouth looked like slits also and had no lips. As soon as it saw me it smiled wide, which was terrifying in its own way, not having lips, and bowed in a fancy flourish, dipping low as it removed its hat and swiped it across the floor, a swish of dust coming up from it. Then it turned around and ran through a hole in the wall. I have never seen it again, but the next day after I had gathered up the nerve to tell my cousins what I saw, we went back up to the attic to search for it. We found no trace, and even the hole in the wall that it had run though was gone. There was no evidence of it ever being there, except the small swish mark in the dust where he had bowed and swiped his hat across the floor. Years later, I told my grandmother what I had seen, and she told me that it was El Duende and that it had come to take me away, but because I had hurt myself on the railing and was bleeding it was satisfied with my penance and left me alone.

The Legend

Duende are considered goblin-like or pixie-like creatures that originated from the Philippines and Latin America, but some have made their way to the United States. They are known for being manipulative and possessive. They are said to live in mounds of dirt like anthills or inside trees.

Spellings and lore differ a bit depending on the culture and local legend, but the word is most widely known throughout Latin America, Portugal, and the Philippines and is often interchangeable with "goblin, brownie, elf, pixie, and even leprechaun in some cases".

In Spanish, Duende is an abbreviation for the term *dueño de casa* or *duen de casa*, which means "possessor of a house" and often refers to a trickster gnome or pixie-type creature that inhabits or "haunts" a home. It will often attach itself to one home or family, or maybe even a bloodline.

There are slight variations in the appearance and intentions of El Duende but it is almost universally accepted that duende are mischievous and vindictive, capable of all sorts of impish, devilish things… even murder. They are often said to play cruel tricks on wayward children, leading them deep into the forest, getting them lost and then leaving them there. There are stories of those Duende that attach themselves to a certain house or family coming out in the middle of the night to groom the sleeping children in the house. They will often cut and style their hair, paint their nails, and apply powders and makeup to their faces… it is said that often these Duende will lose control, whether out of excitement or wicked intent, and a haircut or nail trimming might very well lead to the loss of an entire ear or finger!

The New Oxford English Dictionary tells us that a Duende is a ghost, or an evil spirit and *The Random House Dictionary* describes them as a goblin, demon, or spirit - but the word "duende" can also mean charm or magnetism. It can mean inspiration, magic, or fire, as well.

According to *The Larousse Spanish-English Dictionary*; duende are goblins, elves, or imps, but the word can also mean magic.

Duende will take offense at even those most minor of slights and demand reparations, often in the form of flesh, but can be persuaded to accept alternate forms of payment such as money or prized possessions, though whatever the payment is it will be costly.

Depending on which fable or tale you hear, you may also encounter a Duende that can provide help or even grant wishes - though this comes at the same high cost as an insult or slight - and if you are unable to make good on your agreement or renege altogether it is usually at the cost of your life, or the life of a loved one - should you value their life more than your own.

I can't help but be reminded of the tale of Rumpelstiltskin, as collected and made popular by the brothers Grimm. Rumpelstiltskin was and *is* a purveyor of wishes and desires, often at the cost of flesh, though sometimes not - but always at a cost. I'm not trying to inveigle you to believe that Rumpelstiltskin is Duende, but it might warrant further exploration.

As Real as it Gets

Emilie, the young woman who shared this next incredible story with me of her family's personal and tragic encounter with El Duende actually had her grandmother, her abuela, text this story to me. This is the real-life story of her family's history with El Duende. Fair warning: This tale is a bit alarming.

Here we go -

Abuela always told me and my primos to *never, ever* walk, stomp or destroy any mound of dirt. If we did, the Duende that lived in them would seek revenge on us for destroying their home and family and would possess us in return and take things of ours. And believe me, it worked. To this day when I'm at a park, or on a hike or walk, I will purposely go around any kind of mound or misshapen earthly obstacle in my path, and I make sure whoever I am with does, as well.

She would tell us of a true story that happened to her bisabuela (great-grandmother), my great-great-grandmother, back in the mid-1800s that has been passed down from generation to generation.

The story goes like this (and keep in mind this is an exact English translation from Abuela) ...

It was a midsummer day in Santa Marta, Colombia and bisabuela was out with two of her friends. They were going to go to the beach to relax from the crazy family issues that were going on back home. Keep in mind she and her two friends were only like 16 or 17 at the time. Young, still in high school. It was her, Alejandra and Emiliano. Fast forward a few hours to sunset… they were making their way back home which was a good hour and a half walk. About 25 minutes into walking a horrible storm came through. There was lightning and thunder and it wasn't safe to be out so they had to make their way somewhere safe. Eventually, Emiliano led them to a cave that he had found and they waited for it to pass. Bisabuela felt like hours had passed and felt it was time to head back. They couldn't take the worn path anymore because of the fallen trees and the flooding, so they had to go through the thick trees and vines off the path. Emiliano led the way with bisabuela in the middle followed by Alejandra. The ground was covered so you couldn't exactly see what you were walking on.

After walking for some time, Emiliano tripped on what seemed to be a huge mound of dirt sticking up and it crumbled down. Alejandra was always into superstition and was convinced that it was the home of a duende. Emiliano and bisabuela didn't believe such things and laughed it off as they kept walking. They all reached home well after dark and said their goodbyes, but bisabuela and Emiliano stayed together for a little longer because they were secretly dating. While they were sitting together and walking and talking Emiliano stopped. He seemed frightened. "Do you see that," he asked bisabuela. "What do you mean? There is nothing there," she replied, clearly concerned. "No, I swear there is a creature right there." He pointed out in front of them. "He is about 3 feet tall and kind of like how Alejandra describes her stories to us." Bisabuela was so confused because she could see in the sand that where he was pointing to were obvious prints of someone or *something* standing there but she couldn't *see* anything else. While holding Emiliano's hand she felt him shaking and his eyes grow wide. She asked him, "what is wrong, my love?" He replied saying, "he said that since I have knocked over his home and killed his wife, he wants to take you from me."

Bisabuela was frightened and pulled him inside her house. Everyone was asleep at the time and she had to figure out a way to get rid of this thing. They remembered how Alejandra had said that sometimes a duende will consider money or things of wealth and importance instead of someone you love, so she sent Emiliano out there to bargain with El Duende. He was gone for what seemed like an eternity. He came back and said that the duende had asked for 10,000 COP (Colombian pesos) which is just around $2 in USD (US Dollars) but it was a lot at that time especially for the son of a farmer and tailor. El Duende had given them exactly 3 days to get it or he would come back and take bisabuela from him forever. Throughout the next 3 days, things of value would go missing from Emiliano's house and Emiliano would claim to see the duende outside his window just waiting… watching. The creepiest part was that Emiliano's little brother said that after he came home that first night, Emiliano was not himself. That he had wandered back into the woods and came back with cuts all over his body.

Somehow, they managed to get the money and Emiliano gave it to the duende. Bisabuela and Emiliano thought that it was all over. 20 years passed by and around the late 1800s or the early 1900s Emiliano and bisabuela ended up getting married. They were about to move to the US for a better life. The night before they left, Emiliano confessed something to Bisabuela about that horrible night years ago. He told her how he wasn't able to forge up the money and how he agreed to give El Duende the second-born child of theirs to repay his debt.

Bisabuela didn't know what to say or do. She was just so frightened. After many years and now living in the United States, they had 3 beautiful children Emilia, Yaneilia, Felipe. They had forgotten all about what had happened until Yaneilia turned 7. She came home one day from playing outside with her siblings and told her mother and father that she had made a new friend. They asked what the friend's name was and she said that it didn't have one but that it knew daddy. After that bisabuela and Emiliano kept her inside. They were constantly watching. 3 years later, when Yaneilia turned 10 and everyone was asleep, she snuck outside and she never returned home.

Our family searched and searched and was never able to find her. Ever since then, bisabuela and Emiliano believed that it was indeed the Duende that took her from us. El Duende had made good on his bargain and had destroyed Emiliano's family the same way Emiliano had, that terrible night so many years ago, destroyed El Duende's. That was told from my abuela, Emiliania. I'm Emilie and this is the story of my family's encounter with the Duende.

Another thing she just texted me about is that they sometimes will appear to young children and play with them. Or if a kid encounters one with evil intentions and gives it their name, the Duende will take control over their life and the child will forever become its slave and be taken away. If one is possessed by a Duende, an exorcism will have to be performed by a priest or someone to get the vengeful Duende out of the body.

Wow… Ok, why don't we take a moment here and let that sit. We might need some time to recover.

Time's up!

Conclusion

"Do not go to the bush to cut firewood nor look for coconut husks, or El Dueno del Monte will get you."

This was a common threat in the 1940's and 50's which mom would use when she needed the children at home for some chores rather than going to the bush. The children, of course, preferred going to the bush for the thrill of some adventure. It was not that they liked cutting firewood, but hunting for bird nests and raiding the eggs was a thrill in itself. It also meant drinking fresh coconut water or hunting for coco plums or sea grapes. A trip to the bush could also run you the luck of killing some wild bird, a bush hog or even a deer. Now that was indeed a thrill." - Angel Nunez, "El Duende"- *San Pedro Folklore*

"Be home by supper, or El Duende will get you and take you deep into the forest where I will not be able to hear you or see you"

"Stay in bed until morning, or El Duende will bite off your toes and swallow them whole!"

"Don't make any noise or the Duende will get you"

El Duende is often used as an incentive for good behavior, or really more of a deterrent for bad behavior. The stories have endured decades, even centuries. But are they just stories?

What about Emilie's bisabuela? What about poor Yaneilia? What about the swish in the dust at the top of the stairs?

There is obviously something here...

And that being the case, I feel it my responsibility to equip you with the information, the *tools* that you will need, should you ever encounter El Duende in the wild!

First off, it won't be easy. El Duende are sly… and quick. They are drawn to loud whistles. If you are to lay a trap for one, draw it in with a loud, shrill whistle. Once you have it trapped, be quick! Because El Duende can turn itself into all sorts of inanimate things. A chair, a pair of pants, red clay - these are all shapes and characteristics that El Duende has taken when seen or captured.

Second, as if that won't be difficult enough, you have to do it drunk!

Adults cannot see duende unless they are drunk. So, drink up before you go a'trappin!

Disclaimer here… I said ADULTS! Be responsible and don't drink if you're a minor.

Now you know how to lure it; you know how to see it. What do you do next?

Well, duende will not talk to adults unless *it* is drunk as well! So, make sure you bring enough booze for 2… Offer it some sweet treats to get it thirsty. It will always take treats or food. When it has eaten its fill, offer it the booze. These things are **tiny** so it won't take long.

Now that the Duende is nice and loosened up, you *could* kill it any number of ways. While El Duende is immortal, it *can* be killed and is vulnerable to death by any standard means; guns, blades, fire, a boot… whatever… it'll work, but where is the fun in that!

Here's the kicker guys… if you learn a duende's name, you have control over it. It must do your bidding!

So, after you've gotten the duende nice and liquored up, just engage it in simple conversation. Keep the conversation directed at it. It's life, its deeds, its favorite foods, whatever… make sure its guard is down before you ask. These creatures protect their names most fiercely and I'd hate to see the result of a duende discovering that it was being duped for its name.

Once you've gained its trust, learn its name… once you have its name you have its power!

Again, that kind reinforces the idea that Rumpelstiltskin and the Duende have more in common than we may have once thought? Right?

Good Hunting!

And rest in peace, poor Yaneilia…

CHAPTER 6

The Alaska Triangle

Alaska is home to more than 3 million lakes and is surrounded by 33,000 miles of coastline. More than half of the United States' federally appointed wilderness can be found here. If you were to divide Alaska right down the middle, each half would be larger than Texas. The winters are long and they are dark. For months at a time, the sun will not rise. Snow blankets roads, trails, and tracks leaving those areas - much of which is unmarked anyway - completely oblivious to human presence. Temperatures can easily reach 50 degrees below zero and arctic Northern winds ensure that no matter how many layers you're wearing, you're going to feel it.

Lush, dense woodlands stretch for miles and miles in all directions. Rough and rocky mountains conceal caves and crevasses. Slow-moving glaciers - some the size of football fields and others growing to be hundreds of kilometers long – float in icy waters. Alaska is home to some of the most frigid and dangerous conditions and landscapes known to man. It is also home to many of the largest and most ferocious beasts on earth: Grizzly bears, Polar bears, Moose, Walrus, Wolves, Black bears, and Wolverines just to name a few.

Alaska is wild. It is dangerous. It is untamed.

It is clear that in Alaska, *we* are the visitors. The final frontier is home to many wondrous and unexplainable phenomena. From the Hoar Frost to the Aurora Borealis, from the Light Pillars to Fata Morgana, this last bastion of feral grandeur permits us (humans) passage and even residence, but under no circumstances is it safe.

The Legend

Connecting Anchorage, the state's largest and most populated city, with the small town of Barrow on the very Northern cusp, and then to Juneau, the state's capital - located in the Gastineau Channel - the Alaska Triangle takes up an impressive chunk of real estate. The area also covers the enormous Barrow Mountain range. Also known as the Devil's Triangle, the area is responsible for over 16,000 disappearances since 1988. That is twice the average missing persons rate anywhere else in the United States. Though most of these disappearances could be blamed on the aforementioned rugged and unforgiving terrain, brutal weather conditions, and wild animals - all lending to an eco-system that is anything but merciful - theories abound around the possibility of everything from alien abduction to swirling energy vortexes… to my personal favorite: the evil, shape-shifting Tlingit demon called Kushtaka.

In October of 1972, a private plane disappeared on its way from Anchorage to Juneau. Among the passengers were Alaska Congressman Nick Begich, Russell Brown (an aide to the congressman), U.S. House Majority Leader Hale Boggs, and their bush pilot Don Jonz. The plane and its passengers seemed to simply vanish into thin air. No mayday call, no turbulent weather, and no sign of the wreckage. For weeks hundreds of civilian and official planes, helicopters and boats searched more than 32,000 square miles and found nothing. No plane, no bodies, no survivors, no debris… nothing.

Since then, more and more aircraft have gone down, hikers and hunters have gone missing, tourists and residents alike have simply disappeared. Vanished. Gone. The area has become a playground for conspiracy theories ranging from alien abduction to bigfoot to paranormal or evil anomalies to ghost ships.

Theories

Out of all of these theories, one of the most widely supported is that of the energy vortexes that crash and crackle in the empty spaces of the triangle. These vortexes are swirling gales of concentrated energy that radiates in a tornadic cone-like shape either clockwise or counterclockwise and create positive or negative charges and effects. These impact the natural balance of everything within its influence, including and especially humans. The vortexes can manipulate and affect our emotional, physical, and mental state and awareness.

Upward, clockwise rotations are known as a positive spiral vortex. This enhances the flow of natural energy in that area. It is said that these kinds of vortexes are conducive to life, healing, self-exploration, creativity, and peace. Some of the more well-known places where positive spiral vortexes occur or have occurred in the past are Stonehenge, the Sedona desert, and the Egyptian pyramids.

On the other hand, downward spiral vortexes rotate in a counterclockwise movement. This creates a *vacuum* of positive energy and leaves behind a negative, draining, and impoverished energy. These negative spiral vortexes are known to cause depression, hallucinations, nightmares, and health issues. They also cause visual and audio confusion and interact with electrical equipment to the point of malfunction. The Bermuda Triangle, the Devil's Sea in Japan, and Easter Island are all known locations of Negative Spiral Vortexes… The Alaska Triangle is rife with these energies.

According to Page Bryant, author of *Terravision: A Traveler's Guide to the Living Planet Earth*, "A vortex is a mass of energy that moves in a rotary or whirling motion, causing a depression or vacuum at the center… These powerful eddies of pure Earth power manifest as spiral-like coagulations of energy that are either electric, magnetic, or electromagnetic qualities of life force."

Readings have been taken, analyzed, and scrutinized in the Alaska Triangle for decades and they have found many intense concentrations of magnetic and electric anomalies. These energies have disrupted and manipulated compasses, GPS, and radar equipment to the point of failure. Also, there are numerous reports made by hikers and search and rescue workers that they have experienced audio and visual hallucinations, lightheadedness, and disorientation. Often returning feeling ill and out of sorts.

This energy vortex is just one possible explanation for the disappearances of so many people and vehicles, but it is not the only one.

The Kushtaka or Kooshdakhaa is a shape-shifting demon of lore found in the tales of the Tlingit and Tsimshian peoples of the Northwest. The literal translation is "Land Otter Man". Kushtaka are said to prefer the shape or "form" of an otter. And why wouldn't they? Otters are adorable! It is said that the Kushtaka agree and that they actually use this form to distract and lull victims into a false sense of wonderment and ease. With the otter's naturally playful and curious behaviors, this is all too easy to accomplish.

This is where the legend's paths diverge: on the one hand you have the tale that says that the Kushtaka are cruel and malevolent creatures that would take great joy in luring Tlingit hunters and sailors to their icy deaths, and on the other, the creatures are kind and friendly, often helping those in need by keeping them warm and leading them to safety.

Though the Kushtaka prefers the form of an otter, it is not beyond taking on other forms. It has been known to take the form of a beautiful woman to seduce wayward men. It has taken on the form of a caring and worried mother to entice children into its frozen traps. It has taken the form of children, frightened, hungry, and cold to draw a mother to her doom. A single Kushtaka is a dangerous foe, but a group of them are deadly.

But surely this can't account for 16,000 missing human beings, can it?

Well, hear me out... and don't call me Shirley.

Kushtaka

In the 19th century, Alaska's otter population was decimated by hunters. Their furs and fat were a life-giving commodity and they were quickly hunted to extinction. Now the state population of these adorable little guys is thriving. There are over 26,000 otters in the state of Alaska. You see, Kushtaka are not mindless, senseless killers. They have a goal. A purpose. And they are working in concert with mother-earth to accomplish it.

We've already pointed out that Alaska is the last frontier, that *we* are the visitors there. We are the guest... and what terrible guests we had been by destroying an entire species.

The downward spiral vortex and the Kushtaka have established quite the synergy and this arrangement is something we are not at all equipped to handle. You see, the Kushtaka do not simply kill. They absorb and transform their victims. Their victims are not simply killed and sent to the afterlife, no, they are transformed *into* Kushtaka, their spirits forever cursed to remain here, on this mortal coil. This was an especially frightening tale, as the Tlingit and Tsimshian peoples believed that death was a passage to the next life, where they would be reincarnated. To live again, in some other form, a wiser and more benevolent being than the last, having acquired the experience that they did from the previous life.

The Kushtaka transform their victims *into* Kushtaka, that they, too might add to their ranks. This is why there have been so many disappearances. Because those unfortunate souls have become Kushtaka and now wander the wildlands of Alaska as otters.

This explains the revival of the species - 26,000 and counting.

According to onlyinourstate.com, there is an ancient tale that goes like this: As you're walking through your village, or hunting in woods, or fishing in the sea, a man or group of men approach you. These men look just like kinsmen, and you don't have a clue that they're really the Kushtaka. In some cases, these malevolent creatures appear when you're lost or injured, and claim that they intend to rescue you. However, they lead you deeper into the wilderness and either tear you into pieces or turn you into a Kushtaka, which prevents your soul from being able to reincarnate.

I had stated earlier that the Kushtaka were working in concert with mother-earth, and that is true, but in what way and in what capacity? Yes, she sustains these energy vortexes that cause our navigational and electrical systems to malfunction. Yes, she causes the torrents and gales that blind us and fell our aircraft, but where did these vortexes come from?

We've all been regaled with stories of extra-terrestrial influence and interference. This is such a common narrative that we are often placated with the explanation of "it was aliens" when we ponder such marvels as the Egyptian pyramids or Stonehenge or Easter Island... but how? In what way "was it aliens"?

The energy vortex.

Just as the aliens put into play the spiraling energies that influenced the construction of the coliseum and the iPhone so, too, did they set alight the entirety of the Alaska Triangle with these energies, but instead of the upward, clockwise positive flow that was so used to establish many of the modern-day phenomena that we are unable to explain, they plagued this Devil's Triangle with counterclockwise spiral energies. They saw the destruction of man here and sought to right a wrong, to bring back a lost species and so an alliance was made. A bargain was struck. Through the work of this unlikely triumvirate, balance was restored.

We don't know if this mighty trio has been sated, or if we will continue to see droves of our species fall in order to sustain another, but I guess that is the price we pay for messin' with otters.

Chapter 7

Deadly Valentine's Day

On Thursday, February 14th, 1929 seven men were gunned down in cold blood in the back alleys of the Lincoln Park neighborhood of Chicago's North Side. The massacre happened as a result of the power struggle between 2 heavy hitters of organized crime in the area; The Irish North Siders, captained by George "Bugs" Moran, and the Italian South Side Gang, run by Al Capone.

Moran and Capone had both been vying for gainful control over the Chicago bootlegging gig, with Moran often muscling in on Capone's other dealings, such as the dog tracks, saloons, and speakeasies that were under Capone's control and command. Moran also ordered hits on Jack McGurn, one of Capone's own lieutenants, and *Unione Siciliana* members, Pasqualino "Patsy" Lolordo and Antonio "The Scourge" Lombardo.

The setup was simple: convince Moran that Detroit's predominately Jewish *Purple Gang*, which was tied to Capone, were looking to undercut the crime boss and sell 2 trucks-worth of illegal Canadian whiskey to the North-Siders instead. The plan worked. The Irish North-Siders met at the designated garage on North Clark Street at 10:30 am on Valentine's Day. They were all dressed in their Sunday best, as was the tradition for a meeting such as this.

Two men, assumed at that time to be from the Purple Gang - dressed to the 9s - entered first, followed by 2 uniformed Chicago Police officers. The gangsters pulled .45 Caliber Thompson submachine guns with 50-round drum mags from beneath their coats as the officers pulled Remington 870 pump-action shotguns. The North-Siders were directed to stand against the north wall of the garage and wait. The garage exploded in a cacophony of blasts and bangs as the 7 members of the North-Siders were executed. Before leaving, the assassins checked each body to identify Moran and the rest of his lieutenants. Among the slaughtered were Peter Gusenberg, a North-Sider enforcer, Frank Gusenberg (Peter's brother and also an enforcer), Albert Kachellek (also known as "James Clark"), Moran's Number Two, Adam Heyer (bookkeeper and business manager of the for the North-Siders), Reinhardt Schwimmer, (an optician who, according to Wikipedia, had abandoned his practice to gamble on horse racing and associate with the gang), Albert Weinshank, who covered business for Moran and held an uncanny resemblance to the North-Sider boss and John May, the gang's mechanic.

Not among the deceased were Moran and two of his top lieutenants. They were across the street at a coffee shop.

You see, Moran had been running late and arrived at the garage at the same time as the uniformed officers. He and his men figured it was a sting and hid their faces as their Cadillac drove right on by the garage and parked across the street. The massacre did not take out its intended target, but it was enough to end the North-Siders and give control of the entire Chicago organized crime operation to Capone.

To this day, the men that carried out the cold-blooded killings have never been identified or brought to justice. It is believed that Cosa Nostra hitmen, John Scalise and Albert Anselmi were involved and may have even been trigger-men, acting on the behest of *Unione Siciliana* president, Joseph Guinta. But this was never confirmed and the men were never prosecuted as they were found beaten to death by a baseball bat on a deserted road after having been invited to Capone's house for dinner.

Capone had purchased a baseball bat earlier that day.

The most popular theory is that this massacre was the doing of none other than Al Capone, himself, aided by a corrupt Chicago Police Department that he had gained control over either through blackmail, threats of violence, or offers of a cut of the profit that he was making during this time of prohibition. Whether it was an act of revenge, a pragmatic business dealing, or self-preservation, it was one of Capone's most infamous involvements.

The garage is now a nursing home, and it is said that when it was demolished in 1967 a rich Canadian businessman named George Patey, purchased the entire north wall that the victims were killed against and sold the bricks to various mob-related collectors and museums. Many of these bricks were returned to Patey as numerous owners began to experience rashes of extremely bad luck after purchasing or otherwise acquiring the stones. It is said that a large number of the bricks were purchased by an eccentric owner of a 20's themed gangster club. He is said to have tiled the men's room with them and on opening night, a patron that had had too much to drink peed on the floor of the bathroom.

The club burned down that night!

Epilepsy and Beheadings

Did you know that Valentine's Day was *not* a romantic holiday and that the Valentine's Day as we all know and loathe it, has nothing to do with Saint Valentine at all? In fact, Saint Valentine might have more to do with the *bloody* side of Valentine's Day than the romantic side!

Saint Valentine of Rome was a 3rd-century Roman Saint. He has been associated with love and romance because he used to marry Christians and Romans alike in Christian marriage while the Roman Empire was heavily persecuting those of the Christian faith. He was arrested and beheaded... Martyred, for his blasphemy on February 14th which, from then on, was known as Saint Valentine's Day.

But he is *not* the patron saint of love, or romance... or even platonic relationships... he is the patron saint of epilepsy. As far as Saint Valentine is concerned, February 14th is associated with his martyrdom and has nothing to do with his patronage. According to *The Oxford Dictionary of Saints*: "The connection of lovers with St. Valentine, with all its consequences for the printing and retailing industries, is one of the less likely results of the cult of the Roman martyrs.

Fast forward a thousand years - yes, a thousand years of Feb 14th Saint Valentine's days being a feast to commemorate and remember his martyrdom - to 14th-century English poet and *Canterbury Tales* author Geoffrey Chaucer. Chaucer was a medieval writer who was tasked to compose a marriage poem in honor of King Richard II and Anne of Bohemia's engagement. Chaucer performed his task flawlessly and, as ever was his way, he used birds to tell his tale instead of humans. "*The Parliament of Fowls*" was so well received and struck such a chord that the day it was performed - February

14th, Valentine's Day - would forever after be associated with love and romance and marriage instead of a feast for a martyred saint.

And that's not even the craziest thing I've got for you!

Fertility Whoopins?

It is widely believed that the *actual* origins of the valentine's day that we celebrate in modern times - the traditional gifts between lovers / romantic nonsense - actually originated from an ancient Roman tradition called Lupercalia (Loo-per-cal-ia). Lupercalia was a bloody and brutal tradition held between February 13th and 15th where the men of Rome would bare all (get butt-nekkid), sacrifice goats and even dogs, bathe in their blood, and take the hides of the sacrificed animals on a hunt… though they would not be hunting beasts or prey. They would be hunting women. They would beat the women with the skins of the sacrifices in an effort to implore the spirits cleanliness and fertility to bless them… **That** is the craziest, most messed up thing about Valentine's Day.

So, remember that the next time your significant other wants you to "go all out" on Valentine's Day!

CHAPTER 8

Vampires

". . . Unquenched, unquenchable,
Around, within, thy heart shall dwell;
No ear can hear nor tongue can tell
The tortures of that inward hell!
But first, on earth, as vampire sent,
Thy corpse shall from its tomb be rent:
Then ghastly haunt thy native place,
And suck the blood of all thy race;
Therefrom thy daughter, sister, wife,
At midnight drain the stream of life;
Yet loathe the banquet which perforce
Must feed thy livid living corpse:
Thy victims ere they yet expire
Shall know the demon for their sire,
As cursing thee, thou cursing them,
Thy flowers are withered on the stem.
But one that for thy crime must fall,
The youngest, most beloved of all,
Shall bless thee with a father's name —
That word shall wrap thy heart in flame!
Yet must thou end thy task, and mark

> Her cheek's last tinge, her eye's last spark,
> And the last glassy glance must view
> Which freezes o'er its lifeless blue;
> Then with unhallowed hand shalt tear
> The tresses of her yellow hair,
> Of which in life a lock when shorn
> Affection's fondest pledge was worn,
> But now is borne away by thee,
> Memorial of thine agony!"

The Giaour (Unquenched, unquenchable)
George Gordon Byron - 1788-1824

In this chapter we are going to be immersing ourselves in the dark and desperate world of vampires. Are vampires real? Is vampirism really as sexy as they make it look in modern film and literature? Are the "vampires" that we are familiar with really the vampires of legend and lore? Have we been duped into thinking that vampires wear long capes, have perfect posture and sick one-liners and just want to "fit-in" when really, they are demonic, nefarious creatures of the night?

Answers to all these questions and many, many more may or may not be answered here, depending on how much writing I decide to do. Just kidding! Of course, you'll get your answers! One thing is guaranteed: You are going to get the legend of the vampire told as **only** I can tell it. That I promise!

The Legend:

The earliest translation of the word "vampire" in English - then spelled "VAMPYRE" - was in a travelogue published by The Harleian Miscellany in 1734. The piece was titled *Travels of Three English Gentlemen* and was part of a dissertation published in Duisburg. It was an anonymous manuscript that described the first-ever encounter with vampires. The full title is *The Travels of three Gentlemen, from Venice to Hamburgh, being the grand Tour of Germany, in the Year 1734*. The pages describe a great trek and upon this adventure, the author comes upon one Baron Valvasor in Lubljana, Slovenia. The Baron welcomes the men into his home and bids them stay and rest.

One evening, Baron Valvasor regales them with tales of his land. The Baron is described as a man of good sense and understanding, which makes this tale all the more believable and all the more frightening:

> *"The Vampyres, which come out of the graves in the night-time, rush upon people sleeping in their beds, suck out all their blood, and destroy them. They attack men, women, and children; sparing neither age nor sex. The people, attacked by them, complain of suffocation, and a great interception of spirits; after which, they soon expire. Some of them, being asked, at the point of death, what is the matter with them? say they suffer in the manner just related from people lately dead, or rather the spectres of those people; upon which, their*

> *bodies (from the description given of them, by the sick person,) being dug out of the graves, appear in all parts, as the nostrils, cheeks, breast, mouth, &c. turgid and full of blood. Their countenances are fresh and ruddy; and their nails, as well as hair, very much grown. And, though they have been much longer dead than many other bodies, which are perfectly putrified, not the least mark of corruption is visible upon them. Those who are destroyed by them, after their death, become Vampyres; so that, to prevent so spreading an evil, it is found requisite to drive a stake through the dead body, from whence, on this occasion, the blood flows as if the person was alive. Sometimes the body is dug out of the grave, and burnt to ashes; upon which, all disturbances cease. The Hungarians call these spectre* Pamgri, *and the Servians,* Vampyres; *but the etymon or reason of these names is not known.'*

It was around this time in Trstenik, Serbia that a man by the name of Arnold Paole, a Serbian Hajduk (an 18th-centurey freedom fighter/bandit) was laid to rest. He is credited with post-humously killing 16 people before his body was exhumed. Paole was a freedom fighter in the 18th century and died after falling off of a wagon and breaking his neck. Shortly after his burial, the townsfolk began to report that they were seeing Paole's spectre and were being haunted by him. Days later, the men and women who were making the claims began to die. Rumors began to circulate as more and more people died. Eventually, the townsfolk called upon their Hadnack (a military or administrative leader) to investigate. The grave was dug up and the body exhumed…

They found that the body was not decomposed. There was "fluid-blood" in his veins and there was blood running from his nose and mouth. His shirt and the coffin were covered in blood, as well. His fingernails and toenails had fallen off and new ones, clean and strong, had grown in their place. The Hadnack reported that Paole's body was "flush with life" and that his hair, beard, and nails had all grown. The townsfolk immediately drove a stake through his heart, into and out of the back of the coffin, to keep him bound there. It is said that Paole shrieked and moaned during this procedure, so the townsfolk set the body alight. Once the flames had died down, Paole's head, heart, and lungs were cut out and destroyed. Then the townsfolk repeated the process on all of Paole's post-humous victims.

Though this is one of the first recorded accounts of vampirism, it wasn't **the** first. That honor goes to Jure Grando Alilovic, a 16th-century villager from what we know today as Croatia. Alilovic died due to illness in 1656 but did not stay dead. It is said that he would rise from his grave at night and knock on the doors of the local villagers and whenever he did so, at whatever house he visited, someone there would die within the next few days. One brave villager attempted to subdue and kill Alilovic by driving a stake through his heart after a chase, but failed, as the stake simply broke and could not penetrate Alilovic's chest. A prefect by the name of Miho Radetic had the body exhumed, and much like that of Paole, Jure's body was flush with life and there was a bloody smile upon his face. The villagers immediately ran a *hawthorn* stake through his heart and burned the body. It is said that neighboring villages could hear the screams of Alilovic as he burned. Radetic performed an exorcism while the villager's sawed off the head... and soon after, peace returned to the village.

Alilovic was described and referred to as a Strigoi or Strigun... a word that could translate to vampire, warlock, or sorcerer.

Most vampires we know or think we know today are a form of revenant: a corpse reanimated that haunts or hunts the living. The word is taken from the old French word, *Revenir*, which means "returning" or "to come back" and while, yes, these revenant vampires are real and by far the most popular, they are not the *only* vampires and definitely not the first or most dangerous.

Old Lore (We're Talking Old)

Ancient Babylon spoke of a demon so fierce and so feared... a malevolent demigoddess, the daughter of the Sky God Anu: Lamashtu.

Lamashtu would rob new mothers of their children while they were breastfeeding. She would take them then because she wanted them plump and well-fed as she drained the life from them. She would first drain them of blood, then consume the bodies whole.

Lamashtu is reminiscent of one of the earliest depictions of a vampiric demon: Lilith.

Lilith - or in Hebrew, Lilit - is from the earliest class of demons and can be found in the cuneiform texts of Sumer from the bronze era - one of the earliest civilizations known to man. She can be found referenced in the *Epic of Gilgamesh*, dated 600 BC, and is known to consume the blood of the innocent. According to French Benedictine monk, Augustine Calmet - part of the Duchy of Bar of the Roman Holy Empire - Lilith is considered one of the earliest if not *the* earliest of all vampires and sorceresses in the world.

She is also said to be connected to Lamia, an ancient-Greek monster who fed on children. It is said that Lamia was lovely and that she charmed Zeus into sleeping with her. After Hera, Zeus' wife, discovered this, she forced Lamia to consume her own children - the ones that she had conceived through her affair - and cursed her with everlasting insomnia. Zeus took pity on her and gave her the ability to remove her eyes, a temporary reprieve to the sleeplessness. Lamia became addicted and obsessed with the taste of fresh blood and would forever after be cursed with the need to consume it. She was known to be very beautiful and would often seduce the living to appease her desires.

The tales of Lamia remind us of the Empusa, the ancient Greek spectre that is said to be a woman of great strength and foresight. She is described by the *Crates of Mallus* as a "demonic phantom" and a beautiful seductress. In her natural form, she is hideous and only has one leg - and *that* made of copper - though she has the ability to shape-shift. She often chooses the form of a beautiful young woman, but when not in this form, she prefers the form of either a bat or a wolf. Empusa, daughter of Hecate, is known for seducing men and draining them of their life-blood while they sleep… because of this, she is considered to be responsible for sleep paralysis.

These 4 ancient beings are the true beginnings of what we know today as vampires. Not sure if you caught it, but interesting side note: all 4 of these - the earliest vampires in existence - were women… or at least female. Interesting, ya?

In other histories, we have the Strix, a giant shape-shifting bird that often takes the form of an owl, but will take that of a man when necessary. It feeds on human flesh and blood and only hunts at night.

There is the Lugat, a creature from Albanian mythology. The Lugat is a creature of the night. It hunts in the shadows, avoiding all light. It can fly and will often seduce its victims by taking the form of a very attractive young man. It will lure its victims into a darkened room or alleyway and then consume their blood, often leaving behind a completely drained corpse.

The Manananggal is a hideous and frightening creature - usually female - that will sever its upper torso from its lower half and spring into the night with giant bat-like wings. It uses its long, proboscis tongue to penetrate the hearts of its victims and suck the blood straight from the source. It is said that during this time of hunting and feeding, the lower half of the Manananggal is vulnerable and it can be killed by pouring salt on the open wound where the upper half separated. Its name comes from the Tagalog word Tanggal, which means "to remove" or "to separate".

And, of course, we already mentioned The Strigoi - cursed spirits or beings that have returned from the grave. They are said to receive sustenance and vitality from the blood of the living and are imbued with the ability to change form and become invisible.

All these ancient demons and creatures share common similarities: an appetite and even a *need* for blood, aversion to light (especially the sun), hunting at night, using seduction and beauty to lure their victims, shape-shifting, flight, etc. and ALL these came before the first known vampire… Jure Grando Alilovic

Seriously people… Is this book not the most amazing, most awesome, most well-written and researched book on legend and lore ever?

The Original Gangsters

Although, Alilovic and Paole are the FIRST of what we know today as "vampire", they are far from the most famous. I would venture to say that Vlad Tepes would take that honor, though it is widely disputed as to whether or not that would still be the case had it not been for Bram Stoker - but more on that later.

Vlad Tepes, or Vlad the Impaler was the 15th-century ruler of Wallachia in Romania. He was born to Vlad Dracul in 1428. Dracul was the name his father was given after becoming a member of the Order of the Dragon, which was a high-ranking military order. Dracula is the genitive form of Dracul. The "a" was added as a "son of". So, Dracula was the "son of" Dracul. Vlad was known for his brutality and cruelty. It is said that during his reign he slaughtered tens of thousands in battle and those were the lucky ones! Those that survived or were taken prisoner were impaled alive all about Vlad's homeland. It is said that Dracula would often dine in the presence of his impaled enemies and enjoy their cries of pain during supper. He would often soak his bread in the blood of the impaled as he dined and as they died.

Elizabeth Báthory is another vampire OG. Though she is less well-known, she was just as cruel and heartless as Dracula. Bathory was a noblewoman from the House of Bathory. They owned land in the Kingdom of Hungary, which is now separated into Hungary,

Slovakia, and Romania. Bathory tortured and murdered over 600 young girls and women between 1590 and 1610. She began by killing girls of the lesser gentry who were sent to her to learn courtly etiquette. These girls soon began to disappear and so, too, did hundreds of others by way of abduction. During her trial, eyewitnesses and physical evidence pointed to cannibalism, torture, and vampirism. It is said that Bathory would eat the flesh from her still-live victims and bathe in their blood… like in a bathtub… a bathtub full of blood… (yikes!) all in an effort to preserve her youth. Her station and wealth prevented her from being executed, though she was immured within the walls of Castle Csejte in upper Hungary and died a short time later.

It is because of these *true* stories and those of Alilovic and Paole that we most often think of the areas surrounding Hungary, Serbia, and Romania as the mecca of vampiric energy. And, while that may be true as evidenced by such classic Gothic works as John William Polidori's *The Vampyre*, Joseph Sheridan Le Fanu's *Carmilla*, and Bram Stoker's *Dracula*, that doesn't mean that the US is devoid of all things vampiric!

America's Most Famous Vampire

Mercy Lena Brown was the daughter of George and Mary Brown, 19th-century farmers whose family was struck with tuberculosis - better known as "consumption" at the time. Consumption was a near-death sentence and greatly feared. Mary (mother) was the first to die, followed by their oldest daughter, Mary Olive. Mercy Lena was next to get sick, then her brother, Edwin. Mercy died, but Edwin continued on. He continued on, but never got any better. In fact, he got much, much worse. Edwin withered away to almost nothing. He was constantly spitting up blood and was so weak that he could hardly walk or talk.

Tuberculosis was one of the top killers of the 18th and 19th centuries and like we said earlier, a near-death sentence, but Edwin didn't die… he just kept withering, shrinking, fading into something *other*. Doctors were able to explain the deaths that took, Mary, Mary Olive, and Mercy Lena, but they could not explain why Edwin was not dead, nor why he was not recovering.

The townsfolk, along with George's remaining family and friends were sure that there was something foul afoot. Oftentimes when death or sickness was unexplainable, curses or the "undead" would be blamed. Reluctantly, George eventually conceded to the exhumation of his wife and 2 daughters, as the townsfolk were convinced that the answer lay within the grave.

On March 17th, 1892 in Exeter, Road Island in a graveyard behind a small Baptist church, the bodies of Mary, Mary Olive, and Mercy were unceremoniously wrenched from the ground. The first two caskets were opened and a congressional sigh of relief was let out, as all that was found there were bones and clothing. All attention then turned to the final coffin - the most recent coffin - the coffin of Mercy Lena Brown.

They found inside the flush face and perfectly intact body of Mercy Brown. There was still blood in her veins and in her heart and she was full of color. Blood spilled from her lips and she seemed to be smiling.

The town doctor, Dr. Metcalf, assured the frightened onlookers that this was completely normal for a body that had been in the frozen ground for less than 2 months, that decay had not yet been able to take over… though he said this with very little conviction. The townsfolk, and even George Brown and his family were so taken aback by this that they immediately began to shout "Vampire! Vampire!" They believed that Mercy was siphoning the life from her brother in much the same way that Paole had done centuries before.

Torches were lit and a pyre was erected in short order. Mercy Brown's body was burned to ash, and then the ashes were brought to poor Edwin and mixed with water. Edwin was forced to drink the vile concoction and told that this would remedy his illness. It did not. Two months later Edwin was buried next to his mother and sister.

This was part of a much larger outbreak of tuberculosis *and* vampirism in the 19th-century known as the New England Vampire Panic. It is told that 19 bodies were exhumed and burned in the tri-state area around this time. You see, medicine didn't have all of the answers back then, and one of the most telling traits of someone with consumption was blood from the mouth. Not only from coughing it up, but small lesions would often appear in the mouth, and when those burst, blood would spill forth. Often times, those lesions would not burst until well after the body was buried. So, if a body was exhumed before decay could kick in, there would or *could* be "evidence" of vampiric activity… blood… where there was none before.

Real-Life Vampires in the US

I know this might not be as sexy as some of the vampires we know and love in classic and modern lore, but what if I were to tell you that right here in the United States, right now, there are over 5,000 real-life vampires.

John Edgar Browning, a doctor who has studied every aspect of vampirism from film, to literature, to real-life recently turned his attention to America's vampire population. This isn't a fad or some created culture. This is real-life… and these are real-life vampires. True, they don't have any special powers like some of the modern vampiric anti-heroes we're familiar with, but they *do* consume blood daily and do so in order to survive.

Browning says that vampirism begins to develop around the time of puberty when an individual would find themselves "drained" or "weak". They discover that the ingestion of human blood, even the slightest bit, would provide a boost of energy that they desperately needed. This is called the "awakening" or "coming out of the coffin". Other need to know terms here are: "feed" which is the act of drinking blood, "Elder Vampire" which are those who have been awakened for a longer period of time, and "donor" which are those who willingly give of their own blood.

The New Orleans Vampire Association or NOVA is a local chapter of self-identifying vampires whose purpose is to help other fledgling vampires realize they're true vampiric identities safely and naturally. They are taught how to control their urges and to live a normal life. Browning has stated that these blood urges cannot be controlled and that many need blood to survive. Most vampiric communities keep to themselves and avoid "coming out of the coffin", afraid of the stigma that is no doubt associated with it.

How to Kill a Vampire!

You should know good and well by now that I'm not going to let a chapter like this go without a "How to Kill It" segment!

First and foremost, children… Sunlight! Sunlight will kill a vampire. Let me repeat that: **Sunlight will KILL a vampire**… it WILL NOT turn it all sparkly and glittery. Vampires are not *My Little Ponies* and they are *not* sparkly 22-year-olds playing high school.

Next, is a wooden stake… it can be any kind of wood here, folks, just make sure it's a stake, not a stick, and make sure one side is way sharper than the other. Other than that, just make sure you hit the heart. The key here is keeping the fanged fiend from healing… and you do that by hitting the heart.

Ok, ok… I'm going to let you in on a little secret here - it doesn't matter if it's a wooden stake… it could be an iron stake, a concrete stake, a stake made out of bone… the point here is that it is a stake. The original vampires were staked through the heart *inside* their coffins… they were staked *to* their coffins or to the ground. We're suckers for tradition and traditionally it was a wooden stake… most likely because wood is relatively easy to come by and it's pretty easy to get sharp quickly. But honestly, you could use a knife as long as it was big enough and you can put enough force behind it.

Third - Take the head and watch it burn!! This option does involve 2 steps, so for expediency it may not be at the top of your list, but for style points… you can't go wrong. The rule of cool definitely applies here. You can be as creative as you want to be, just make sure that A. The head comes completely off and B. That the fire is hot! This goes back to the not letting it heal thing. The head is severed from the body. Good. But what's to keep it from attaching right back on?!!? Fire! Fire will cauterize the wound and not allow reattachment. Now this will work for other appendages too, arms, legs, fingers, toes… whatever, but we're' talking about killing it, not maiming it.

And on the subject of maiming, garlic, holy water, a crucifix… cute… you wanna piss it off, load up your duffle with some cloves, a water gun, and a cross… these things will slow it down, they will hurt it, but they will *not* kill it.

If you want the **vampire** dead and *you* alive - sunlight, a stake through the heart, or decapitation and fire… some might argue silver here… ok, great argue away… but A. Do you know who you're talking to? And B… the only way silver will kill and not maim is if it's through the heart, and we already established that anything sharp will do here… it's called a stake, and its option #2… so save yourself the money and quit arguing with me.

Whew… ok… I think that's it!

I'm sorry I got a little worked up there, but I get really fired up when people argue with me…

CHAPTER 9

The Pope Lick Monster

What started out as a day of adventure and romance quickly turned into one of tragedy and death.

David Knee and Roquel Bain had just begun dating. They were young, athletic, audacious and in love. Knee was a world-class martial arts instructor and criminal justice student. He was also working on his pilot's license. Bain was a surgical assistant and a mother of a young boy named River. She was known as "Rocky" to her friends and co-workers due to her "never die" attitude and fearlessness. She was kind and welcoming. She even had a group of "popular unpopulars" that she would often invite outsiders or outcasts to join, ensuring that *no one* felt left out. They had their whole lives ahead of them and were ready to take on the world... *and* the Pope Lick Monster. Unfortunately, the curse of the infamous Kentucky Goatman changed all that.

"It's just so sad - a very pretty young girl who had her life in front of her," the deputy coroner told the local newspaper. "It's just so preventable."

On April 23rd, 2016 Knee and Bain booked a 2-hour paranormal tour in Louisville, Kentucky. Both being avid hikers and both having a love and curiosity for all things supernatural, they decided on a detour to kill time before the tour started. Bain had seen stories of a preternatural beast that made its home on an old trestle bridge in the Fisherville area of Louisville.

"When I saw that bridge, the thing looked so rickety. I thought it was out of service." Knee told officials during their investigation. "It was Russian roulette to try and walk across that."

But when Bain extended her hand, eyes full of encouragement and promise, Knee took hold.

The dirt and gravel path was overgrown. It was apparent that there had not been much foot-traffic here for some time. But there had been some, at least… because despite the numerous "no trespassing" signs and the 6-foot fence topped with barbed-wire, there was an easily-enough perceivable path through the growth leading to a weak point in the fence that one could easily push through.

Before they knew it, Bain and Knee were standing at the edge of a 100-foot tall, 742-foot-long trestle bridge.

Bain regaled Knee with tales of the Pope Lick Monster that she had seen online, including a 1988 short film, and while she was not convinced that the monster was "real", she was eager to do everything in her power to prove it one way or the other.

Knee later said. "We only dated a month, but I've never been impacted by anyone as much as her. She was one in a million."

Bain had read that one must cross the bridge in its entirety, East to West in order to summon the Goatman, so that's exactly what they did.

About half-way across the Pope Lick Trestle the old bridge began to shake... the iron rails began to rattle. A train was coming. David would later state that they never even heard the train until it was too late.

Knee and Bain began to run but soon realized that they would never make it in time. Knee leaped over the side and wrapped his arms and legs around the metal edge of the structure. He rode out the horrendous event from beneath the bridge, able to walk away with nothing more than a scar on his arm where the train connected with him for just a moment. Bain was not so lucky. She never made it to the safety of the under-bridge. She was struck head-on and thrown off the side of the bridge. Knee was forced to watch her body plummet 100 feet to the ground below.

"Out of the corner of my eye I saw her body go flying," he said. "It's a nightmare waking up each day and realizing it's not a dream."

Was this just sheer bad luck? Was this just another example of what happens when you don't heed the warnings? Or was this the act of the hideous and heinous Kentucky Goatman?

Now let's get down to business… and get learnt about the Pope Lick Monster!

The Legend

The Pope Lick Monster is a half-man, half-goat creature that is reported to inhabit the Fisherville area under the Norfolk Southern Railroad Trestle that spans Floyds Fork Creek in Louisville, Kentucky. The trestle in this case is a metal-framework elevated bridge used by the Norfolk Southern Railroad. The Norfolk Southern Railroad has been in business a long time, since 1827 in fact, and has seen its fair share of death and tragedy. From derailments to switching accidents to suicides, Norfolk Southern has a long and storied history of calamity and misfortune. But that could be said about any railroad or railroad company… I mean, when you have a million tons of speeding metal flying down train tracks that pass through cities and tunnels, over crossroads and bridges… you're bound to have a few accidents.

The devastating catastrophes that plague this particular stretch of railway is not attributed to accidents or felo-de-se, but instead is believed to be caused by the odious creature that haunts it.

This mythical, mysterious, and murderous monster is known as the Pope Lick Monster (named after the area that it is said to dwell) or The Goatman. It is a bi-pedal humanoid beast that is said to stand 6 to 7 feet tall. With the misshapen torso and arms of a man, long and crooked goat legs (complete with cloven hoofs and a tail) and a great horned head in the shape of a goat or sheep. It's easy to see why this creature would be feared simply because of its menacing and sinister visage. But unlike the majority of cryptids - some of which we've already covered - that are content and even *prefer* to leave us well enough alone, this creature is much more akin to the malevolent and vicious Wendigo. It is driven not only by a need to kill, but also a desire to.

This has been proven time and time again, not only by the numerous deaths that have occurred on the Pope Lick Trestle - as recently as May of 2019 when a young girl and her friend, determined to suss out the truth behind this local legend, climbed the scaffold-like structure and began to cross. The girl, 15-year-old Savannah Bright, perished that night and her friend ended up in the ICU for months. Police, parents and neighbors are fed up with and at a loss as to why these deaths keep occurring - why do people still insist on going into these woods and climbing this 100-foot-tall bridge in the middle of the night? - and also by the gruesome unexplained deaths and dismembered bodies that have been found in the area.

The beast is said to have hypnotic powers. It is able to seduce its victims telepathically from any distance, as is the case with David Knee and Roquel Bain. They were from Ohio and ended up victims of the Pope Lick Monster in Louisville, Kentucky. It is said that all it takes is a passing interest, just a spark of fascination and he has you.

He has been referred to as the Siren of Pope Lick.

The History

This obviously refers to the sirens of Homer's *The Odyssey Book XII* where Odysseus encounters beautiful maidens off of the coast of what is now known as Italy, near Naples on the Rocks of Scylla. Homer describes these daughters of Phorcys as dangerous creatures that would lure sailors to their deaths by a beautiful and hypnotizing song. Of course, Odysseus - warned by the sorceress, Circe - was able to endure the sirens' song and survive his encounter by stuffing wax into his ears and tying himself to the mast of his ship as he passed.

The Pope Lick monster may be a variation of siren or at least possess certain similar attributes, as he often lures victims to their deaths by enticing them with the promise of thrills and adventure atop the trestle, only to be killed by a passing train that they do not hear or notice until it's too late.

Although this may seem like an efficient and satisfactory way to kill, and by all accounts it is, it is not the Pope Lick Monster's *only* way to kill, and it may not even be his **preferred** way.

There have been reports of mutilated bodies and severed limbs just randomly appearing around the area. Many of these bodies and limbs are never claimed, but are reported to have been caused by a sharp-edged tool such as an axe or a machete…

In many instances, the creature is described as carrying an axe or hatchet, though this is no ordinary thing. It is speculated that the axe that this Goatman wields is none other than Labrys!

Labrys is the mystical axe that Hephaestus used when he ruptured the head of Zeus to cure him of a great headache. Labrys came down upon the head of Zeus, splitting his headache, and out came a fully grown Athena!

This theory is more than just speculation, though, as it directly ties into the idea that the creature is some long-lost descendant of the Sirens of old.

This is a pretty powerful being for just some random cryptid in the middle of the US… at least that's what I thought... until I did a little more research and started seeing the comparisons between this, The Pope Lick Monster and The Maryland Goatman.

The Maryland Goatman is an axe-wielding, bi-pedal humanoid half-man-half-goat creature that roams the back roads of Beltsville, Maryland.

Ok, so what, just another cryptid... save it for a different chapter, right?

Wrong.

If you do your due diligence here, as I have done, you'll soon find the breadcrumb trail leading to the Lake Worth Monster just outside of Fort Worth, Texas. This monster is, you guessed it, a half-man-half-goat beast that hunts and kills in the Lake Worth and Greer Island area. It is also said to wield an axe and possess hypnotic powers...

So, what do these 3 goatmen have in common outside of the obvious? Well, they are the only 3 axe-wielding bipedal, humanoid goatmen in the United States. Also, if you point out their locations on the US map, you will get a near straight line from Lake Worth, Texas through Louisville, Kentucky all the way to Maryland... a straight line.

So what, right?

Wrong again, fool!

That straight line just happens to land smack-dab on one of the most prevalent ley-lines in the United States!

Your Money's Worth

A ley-line is a mystical, magical line between two or more points that carry with it earth energies from sacred and important sites or locations such as Stonehenge, the Egyptian Pyramids, and the Great Wall of China. The powerful "lines" are all across the globe and they are all connected by the energies and magics of the earth.

Now the particular line that these three goatmen all seem to touch is special because it actually *crosses* the Pacific Ocean and connects to a sacred place of worship on the Temple Mount in Jerusalem. This location will come up again, as I discuss it in great detail in my Friday the 13th chapter.

> The true beginning of Friday the 13th came in 1307 when King Philip the IV of France had his officers arrest hundreds of the Knights Templar! The Knights Templar or simply, the Templars were (or some believe, still are) a military order established in 1119 at Temple Mount in Jerusalem. They were also known as The Poor Fellow-Soldiers of Christ and of the Temple of Solomon or the Order of Solomon's Temple. They were among the most skillful fighters and

heavily associated with the Crusades. That and rumored initiation practices along with many, many secrets made them a feared and often mistrusted organization. King Phillip the IV was in great debt and leaped upon the opportunity to play upon the public's growing mistrust of the Templars while at the same time ridding himself of the nuisance. He had them arrested, tortured until they gave false testimony and then burned at the stake. He did all this under the guise of eliminating a criminal organization, but really it was to eliminate his debt… and his enemies.

One of the main atrocities that the Templars were accused of was worshipping the half-goat-half-man god Baphomet. Baphomet is known as the Sabbatic Goat and represents the equilibrium of opposites. It represents balance, but is steeped in pagan ritual and religion. The name Baphomet comes up multiple times in the recorded confessions that were forced and tortured out of the Templars when they were tried for apostasy. Part of the initiation rites of the order was apparently the sacrifice to and worship of Baphomet.

According to Jules Michelet in his *History of France* - "all the provinces, they had idols, that is to say, heads, some of which had three faces, others but one; sometimes, it was a human skull … That in their assemblies, and especially in their grand chapters, they worshiped the idol as a god, as their savior, saying that this head could save them, that it bestowed on the order all its wealth, made the trees flower, and the plants of the earth to sprout forth."

An ancient text was found near this site with the words "Adore this head—this head is your god and your Mahomet." inscribed within. Mahomet is the Old French word for Baphomet.

Baphomet is the titular "goat's head" that we so often think of when we think of the occult and its pentagram or goat-head. He often appears in tarot or items associated with the witches sabbath as a goat with a candle between its horns according to medieval witchcraft records.

Now, I know you're incredibly tired of reading by now and are super bored with this exacerbating tangential nonsense, but bear with me a moment or 2 longer… I promise, we're getting there…

- That was sarcasm. This stuff is gold!

According to Ancient Greek Historian, Herodotus, Baphomet is the Goat of Mendes or Goat-god and is depicted with a goat's face and legs. This Goat of Mendes is a pivotal figure within the cosmology of Thelema.

That should sound familiar, and here is where I need you all to hold on to your hats, boys and girls… The mystical order of Thelema was created by none other than the one and only Aleister Crowley. Yes, *that* Aleister Crowley - "the wickedest man in the world" Aleister Crowley. In Book 4 of his magnum opus, *Magick*, Crowley says this of Baphomet, that he is "the hieroglyph of arcane perfection" which resembles balance. "What occurs above so reflects below, or As above so below"

Baphomet is a powerful deity to be sure, and he also has been known to wield a mighty glaive named Heart Cleaver. What is a glaive you may ask... it is an axe.

Tada!

Baphomet utilizes the power of the ley-lines to travel from the place of its birth on the Temple Mount in Jerusalem across the ocean to the United States and takes on the forms of these local legendary cryptids. The pagan god of balance and ancient Greek deity, Baphomet - imbued with ancient powers of mind-altering, telepathic seduction and carrying the god-splitter, Heart Cleaver - roams the backwoods of the rural united states. There is no other explanation for the power and brutality that is regularly on display at the Pope Lick Trestle. But it isn't just here in Kentucky.

We've already established that he is able to use the ley-lines to travel between Kentucky, Texas, Maryland and back home to Jerusalem, but if we follow the ley-lines and the trails of broken and bloodies corpses, my hunch is that we would find even more evidence of

Baphomet's activities and even *more* urban legends about the malicious and menacing... Goatman.

CHAPTER 10

Bloody Mary

Subject: Death by Bloody Mary

THIS EMAIL HAS BEEN CURSED - ONCE OPENED YOU MUST SEND IT.

You are now cursed. You must send this on, or you will be killed. Tonight at 12:00am, by Bloody Mary. This is no joke. So, don't think you can quickly get out of it and delete it now because Bloody Mary will come to you if you do not send this on. She will slit your throat and your wrists and pull your eyeballs out with a fork. And then hang your dead corpse in your bedroom cupboard or put you under your bed. What's your parents going to do when they find you dead? Won't be funny then, will it? Don't think this is a fake and it's all put on to scare you because you're wrong, so very wrong. Want to hear of some of the sad, sad people who lost their lives or have been seriously hurt by this email?

CASE ONE –

Annalise [Surname Removed]: She got this email. Rubbish she thought. She deleted it. And now, Annalise is dead.

CASE TWO –

Louise [Surname Removed]: She sent this to only 4 people and when she woke up in the morning her wrists had deep lacerations on each. Luckily there was no pain felt, though she is scarred for life.

CASE THREE –

Thomas [Surname Removed]: He sent this to 5 people. Big mistake. That night Thomas was lying in his bed watching T.V. The clock shows 12:01 am. The T.V mysteriously flickered off and Thomas's bedroom lamp flashed on and off several times. It went pitch black, Thomas looked to the left of him, and there she was, Bloody Mary standing in white rags. Blood everywhere with a knife in her hand then disappeared. The biggest fright of Thomas's life.

Warning... NEVER look in a mirror and repeat - 'Bloody Mary. Bloody Mary. Bloody Mary... I KILLED YOUR SON' Is it the end for you tonight! YOU ARE NOW CURSED

We strongly advise you to send this email on. It is seriously NO JOKE. We don't want to see another life wasted. IT'S YOUR CHOICE… WANNA DIE TONIGHT? If you send this email to…

NO PEOPLE – You're going to die.

1-5 PEOPLE – You're going to either get hurt or get the biggest fright of your life.

5-15 PEOPLE – You will bring your family bad luck and someone close to you will die.

15-25 OR MORE PEOPLE – You are safe from Bloody Mary

This was a chain letter that was sent out over and over again in the infant stages of email… Circa 1994. It could show up on your work email or at your AOL account. There was really no telling when or where you would get it, but you were definitely going to get it one way or another.

This was often many people's first encounter with Mary, but for the unfortunate… it wasn't the last.

It was a hoax, of course… but why Bloody Mary?

The Legend

Bloody Mary, Bloody Mary, Bloody Mary.

A dimly lit room, a mirror… and usually a number of giggling teens or pre-teens all gathered in so closely that even if she did appear, she wouldn't have any room in the mirror as all that reflective real estate would be taken up by pushing and pulling adolescent exuberance, all trying to catch a glimpse… but a glimpse of what?

The ghostly spectre of their future love? A demonic she-devil portending their end? A phantom skull floating in the ether, an auger of things to come? A broken and bloodied revenant cradling a lost child? A jealous and hateful witch? A Heart-Broken and mutilated crash victim?

Yes.

The legend says that if you stare into a mirror in a dimly lit room and call out the name of Bloody Mary 3 times, she will appear in the mirror. She may be benevolent or she may break through the glass and eat your face. And this isn't a Santa Claus type thing where if you're good you get a good gift and if you're bad you get coal… it's a toss-up. No one knows which Mary you're gonna get until it's too late. And let me tell you, more often than not, you're not gonna get the good one.

Why would anyone want to summon Bloody Mary? Who is she? Where did she come from? And why a mirror?

Let's start with the last first.

Catoptromancy, also known as enoptromancy or captromancy is the art of divination through the use of a mirror.

Pausanias, a great Greek traveler and chronicler born in 110 AD and known to be the first to document the ruins of Troy, says this of the origins of Catoptromancy:

> "Before the Temple of Ceres at Patras, there was a fountain, separated from the temple by a wall, and there was an oracle, very truthful, not for all events, but for the sick only. The sick person let down a mirror, suspended by a thread till its base touched the surface of the water, having first prayed to the goddess and offered incense. Then, looking into the mirror, he saw the presage of death or recovery, according as the face appeared fresh and healthy, or of a ghastly aspect."

Here is where we can safely say that the origin of, at least the mirror aspect of, Bloody Mary took root. Let's fast forward a number of centuries and see how this act of catoptromancy has evolved.

Sometime in the 16th-century a form of the Catoptromancy ritual was taught to young women as they were seeking guidance on marriage prospects. They were instructed to invoke the fates by walking up the stairs in a dimly lit home holding a candle and a mirror. They would do this backwards. As they ascended the steps slowly, in the dark, they would focus all their attention and intention on the mirror. The flickering flame from the candle would cast shadows to dancing across the walls in a maniacal show of chaos and spontaneity. As they regarded the mirror with complete focus, they would catch a glimpse of their future husband's face. There was a possibility here, though, that they would *anger* the spirits and see instead a floating, disembodied skull. This was a portend to their death. It is often thought that this was the Grim Reaper himself coming to mark the young women as his.

So, if this is where the mirror comes into play, where does the "Mary" come from?

Mary Tudor

The most closely associated historical being to the legend of Bloody Mary is, no doubt, Mary Tudor. Mary Tudor was the daughter of King Henry VIII and his first wife, Catherine of Aragon. Mary's life was not an easy one, especially for a "princess". She was the only heir to the throne of England, but this *true* claim was constantly threatened, along with her life, as King Henry VIII's multiple marriages - in an attempt to produce a male heir - pushed her further and further from his graces and the throne. Mary's mother was exiled and Mary would never see her again. King Henry then married Anne Boleyn (Catherine's maid-of-honor) who was beheaded for treason, incest, and of course, not bearing a son. It is believed that Anne's charges and subsequent execution were set up by one of her own former confidants, Thomas Cromwell.

Cromwell and Boleyn were close. In fact, it was Cromwell who comforted Boleyn when King Henry began to court his future wife while still married to her. There is no motive for Cromwell's betrayal, but it is said that in the last days of Anna Boleyn's life, Cromwell and Mary became quite close. Shortly after, Boleyn was accused.

Mary's father (the king) would go on to have 6 wives, divorcing or beheading them as he went. All in search of a male heir and political supremacy. This did little to improve his already tenuous standing with the Roman Catholic Church and led to him being excommunicated by Pope Paul III.

Throughout all of this, Mary was living in constant fear for her life and dealing with melancholia, depression, intense menstrual pains and irregular cycles resulting in massive blood loss at times, rendering her weak and near death. Despite all of this, including being declared legally illegitimate by Parliament at the behest of Anne Boleyn, Mary took the throne in 1553. During her short life she would become known as Bloody Mary due to the vicious and violent persecution she wrought upon the Protestants - a result of her father's excommunication. She would have men and women bound and either burned alive or beheaded.

Mary's tragic and brutal life, short as it was, is a well-known historical account.

But what comes next - the lesser known more private details of her woeful existence - may help connect her to the Bloody Mary of urban legend.

Immediately after taking the throne, Mary took a husband - Philip of Spain. Phillip was more interested in power and position than marriage but that did not stop Mary from claiming what was rightfully hers. Desperate for her father's attention, broken from years of abuse and resentment, Mary *would* produce a male heir to the throne. She *would* earn her father's love. It is said that Mary would "lavish all her frustrated emotions on" Phillip and eventually she conceived! A mere 2 months after her marriage Mary was with child.

Mary's pregnancy was a joyous announcement to be sure! She would spend hours in front of a mirror, watching her body change. But that joy soon turned into scrutiny and suspicion as Mary's due date came and went. Her stomach and breasts had grown, she had that glow that only shines from a woman with child, but no child ever came. There was no miscarriage. Mary's stomach and breasts began to shrink and she began to take on a more sickly and sober visage. It was determined that this was a punishment from God and ushered in the Marian Persecutions.

Mary's is quite possibly the most notorious case of supposed pseudocyesis ever recorded. Pseudocyesis or "phantom pregnancy" is a disorder where women (or even men) believe so whole-heartedly that they are pregnant that they experience *all* the symptoms, both physical and mental, of an *actual* pregnancy - except there is no baby. Such a rare and devastating delusion is *still* an enigma to scientists and doctors but is often the result of catastrophic abuse either mental, physical or sexual, all of which Mary was intimately familiar.

Years later, Mary would again announce herself with child, and show all the physical and mental symptoms associated, only to discover 9 months later that she had instead entered menopause and would never conceive.

It is said that upon receiving this news, she broke every mirror in the castle so that she would never again be able to see herself in them.

Mary Worth

Mary Worth lived on Old Wagon Road in Chicago, Illinois in the middle of the 19th century. She lived in the forest in a small cottage and sold herbal remedies, dyes, and potions. She seemed kind enough and was often asked to speak with the dead or with animals when a crime was unsolvable… Oh, and she was a witch. She was old and seemed harmless enough, although the townsfolk would avoid her, for fear of being cursed and because any who would associate with her or use one of her potions would be shunned and accused of associating with a devil.

A short time after the Civil War, young girls began to go missing. Not only girls from town, but girls from all across Chicago. Over the course of weeks, with no end in sight for the disappearances, people began to get suspicious of Mary. It is reported that she began to be noticeably more agile and youthful. Even her gray hair and wrinkled face had begun to take on a more vernal appearance.

Eventually, and with little else to go on, the townsfolk gathered enough courage to confront Mary. At first, they were deterred by the conviction in Mary's denial, but after a while, fed up and with no other leads, the townsfolk returned. What they found when they stormed her quiet little cottage was the stuff of pure nightmare.

The broken bodies of the missing girls were strewn about a large underground cellar directly beneath Mary's home. Not only that, but it was discovered that during the Civil War, Mary had been harboring runaways in her home, promising them safety, only to slaughter them. Mary had tortured and killed hundreds in her rituals. It was discovered that she was involved in the slave trade and had used that to fund her witchcraft.

So disgusted and furious were the people of the town - the mothers and fathers of the missing girls - that they took the law into their own hands right then and there. They dragged Mary out into the forest and hanged her until she died.

It was improper to bury a witch on sacred ground, so instead of burying Mary in the cemetery, they dug a shallow grave near the cabin and tossed her corpse into it, along with a broken mirror that they had found in the cellar. The mirror was to remind Mary for all eternity of the atrocities that she had committed while here on earth. The grave was topped with a large stone and Mary was forgotten.

A little more than 100 years later, the forest was torn down, along with the remains of a dilapidated little cabin, and a subdivision was built. The construction crew gathered stones from the excavation and used them in paving walkways for the homes. One home is said to have experienced nothing but bad luck since the time it was built. Cracks in the foundation, dishes would inexplicably crash to the floor. It even burned to the ground... twice. The house was never rebuilt after that. It is said that the stone of Mary's grave from all those years ago was one of the stones used in the pathway of the house and that Mary was the reason for all the misfortune there.

The Miller's Daughter

There is a story told of a miller and his wife who lost their daughter to a witch in the woods. The miller's wife had recently purchased a salve from the witch for a very bad toothache. The miller did not have enough money to pay for the salve outright but was assured by the witch that she would collect at a later time. He was told to go home to his wife and daughter and to give his wife the salve.

That night the miller was awakened by a horrible scream. He ran to the front door to see his wife running out into the fields. A little further on was their daughter, floating out towards the woods. The miller grabbed his pistol and ran after his wife and daughter. They screamed for her to stop, to come back, but she was entranced. She could not hear them. She was being pulled to the forest by an unseen force. The miller noticed an eerie, unnatural blue light coming from the tree line, more specifically, from a large dead oak tree. He saw that standing beside that oak tree was the witch from the woods. She was grinning wildly, hand outstretched toward his daughter.

The miller fired all 6 rounds at the witch and then continued running. He caught up with his wife and they soon made it to the tree line, but by that time the witch and their daughter were gone. He immediately ran to the large oak and found 5 marks made by the rounds he had fired. He did not see the 6th but he found blood on the ground next to the tree.

They roused the village and made their way to the witch's cabin. There was no trace of the witch, but the miller found his daughter lying dead at the threshold of the witch's home, a single bullet wound in her chest. Laying atop the miller's daughter was a mirror and written on it in blood was the word "Murderer". The miller stared into the mirror, tears in his eyes, accusation written in blood and saw the countenance of the witch staring back at him... The witch's name was Mary Worth.

Years later, the miller found Mary. He had never given up searching for her and had, in fact, dedicated his life to finding and killing her. He got his chance one fateful night as he stalked her in her new dwelling. So many times before he had been so close, but she had always evaded him. She had always been just one step ahead. But this time, instead of lead bullets, he had silver, and instead of a revolver he carried a Henry repeater.

The Miller caught her in the hip with his first shot as she ran. She fell to the ground screaming and cursing. With zero hesitance and zero remorse the miller plunged a stake deep into her chest. She writhed and thrashed as he dragged her back to her home. He doused her and her home in gasoline and lit her on fire. She screamed as she burned, cursing him and the village that they were in. Her last curse, and maybe her most unrelenting, was that if any would ever summon her by calling her name and staring into a mirror she would be loosed again and exact her revenge.

After the witch had died, the townsfolk came to see what they could discover. The miller told them his story and was not surprised to hear that many of them had similar ones. They began to search the property and before long found a path in the woods leading to an alcove deep in the forest. There they found rows and rows of unmarked graves… each grave held the body of a missing little girl.

Modern Mary

There are fringe theories that Elizabeth Bathory is the original Bloody Mary, but I have chosen not to include her here, because A. She is *definitely* one of the most notorious original vampires of all time, and nobody gets to be an OG of two Urban Legends. And B. We already talked about her in our Vampire chapter… Oh and C. I just don't believe for a second that she has anything to do with Bloody Mary.

There is one modern story that I'd like to take a little closer look at and although I know this is more of an urban legend *inside* of an urban legend… an urban Turducken, if you will… I think it bears taking a closer look.

There was a beautiful young woman not too long ago who was in a terrible car crash. This left her face horrendously mangled and her body mutilated. Before this, it is said that she was very vain and would often spend her afternoons in front of a mirror admiring the beauty in her own reflection. After the accident, her reflection became the bane of her existence. Every mirror that she saw she would destroy. Eventually, she began to lose her mind. She started losing touch with the people around her and with reality. One day, she decided that she could no longer bear to ever see her reflection again, so she walked *into* the mirror and terrorized her victims from within. This young woman's name was Mary.

So, there you have it… the history… or *Herstory* (pause for dramatic effect…) of Bloody Mary.

Chapter 11

The Abominable Yeti
And Shambhala

The yeti is said to stand 8 to 10.5 feet tall. It has a coat of brown, reddish or black hair and resembles a large ape or man. It is believed to have been popularized by the Sherpa people who reside in eastern Tibet in the Nepal and Himalya regions. For 700 years the Sherpa people have lived in the Himalayan Mountains, though they also live in China, Bhutan, and the United States. Pre-dating even the Buddhist beliefs that the Sherpa people hold to, the Yeti or Yah-Teh or even Meh-Teh was worshipped by the Lepcha people as the God of the Hunt and was known simply as the "glacier being" at the time.

Through spoken word and folklore passed from generation to generation, the yeti proved itself a mighty force to the Sherpa and Lepcha people. Lore is often used as a way to impart wisdom or continue tradition and so it was with the yeti. Over time, however, the yeti went from a vehicle for these stories and traditions to the story itself.

Shiva Dakhal published a book of short stories, a collection of yeti lore, wherein the yeti is always a point of danger and trouble. In these tales the yeti is a villainous and vile fiend - murderous and barbaric. There are 12 stories in all and they do not paint the yeti in a positive light whatsoever. But, where did this image of the yeti come from? When and why did the yeti go from mascot to murderer, from friend to foe... or did it?

The Proof

In 1921, Lieutenant-Colonel Charles Howard-Bury, headed up the 1921 British Mount Everest Reconnaissance Expedition, which was formed to explore access to Mount Everest, to chart accessible routes for ascending the mountain, and – if possible – attempt the first ascent of the mountain - the highest in the world. Nepal was closed off to foreigners at this time, so the party had to approach from Tibet. It was a northeastern route up the Kharta Glacier and across the Lhakpa La pass. The expedition was successful as a recon mission, but they were not able to breach the summit of Everest from that direction.

Lieutenant-Colonel Charles Howard-Bury wrote a book on his adventures during the expedition and in it he recounts his findings near the Kharta Glacier at 21,000 ft where he discovered large prints in the snow. He says in his book that they "were probably caused by a large 'loping' grey wolf, which in the soft snow formed double tracks rather like those of a bare-footed man". Howard-Bury's Sherpa guides "at once volunteered that the tracks must be that of 'The Wild Man of the Snows', to which they gave the name 'metoh-kangmi'."

"Metoh" means "man-bear" and "Kang-mi" means "snowman".

Later, another explorer by the name of Henry Newman chronicled his own adventures in the Himalayas and noted that he, too, came across large, unexplainable tracks. He referenced Howard-Bury's experiences with his own while penning his story to submit to the papers under the pen-name, Kim, but misinterpreted or mistranslated Howard-Bury's use of the word "Metoh" to mean "filthy" instead of "man-bear". Newman, disliked the word "filthy" and out of artistic license changed it to "Abominable". So, the papers got a story about an "abominable snowman" instead of a "man-bear Snowman". Thus, the Yeti became the Abominable Snowman.

This was about the time that the yeti, or the abominable snowman, began to gain a wider audience, but was not the first mention of it outside of the indigenous mountain peoples.

James Prinsep's *Journal of the Asiatic Society of Bengal* was published in 1832 and in it was noted explorer, B. H. Hodgeson's experience in northern Nepal. Hodgeson and his guides reported that they came into contact with a large bi-pedal beast with long, dark fur. Hodgeson would later argue that this was an orangutan, but without solid evidence - even then - the imaginations of the readers pointed to something more mysterious, something more cryptic... the yeti.

The legend of the yeti really took off when, in the early 20th century, not too long after Howard-Bury's expedition, the borders of Nepal were opened and would-be climbers from all across the globe flocked to the Himalayas to attempt to climb Everest.

A photographer by the name of N. A. Tombazi, who also happened to be a member of the Royal Geographical Society, reported this in 1925 of his encounters: "Unquestionably, the figure in outline was exactly like a human being, walking upright and stopping occasionally to pull at some dwarf rhododendron bushes. It showed up dark against the snow, and as far as I could make out, wore no clothes."

In 1951, photographer Eric Shipton took photos of yeti prints that are still being studied and scrutinized to this day. These prints are considered by some to be the single most telling evidence of the yeti's existence.

In 1954, leader of the Daily Mail Snowman Expedition, John Angelo Jackson, found symbolic paintings of the yeti in a Khumbu monastery. He would later document many unexplained and unidentifiable footprints in the surrounding areas.

Later that year the Daily Mail obtained what they reported as yeti fur from another monastery in the area. The hair was analyzed and tested by Professor Frederic Wood Jones, an expert in human and comparative anatomy. Professor Jones compared the analysis to every known specimen from that area and could not identify the tuft of fur.

Sławomir Rawicz states in his book, *The Long Walk* that he and his party were halted for hours as 2 bi-pedal snow creatures blocked their path. They did not attempt to harm the group, but neither did they seem eager to allow them passage.

Later, feces and a hand - both from a yeti - were discovered and sent to the United States for analysis. It was determined that the feces and hand were **not** from any known species! The yeti articles were sent back to the Nepalese government and seemed to be enough evidence that the US declared 3 rules for any US citizen that would being attempting to climb Everest or find a yeti: 1. Obtain a Nepalese permit, 2. Do not harm the Yeti except in self-defense, and 3. Let the Nepalese government approve any news reporting on the animal's discovery. This decree was broken by none other than legendary actor James (Jimmy) Stewart. When on location, Stewart smuggled away the yeti hand, hiding the it in his luggage.

The reports and stories go on and on. In fact, in 2011 a group of scientists and anthropologists from all over the world gathered in Russia and determined that they had "95% evidence" of the yeti's existence.

But what is it? This mountainous cryptid is real. We know that, but what is it? Is it a cousin to bigfoot? Is it a large ape? A bear?
And what does it want? Is it dangerous? Is it lonely?

Is it magical?

Ever heard of Shambhala? Could these cryptic snow monsters be the key to finding the lost paradise of Shangri-La?

Should we be afraid? Should we leave it alone?

Shambhala

Marco Polo? Heard of him? He is known the world over for his travels both on land and sea. These adventures are chronicled in the book *The Million* or *The Travels of Marco Polo*, also known as the *Oriente Poliano* (the Orient of the Polos) and *The Description of the World*. Marco Polo learned about trading and traveling from his father Niccolò and his uncle Maffeo. He journeyed extensively throughout Asia, returning to Venice 24 years later. Polo was imprisoned during the war between Venice and Genoa and dictated his stories to a cellmate who wrote them down for him. Polo married and had 3 children after his release and became one of the most famous merchants and traders in history. He died in 1324.

What you may not know about Marco Polo and what was definitely *not* included in the published versions of his chronicles was that he was one of, if not the first and only, outsider to ever have, not only found the hidden entrance to Shambhala, but set foot in the wondrous kingdom!

Marco Polo was the first to discover the city as he and his caravan were returning from Kublai Khan's court. The entrance to Shambhala is hidden inside an abandoned Surya Samadhi monastery in Tibet and guarded by monstrous creatures. Polo was able to escape with his life and, it is said, even a portion of the lost city's treasures!

In a series of Buddhist texts known as the *Kalachakra Tantra* there is mention of a mythical kingdom called Shambhala. This land is to be the birthplace of Kalki or Kalkin - the 10th and final avatar of Vishnu - who will usher in the new age. Shambhala is to be ruled by the future Buddha Maitreya. This magical kingdom and eschatological prophecy were introduced in the 11th century when King Manjusri Kirti ruled over a kingdom of 300,000 followers of the ancient Mleccha religion. Of those 300,000 followers, some chose to cling to Surya Samadhi or "solar worship" and worshiped the Sun rather than convert to Kalachakra or "Wheel of Time"

Buddhism.

The King expelled 20,000 people from his domain who held fast to this solar worship. The king soon realized that these exiled few were the wisest and best of his people and that he was in need of them. He asked them to return to his kingdom. Some returned. Others did not. Those who did not return are said to have established the wondrous city of Shambhala.

Shambhala remained a Tibetan Buddhist secret for centuries, but eventually word of this hidden paradise spread to other parts of the world. In 1924 a clandestine expedition made up of Soviet Secret Police, cryptologists and writers from the Soviet communist party made its way to the Tibetan mountains in an attempt to discover Shambhala and harness its rumored powers to create the "perfect communist human beings". There were even labs set up to experiment with Buddhist principles and practices to accomplish this goal.

The expedition was unsuccessful, but not for the reason you may have thought… many would assume that the failure was due to never having found the secret entrance to Shambhala, but that is incorrect. The mission failed because the entire expedition disappeared. There was frantic radio chatter calling for aid and describing giant humanoid beasts that were well organized and stronger than anything that the group could handle. The group was never heard from again, and never again has anyone come close to finding the lost city.

It is believed that the beasts reported over the broken radio calls were yeti. It is also believed that the yeti were... and still *are*, the few Manjusri Kirti followers who did *not* return to King Manjusri Kirti. Those followers were transformed by Surya Samadhi into the guardians of Shambhala... into Yeti.

In the 1933 novel *Lost Horizon*, British author James Hilton describes a "Paradise on Earth" hidden in a Tibetan valley. This legendary paradise is known as Shangri-La. Shangri-La is a hidden oasis, a Himalayan utopia where time stands still. This is largely believed to be because this is the sanctuary of the Tree of Life or in some translations, the Fountain of Youth. It is a harmonious paradise isolated from the rest of the world. It is also rumored to be located in the Ngari Prefecture - which is where the entrance to Shambhala is believed to be. It is on the peaks of Mount Kailash, where these two legendary cities reside. It is also believed that these two cities, these two legendary and mystic plains: Shambhala and Shangri-La - are one and the same... and that they are forever watched over by Surya Samadhi sentinels... The Yeti.

Yeti Sanctuary

There is a country, a kingdom, nestled deep in the Himalayas called Bhutan. It is a tiny kingdom set in between India and Tibet and is known as "the last Shangri-La" due to its unspoiled natural habitat. The mountain ranges with their snow-covered ridges, sprawling fields and foothills flush with flora and fauna - vivid greens and blues and purples… Its dense forests, a wooded bastion for numerous creatures large and small… the ancient steeples and hidden roofs of centuries-old monasteries… The kingdom of Bhutan is truly an oasis without equal.

The Bhutanese government manages the Sakteng Wildlife Sanctuary, a 253-square-mile sanctuary specifically to protect and cultivate the habitat of the yeti. This massive environment protects a number of endemic species including the eastern blue pine and the black-rumped magpie, and is about 500,000 times as big as Manchester Cathedral, just to give you an idea of the size and scope of the place!

The Kingdom of Bhutan believes so strongly in, not only the existence of the Yeti, but in its contribution to the local ecosystem and its innate calling to protect Shambhala, that it has dedicated a large percentage of its national budget to this sanctuary. They also believe that the yeti, known here as the migoi is as mystical as its legend implies. Bhutan migoi experts claim that the yeti stands just over 8 feet tall, walks backward to evade trackers and can even make itself invisible! Which would, of course, illuminate for us the mystery as to why so few people have actually seen one.

This fascination with and dedication to a mountainous cryptid that most of the world sees as fanciful at best, may be frowned upon by many countries around the world, but the King of Bhutan has said that he is more interested in the Gross National Happiness rather than the Gross National Product of his small kingdom

Encounters

According to The Serbian Times Reporter (TheSerbianTimes.com), Andrey Lyubchenko claimed that he came face to face with an Abominable Snowman just recently. He states that the yeti posed for him and allowed Andrey to draw his picture on birch bark. Andrey further claims that the pair even "spoke" to one another.

> 'It happened so unexpectedly and fast that I had no time to get scared,' he is quoted as saying. 'There was a clear feeling that this was a thinking creature, I felt he was trying to 'talk' to me.
>
> 'The Yeti was about two and a half metres tall, with thick, dark, brown hair like a bear's - but a lot softer. He was holding a wooden stick, with bits of hair wrapped around it. But the main thing was his eyes, they were just like light-coloured human eyes.'
>
> 'I went out onto a small open patch, and

there I felt the Yeti's presence. I turned back and saw him standing up, deeper in the woods, not going away… and trying to communicate'.

Andrey explained: 'I am saying 'He' because of the shape of his body, his gestures, his behaviours were clearly male. His body was very toned, with lots of visible muscles. His hands and feet were proportionate to his body, the same way as with humans. His face was expressive, too, just like his eyes. Also, I remember that he had huge legs'

He suggests that the Yeti's feet were about 18 inches long.

'I can't describe or understand how we spoke, because - well because it sounds unbelievable. It felt like we heard each other's thoughts, as if it was telepathy. There was only one word that the Yeti actually said when I asked his name. His voice was low and chesty, and the name sounded as if somebody hit a tambourine twice - 'Ta-ban'.'

Andrey sought out a translator after his encounter and was told that Ta-Ban translated to 'a soul' or 'the one that wasn't discovered'.

Andrey states that he 'talked' to the Yeti for about 40 minutes.

"I always carry a pencil and something I can draw on. This time it was a piece of birch tree bark. I made a drawing of the Yeti and showed him. The Yeti studied it really carefully for a while, and then drew a symbol next to my drawing.

'I still can't find what this symbol means, I've been going through books and the internet, but found nothing similar. There is a similar looking symbol of friendship, but I am not sure this is it.'

When asked why he was chosen by the Yeti, Andrey stated:

'I guess it was a pure coincidence. Or perhaps it happened because I sincerely believed in the Yeti's existence and imagined how one day I'd meet them. I've been dreaming about meeting them, to be honest. I also don't think that I am the only person that met Yeti. Others simply don't speak about it, rightly fearing they might be called insane.

'All I can say about myself is that I am as normal as one can find, I am physically and mentally healthy, I don't drink or take drugs. I think one day I'll get back to the place where we've met… I think we might see each other again.'

Researcher Myra Shackleyin writes this in her book,

Still Living? Yeti, Sasquatch, and the Neanderthal Enigma, of an encounter had by a pair of hikers in 1942:

> "Two black specks moving across the snow about a quarter mile below them." Despite this significant distance, they offered the following very detailed description: "The height was not much less than eight feet ... the heads were described as 'squarish' and the ears must lie close to the skull because there was no projection from the silhouette against the snow. The shoulders sloped sharply down to a powerful chest ... covered by reddish brown hair which formed a close body fur mixed with long straight hairs hanging downward." Another person saw a creature "about the size and build of a small man, the head covered with long hair but the face and chest not very hairy at all. Reddish-brown in color and bipedal, it was busy grubbing up roots and occasionally emitted a loud high-pitched cry."

Anthony Wooldridge, during a hike in 1986, observed a yeti and happened to capture two shots with his camera before the creature took off. The pictures were later analyzed and proven to be real, genuine and legitimate pictures of a real-life yeti! John Napier, the Smithsonian Institution's director of primate biology, anatomist, and anthropologist certified these pictures as authentic and backed Wooldridge's claim that this was, indeed, a yeti. This bolstered the confidence of many in the bigfoot community as to the existence of the yeti and was considered quite the boon for cryptozoology in general.

    The Yeti has been featured in over 50 films, books, and video games. It's easy to say that popular culture has a soft-spot for this mysterious and mythical being. I know I certainly do. How could you not?!? I mean, ancient Buddhist monks turned immortal protectors of Shambhala?!?! What's not to love!?!?

    I hope that if you are a believer, I've renewed or buoyed up your convictions and if you are not or were not, maybe I sprinkled in just enough magic, just enough wonder to plant a seed… maybe your imagination has been awakened to the possibility of something… other.

Micah Campbell

CHAPTER 12

The Jersey Devil

The wind it howled through dark of night
Father stammering in paralyzing fright
He hid me deep in closet bare
Eyes wide open through slats I stare
~
The growl it came on putrid breath
I feared the end a gruesome death
Father held tight as the door it rattled
Futile to fend an unnatural battle
~
Slowly the door it did part from its frame
Demon's eye I see glowing red as a flame
Father held tight, just as tight as he could
But he knew in short order his strength fail it would
~
The beast it did shriek as father fell to the floor
Claws round his throat he threw father at the door
With a horrible thud bleeding and prone
Father lay silent and I cowered alone
~
I could see cloven feet moving this way and that

Flapping leathery wings as if clipped from a bat
It spit as it growled from between fang laden jaws
Destroying our cottage with yellow curled claws
~

Its face was not human, nor of beast of the earth
Larger than a man in its height and it's girth
The horns that did sprout from the top of his head
Certain in a moment I surely be dead
~

It clawed at the closet breaking slat after slat
'til the drool from its fangs fell inside pitter-pat
I curled in the corner as best that I could
Live another night I prayed to God that I would
~

The stink of the devil almost more than I could bare
As lice and maggots fell from his feathers and his hair
With one longing screech as spit ran down the wall
I closed my eyes and held my breath as the satan's tail did fall
~

Then as fast as it came it turned and did run
Back into the pines from whence it did come
Leaving claw marks and stench behind in its wake
This night we were lucky for no life did it take
~

Battered and bloodied was my father it's true
No worse was I for the terror gone through
This story's been told, handed down through the ages
Written in books filling volumes of pages

~
Still there are those who refuse to believe
'til receive they a visit on one dark moonless eve
Jersey Devil of the pines unannounced makes his call
The season matters not winter, spring, summer or fall
~
The son of Mrs. Leeds, cursed long before birth
Banished to the forest amongst pine and marshy firth
Spawn of the Devil to live immortal life
It's best to guard your sons and daughters and your wife.

A poem by Dominic R. DiFrancesco. An ode to the oldest and longest lasting legend in New Jersey: The Jersey Devil.

The Jersey Devil is often described as a bipedal creature resembling a kind of warped kangaroo-like or wyvern shape. It has the head of a horse or goat, cloven-hooves, leathery wings like that of a bat - clawed skeletal hands included - and a forked tongue and tail. It is very fast and has a blood-curdling scream, like millions of tiny nails raking across a chalkboard applied to the nth degree. It was also once human.

The Jersey Devil is also, and actually was *first*, known as the Leeds Devil.

An article from a local paper reported *this* all the way back in 1887 of a farmer and his recollection of the

Devil of Leeds and his having been told of the monster for years:

> "Whenever he went near it, it would give a most unearthly yell that frightened the dogs. It whipped at every dog in the place. "That thing," said the colonel, "is not a bird nor an animal, but it is the Leeds devil, according to the description, and it was born over in Evasham, Burlington County, a hundred years ago. There is no mistake about it. I never saw the horrible critter myself, but I can remember well when it was roaming around in Evasham woods fifty years ago, and when it was hunted by men and dogs and shot at by the best marksmen there were in all South Jersey but could not be killed. There isn't a family in Burlington or any of the adjoining counties that does not know of the Leeds devil, and it was the bugaboo to frighten children with when I was a boy."

The origin of the Devil of Leeds, or what we know today as the Jersey Devil, can be traced back to 1735.

And oh, what an origin it is!

The Legend

Jane Leeds was known as Mother Leeds in her hometown of Pine Barrens in South New Jersey. Mother Leeds had 12 children and loved them each dearly, but was distraught to find out that she was pregnant with another. She cursed the day that she found out and cursed the child, for what child would bring such misery and despair upon a mother whose womb had born 12 already!

She couldn't bear it

On a sinister and stormy night in 1735 Mother Leeds bore the child, but would not look upon its face. Her husband, children and friends were all gathered 'round and were witness to all the devilish and disturbing things that happened next.

The child was born as a happy and healthy baby boy, but it was cursed. Cursed by its mother, who wanted nothing to do with it and cursed by its very bloodline - it's very birthright - for though Mrs. Leeds was indeed the boy's mother, Mr. Leeds was *not* its father. Its father was the devil himself.

The child's cries, as it was jettisoned into this mortal coil, quickly took on a high-pitched and horrific tambour! Its scream was so loud that it shattered the ceramic bowl full of Luke-warm water and bloodied towels next to the birthing table. As blood and water flowed, so, too did the mortal restraints that held the boy. Windows fractured and the house shook as the storm raged outside as well as within.

Before terrified family and friends, the child began to change. Its legs elongated and stretched, bones snapped like hollow husks, and reshaped in an unnatural convex direction. Its feet turned to hooves. Its rib cage cracked and its spine shifted to make way for the leathery wings to sprout forth. Its spine reformed and erupted from the babe's tail-bone, taking the shape of a forked tail. It began to growl as the rest began to scream and run. And then its head… its head began to move, began to swim, to somehow become malleable and shapeless, like clay over-saturated. The head took the shape of a goat, slit eyes and horns

It is said that the demon-child beat its wings and took to the air, attacking *everyone* within the small home with its claws and tail, before rushing out into the night to take refuge in the forests of the Pine Barrens.

The demon-child still haunts the areas of South Jersey and Philadelphia to this day. It is said to be immortal and impervious to all forms of weapon and religion. Local clergymen have even attempted to exorcise the beast from the region multiple times, to no avail. These attempts do nothing but anger the devil and remind it of the pain that it went through at its birth. The Jersey Devil has been known to topple trees onto unsuspecting victims, killing them instantly. It is also known to call upon its hellfire and boil those he catches swimming in the lakes, ponds and rivers in the surrounding area.

The Leeds

Though the corrupt origin of this fiendish cryptid is well known, the identity of Mother Leeds is somewhat an area of contention amongst the scholars and researchers of the Leeds Devil. Mother Leeds is often referred to as Jane Leeds, though there are no documents to support this woman ever having lived in the Pine Barrens area at that time. A more substantive identity would be that of Deborah Leeds, who did, in fact, live with her husband, Japhet Leeds, and their 12 children in the Pine Barrens in the early 18th century. This is evidenced by a will written by Japhet Leeds in 1736 that included Deborah and his 12 children. However, a 13th child born to the Leeds family in 1735 was stricken from the will.

Now that is interesting enough, but for this book... for my readers... I am not satisfied with "interesting enough". I want "interestinglyer the most" or "the interestinglyest of all!" so let us go back even *further*, to the 17th century where Japhet's father, Daniel Leeds, battled his arch-nemesis in "colonial-era political intrigue".

Daniel Leeds was an almanac publisher and politician whose main competition and rival was none other than Benjamin Franklin! Leeds was no match for Franklin and was easily painted as the "bad guy" by Franklin, even so much so as to be labeled a "monster" by Franklin supporters.

Oh, politics.

This moniker followed Leeds for the rest of his life and seemed to be one that would continue to haunt his legacy, as Japhet Leeds would learn: The sins of the father are to be laid upon the children.

Daniel Leads was an English Quaker but was swiftly ostracized from his congregation after an article that he had published containing astrological elements was brought to the congregation's attention. The Quaker community seized and destroy all of Daniel Leeds's works, citing them as pagan and blasphemous, thus cementing his reputation as a "monster".

Interesting fact: Daniel's 3rd wife (and Japhet's) mother bore 9 children, his 2nd wife died in childbirth giving birth to a baby girl, who also died. Daniel's 1st wife bore 3 children. 9 + 3 living children = 12 and 1 dead child makes 13.

Leeds continued writing his astrological almanacs and even began writing anti-Quaker works and rhetoric. His and Franklin's rivalry continued well after his death, as his son, Titan Leeds took up the mantle and continued the Leeds assault on the Quaker's and Franklin. Titan and Franklin became so embittered toward one another that they released continuing, sparring writings accusing one another of more and more heinous and unsavory acts.

The coup de gras was after Titan's death. Franklin reminded the people of the Leeds's blasphemous and occultist reputation and also of their stance on monarchy, being heavily pro-monarchy in a largely anti-monarchy community. Titan also had begun using his family crest to sign his works and the works of his family. The crest is that of a wyvern, a dragon-like beast with large, leathery bat-like wings and razor-sharp claws. Not unlike certain aspects of the Leeds Devil, this crest was likely the linchpin in the Leeds "monstrous" and "evil" legacy.

So, when did the Leeds Devil or the Devil of Leeds become The Jersey Devil that we are all familiar with?

According to Brian Regal, a Kean University historian of science it was in the dawn of the 20th century. 1909 to be exact. He states:

> "During the pre-revolutionary period, the Leeds family, who called the Pine Barrens home, soured its relationship with the Quaker majority ... The Quakers saw no hurry to give their former fellow religionist an easy time in circles of gossip. His wives had all died, as had several children. His son Titan stood accused by Benjamin Franklin of being a ghost ... The family crest had winged dragons on it. In a time when thoughts of independence were being born, these issues made the Leeds family political and religious monsters.

From all this over time the legend of the Leeds Devil was born. References to the 'Jersey Devil' do not appear in newspapers or other printed material until the twentieth century. The first major flap came in 1909. It is from these sightings that the popular image of the creature—bat-like wings, horse head, claws, and general air of a dragon—became standardized."

The Encounters

So, we've covered the Legend, we've covered the Leeds...

But I don't think that this chapter would be complete without a look at some of the most curious encounters with the beast. First and foremost being the Bonaparte Incident.

The King of Spain, Joseph Bonaparte - yes, Napoleon Bonaparte's brother - tucked tail and ran after his defeat to the English in the Peninsula War. He ran all the way to New York. After spending some time there and in Philadelphia, Bonaparte landed in Bordentown, New Jersey, where he erected a large mansion on a sprawling estate. It is said to have been a little piece of France right there in Jersey. Acres and acres of forest with a King's Road winding throughout, lavishly manicured gardens and lawns... even its own lake.

During the winter of 1813 Bonaparte went hunting in his forest. He said that he came across the most peculiar set of prints in the snow: They were prints of a donkey, but it was only one set, like the donkey was walking on 2 legs as like a human would. A sound behind him sent him spinning around to stare directly into the face of the devil. He described it a "huge creature with a horse's head and wings". He took a shot at the beast hitting it directly in the chest, but causing no damage. The creature took to the sky and let out an ear-piercing screech that had Bonaparte on his knees, reeling. Later that day, he swore to all at his estate that he had encountered the devil.

According to HistoryCollection.com:

Back in the 1800's, people who lived in the middle of the Pine Barrens were given the nickname "Pine Rats", because they were often living in huts and cabins in the middle of nowhere, scavenging for supplies whenever they could find it. Today, they're called "Pineys", or, like everywhere else in the country, just plain out "rednecks". The woods were filled with moonshiners, criminals on the lamb, runaway slaves, and men who deserted the draft. Basically- everyone was hiding in the wilderness from something, and it was even more of a reason to give them a rude nickname. Most Pine Rats were superstitious, and told a lot of spooky campfire stories about local legends, especially during the 1800's. So, it was very rare for residents to go out into the woods after dark, for fear of the Jersey Devil.

In an issue of *The Atlantic Monthly*, a woman named Hannah Butler, who was labeled to be a "pine rat", was drinking a strong apple cider that was known as "Jersey Lightning". She drank so much that she lost her fear of night and started walking in the forest. Sure enough, the one time she decided to go out she heard the blood-curdling screams that the Jersey Devil had become famous for. She came face-to-face with the Jersey Devil and described it as having black fur and hooves. Its face looked like a horse or a goat, but it stood on only two legs, and had large leathery wings.

According to WeirdNJ.com:

> "The most infamous of these incidents occurred during the week of January 16 through 23, 1909. Early in the week reports started emerging from all across the Delaware Valley that strange tracks were being found in the snow. The mysterious footprints went over and under fences, through fields and backyards, and across the rooftops of houses. They were even reported in the large cities of Camden and Philadelphia. Panic immediately began to spread, and posses formed in more than one town. Fear and intrigue grew even greater when it was reported that bloodhounds refused to follow the unidentified creature's trail in Hammonton. Schools closed or

suffered low attendance throughout lower NJ and in Philadelphia. Mills in the Pine Barrens were forced to close when workers refused to leave their homes and travel through the woods to get to their jobs.

    Eyewitnesses spotted the beast in Camden and in Bristol, Pennsylvania, and in both cities, police fired on it but did not manage to bring it down. A few days later it reappeared in Camden, attacking a late-night meeting of a social club and then flying away. Earlier that day it had appeared in Haddon Heights, terrorizing a trolley car full of passengers before flying away. Witnesses claimed that it looked like a large flying kangaroo. Another trolley car-full of people saw it in Burlington when it scurried across the tracks in front of their car. In West Collingswood it appeared on the roof of a house and was described as an ostrich-like creature. Firemen turned their hose upon it, but it attacked them and then flew away. The entire week people reported that their livestock, particularly their chickens, were being slaughtered. This was most widespread in the towns of Bridgeton and Millville.

The marauding misanthrope reappeared later in the week in Camden, where a local woman found the beast attempting to eat her dog. She hit it with a broomstick and it flew away.

These are just a few of the myriad reports and encounters that surround this centuries old cryptid. I hope you enjoyed learning a bit about this creature, this Jersey Devil. I know I certainly did! I had a wonderful time researching and reading up on this legend.

Chapter 14

Area-51

Super Serious Introduction (Seriously)

Located in Groom Lake Valley in the Tonopah Basin is a lake. It is a dry lake, also described as a salt flat. Groom Lake sits at an elevation of 4,409 ft and is approximately 11.3 miles in circumference. This dry lake was discovered in 1864 along with a series of mines that produced Silver and Lead. Multiple other mines were then found around the same area. These mines included Maria, Willow and White Lake. Groom Lake is also a B-rated (at best) science-fiction film written by, directed by, and starring the final frontier's leading man and resident heart-throb, William Shatner. And as much as I'd like to dive into that beautiful pile of Syfy-feces face first, I couldn't stop laugh-crying enough to sort out or formulate a single cohesive thought…

So, there will be no humorous or sarcastic overtone in this chapter. There will be no pop-culture summary in the guise of a documentary or educational segment. There will be no jokes or stories veiled as truth. We are going to look at nothing but the cold-hard facts. We are just going to have to focus on the *second* most widely known aspect of Groom Lake Valley (Shatner's atrocity being the first... obviously). It is where a Top-Secret Air Force base, approximately the size of Connecticut is located. It is where 90% of the United States nuclear bomb testing takes place. It is completely restricted to civilians and guarded 24/7 by highly trained, heavily-armed military personnel. It is a no-fly zone and is impossible to approach by land or air without permission. It is where our government experiments on UFOs and extraterrestrial life, performs experiments and autopsies on aliens, controls the weather, builds energy weapons, develops future transport and houses the "majestic 12" ... It is Area-51.

Aliens, space, Area-51... not my wheelhouse. I'm a fantasy guy. Elves and magic. Monsters and demons... Ghosts... Wizards... you know, the "cool" stuff. I have never, ever gotten into the alien/UFO stuff, so this will be a great chapter to wet my whistle and make me an **expert** on all things Science-Fiction!

Bob Lazar

We all know that UFOs run on antimatter. This is fact. There is no room for debate here. None. Antimatter is the same as "ordinary matter", that is, it occupies the same mass as ordinary matter, but provides the opposite electric charge of ordinary matter... i.e. antimatter. There are other more advanced variables and characteristics to be explained here in a quantum capacity, but we will leave that for the nerd books and Shatners of the world to provide *that* fake news. I'm here to bring you the *real* news... the truth... we separate fact from fiction, child from adult... so here, we'll stick with what we know to be true. UFOs run on antimatter.

    The foremost authority on this matter is Robert Scott Lazar. Lazar (probably pronounced Lah-zar, not Lay-zer) is the owner of United Nuclear Scientific Equipment and Supplies, a world-renowned and disavowed physicist, and a conspiracy theorist. He **is** the authority on this matter. He was also busted and convicted of aiding and abetting an illegal prostitution ring and for violating the Federal Hazardous Substances Act. That doesn't mean this dude's first-hand account should be discounted, it means he's REAL.

    Lazar says that in the 80s he was hired by the men in black to reverse-engineer extraterrestrial tech, including UFOs. He states that he was sequestered to a top-secret location within Area-51 known as S-4. He was actively working on a UFO that was powered by antimatter known as element 15, which we all now know is Moscovium. Moscovium at that time had not been synthesized yet, and in fact wouldn't be for another 20 years when, in 2003 a team of Russian and American scientists did so at the Joint Institute for Nuclear Research. It was later recognized as one of four new elements by the Joint Working Party of International

Scientific Bodies. This antimatter, Moscovium, is an extremely volatile radioactive element and is therefore perfect for (FSP) or flying saucer propulsion. FSP is trademark pending Micah Campbell 2022.

While under the employ of Uncle Sam, Lazar was privy to a number of classified US documents that described extraterrestrial involvement in human affairs for the last 10,000 years!

Peabody and Emmy award-winning journalist, George Knapp, interviewed Lazar in 1989. This interview brought to light many of the conspiracies that we know today as truth. Lazar revealed that in the Papoose and Groom Lake region, there are massive aircraft hangars built into and hidden by the large mountain ranges. These hangers do not, however, house the US Air Force fighter and spy aircraft that we are familiar with… they house 9, yes 9, flying saucers of extraterrestrial origin. At least one of these unidentified flying objects was constructed by some form of foreign alloy, similar to touch and appearance to stainless steel. Lazar clued us all into the gravity wave that not only allows the aircraft flight, but also bends the light around it, making it invisible to the naked eye. He explained that this was accomplished by an intricate combination of gravity amplifiers and gravity emitters which were housed within the UFOs.

Lazar also pointed out in this interview that certain documents that he had access to, whether legally or not, exposed and confirmed what we have known all along. That aliens have been among us for a "decamillennium" or 10,000 years. These classified documents describe the extraterrestrial beings as "grey aliens from a planet orbiting the twin binary star system Zeta Reticuli." He also confirmed the size and shape of these extraterrestrial beings as being small, child-sized with long arms. He confirmed this in his reports on the size of the seats in the alien aircraft and also from personally witnessing alien cadavers being experimented on. He even states that as he was walking down the hall, he witnessed 2 men in white lab coats carrying on a conversation with a small, child-sized being strapped to a table.

Lazar's testimony has been praised by alien and UFO proselytes for decades, but he has also been met with some intense scrutiny, hatred and even character assassination!

Lazar has a master from MIT in physics and a masters in electric technology from Caltech, but guess what… neither Caltech nor MIT have any record of him *ever* attending their schools…

Cover-up? I think so!

He was employed as a physicist at Los Alamos Meson Physics Facility, in the Los Alamos National Laboratory. The Facility denies having employed him or having any record of him.

Cover-Up? I think so!

Same goes for EG&G (a private national defense contractor). Lazar worked for EG&G and the US Navy, but all records of his employment are denied.

Cover-up? Of course, it is!

And then, of course, there's the outrageous false arrests and convictions involving aiding and abetting an illegal prostitution ring and stealing element 15 from a government site.

Lies!

All Lies.

Lazar appeared on the Joe Rogan Experience on June 20th, 2019 and explained to Joe that the government had his birth certificate, employment records, and college transcripts wiped from existence, completely discrediting him. It was actually this interview that sparked the idea to "storm" Area-51. Do you all remember this? There was a social media movement that saw hundreds of thousands of participants sign up to rush into area-51. I believe one of the slogans for the event was "they can't shoot us all". That's crazy, but it goes to show how much people want the truth.

Bob Lazar is an American patriot who has been punished… silenced for bringing us the truth… But why? Why is it so important to silence the brave men and women, the fearless Americans who expose the truth? Why did this joker get canceled faster than a conservative on social media?

Well, it's because what he was saying was true!

If it were conspiracy or *false*, the powers that be would not go to such extreme measures to silence him.

But what are they trying to hide?

Well, surprisingly, not just aliens.

Area-51

Area-51 is located 120 miles northwest of Las Vegas, in the Nevada desert. There is very little around, including reception. It is a dead-zone and that is quite by design.

In 1954 President Dwight Eisenhower tasked the CIA with locating a remote and easily guardable location to begin testing "high-altitude recon programs" … i.e., spy planes. The goal was to develop aircraft that could fly high enough and fast enough over foreign territory and not get shot down. It didn't take the agents involved long to find the perfect location. According to

Nellis.af.mil: "The Air Force-operated Nevada Test and Training Range is the largest contiguous air and ground space available for peacetime military operations in the free world."

There is the NTTR and little else. The majority of the testing being performed by the NTTR here was of a nuclear variety.

Annie Jacobsen writes in her book: *Area 51: An Uncensored History of America's Top Secret Military Base:* "They discovered the perfect fulfillment of the presidential request which was a secret base centered around a dry lake-bed in the middle of Nevada that happened to be located in an already classified facility where the government was exploding nuclear weapons. There was no way that anyone was going to try to get into this facility, especially because nuclear bombs were being exploded there."

Jacobsen goes on to say that, "It wasn't long before a mix of engineers, spies, and uniformed military turned the facility into the birthplace of overhead espionage for the CIA."

There were 2 aircraft that were developed here in the early days: The U-2 Spy Plane and the SR-71 Blackbird. These planes and this initiative were of utmost national concern and import because at this very time the Soviet Union were conducting secret experiments and programs of their own. Atomic programs. The U-2 cost millions and was found lacking, as it was brought down by the soviets.

But where the U-2 failed, the SR-71 excelled. It flew so high and so fast that it was completely undetectable and impossible to bring down. It was able to travel 30,000 miles, 80,000 feet high, at 2,100 miles per hour without the need to refuel and carried upwards of 700 lbs. of high-resolution cameras. The location of this program soon became known as Area-51 because of its location in the sprawling Nevada Test and Training Range. Areas 1-50 had already been taken. Though you will never see it on an NTTR map.

A massive, coordinated effort began to build out and expand area-51 to accommodate all of the engineers and agents that were being brought in, but since there was no room to expand out, they went **into** the mountains and **down** below ground. The SR-71 was being manufactured only in Area-51 and parts for the aircraft were brought in in secrecy and built underground. Observers and those "not in the know" would see planes appear on runways, seemingly out of the blue. These planes were so futuristic and fast that many didn't have a name for them. The CIA encouraged the term Unidentified Flying Object and even facilitated rumors of extraterrestrial involvement or activity, so as to throw any spying eyes or ears off the scent of what they were really doing.

This kind of counter-intelligence still goes on today. Though some things that go on here are known to the wider audience, most of the goings on inside Area-51 are still secrets that our government holds tightly to its chest. There is a private security team contracted by the government to ensure that no one is watching, listening or attempting to access the grounds. They are known as the "cammo dudes" and they drive around in white jeeps and trucks keeping an eye on the base. They are heavily armed former-military personnel and they take their job very, very seriously.

So outside of the SR-71s there are stealth bombers, drones, the military training, weapons testing, spy technology, anti-intelligence programs, and tactical air maneuver testing. What else is going on here that they don't want us to know?

Aliens

Aliens are real. We know this. John Lear, heir to the Lear jet fortune described Area-51 as "one of this nation's most secret test centers" and told us that the facility had actually been built with the help of aliens. He called the aliens "Grays" and reported that aliens were kept there against their will and experimented on. He also accused the government of feeding the Grays kidnapped children and mutilated cattle.

That's a bit morbid, but it *is* our government... should we really be surprised?

July 1947 - Roswell, New Mexico. An unidentified flying object - an extraterrestrial flying saucer - went down near a ranch outside of the small town. The government and military were quick to act, assuring the locals and the news outlets alike that this was simply a nuclear test surveillance balloon from Project Mogul (a top-secret military program that involved high-flying balloons equipped with high-powered microphones meant to spy on soviet atomic testing. They said that the balloon launched from Alamogordo Army Airfield 30 days prior to the crash.

This may have done a fine enough job to assuage the average American Joe, but for those who see more, for those who are not blindly led by lies and false narratives, it wasn't nearly good enough. They would need much more. This story was repeated multiple times over the next 40 or so years but seemed to have the opposite effect than intended. Conspiracies and theories began to take shape. More and more evidence was uncovered, not just concerning Roswell, but from all over! It was clear that there was a cover-up afoot, and as the years went on and technology got better and we got wiser, it was also becoming clear who was in charge of that cover-up and why.

When the military steam-rolled that ranch outside of Roswell in '47, where do you think they took all the evidence of the crash?

Any guesses?

Exactly - Nevada Test and Training Range. Future home of Area-51.

You see, the government has been covering up alien activity since there was such a thing as a government. Far before Area-51. Far before the Roswell UFO Incident. Bob Lazar's documents show evidence of extraterrestrial involvement for the last 10,000 years!

In the early 90s via the Freedom of Information Act, numerous documents were released that evidenced at least *one* extraterrestrial UFO crashed near Roswell, alien bodies *had* been recovered, and a government cover-up of the incident *had*, indeed, taken place.

In 1995 a film that appeared to have been shot by the US military showing an actual alien autopsy was released by Ray Santilli. It was dated September of 1947, just 2 months after the events near Roswell. This footage made its way around the world as it was covered by nearly every local, national and international news outlet.

Conclusion

Whether it is for power or protection, greed or guilt, the fact of the matter is that the government has spent years and years keeping their secrets regarding alien existence, UFOs and everything extraterrestrial.

They have done this behind the impenetrable and unassailable walls of Area-51. We may never know everything, we may never have all of the answers, but we are getting there. We are getting closer every day. We know more than our fathers before us, and our children will, no doubt, learn much more than we. All we can do is continue to seek the truth and never stop believing.

Check this out!

Annie Jacobsen had a source that provided evidence of a Nazi doctor surgically enlarging the heads of teenagers that they kidnapped, in order to make them look like aliens. This was ordered by Joseph Stalin. Stalin and his Nazi officers then forced the teenagers to fly flying saucers over the US. This was intended to be a scare tactic to incite an all-out War of the World type reaction. It did not, but the UFOs and the large-headed teens did crash and were taken to Area-51 for experimentation.

Crazy!

Urban Legends, Ghost Stories, and Folklore

CHAPTER 15

Boy Scout Lane

Nestled between Cemetery Road and Little Chicago Road in Stevens Point, Wisconsin is an unpaved stretch of packed earth and gravel that runs North off of River Drive and disappears into the River Run Woods. It was once owned by The Boy Scouts of America and was intended to be the sole entry point into the large, wooded area where the organization had planned to host their camps. Unfortunately, that never happened. That land and Boy Scout Lane is now privately owned and off-limits to all. Signs that warn trespassers to steer clear are posted all along the road and into the woods, but that hasn't stopped thrill-seekers, paranormal investigators, and bored teenagers alike, from sneaking their way in only to be frightened and chased off again, not by the owner of the property, but by a troop of Boy Scouts that perished there in the mid-1950s

The Legend

Boy Scout Lane has earned itself a spot on many

"Most Haunted Roads" lists and for good reason. You wouldn't think that an unassuming, plain gravel road less than a mile long and surrounded by farmsteads would have that sinister a story, but this one does. As all legends do, this one varies and shifts over time and depending on who is telling the tale, but nearly everyone can agree: it happened in the late 50s and it happened on Boy Scout Lane.

It was fall. The trees had already donned the best of their festive oranges and brilliant reds when a local scout troop, led by their scoutmaster, went for a weekend excursion in the River Run Woods. This was no ordinary weekend retreat, though. This was the troop's first opportunity to explore and camp in the newly purchased bit of land that the Boy Scouts of America had just acquired with the intention of making it their new local camping ground. They had barely breached the forest proper when they decided to set up camp. Tents were erected and fires brought to life with competency and efficiency. There was an eagerness… an anticipation in the air that was almost palpable.

There's not much information about what the young men and their troop master did that evening, but I imagine that it involved talking about girls, roasting marshmallows, farting into the fire, whittling sticks, tying knots, reading *Urban Legends, Ghost Stories and Folklore* by Micah Campbell around the fire, making dirty jokes, etc.

The next morning the scoutmaster wakes up, brings the fires back to life and puts on breakfast - bacon and sausage sizzling... got that coffee brewin... maybe even some flap jacks bubblin on the cast iron... and then proceeds to wake the camp with a rousing rendition of Reveille, the Scout bugle call for "Get up and get you some bacon".

Expecting a swarm of hungry hikers ready to take on the trails, he was instead met with an eerie quiet. The ground undisturbed, still wet with dew that glistened off of the bright, blurry rays that broke through the trees, smoked and steamed as the temperatures rose with the sun. The temperatures rose, but his campers did not. The troop leader rushed from tent to tent, panic beginning to take firm hold of his thoughts as worst-case scenarios played through his head. His frantic search took him from the campgrounds into the forest of River Run. He shouted. He screamed. He called each of them by name... but received no response.

Exhausted and out of options, he made his back to camp. The only vehicle that they had was the old yellow school bus that the local troop had raised money to purchase at an auction years ago. It was rusty, smelly and missing half the seats, but it did its job. It was also gone. The driver, who was a good friend of the troop and offered his services on the weekends, had opted to sleep in the bus instead of on the cold hard ground. He was gone, as well.

The troop master made his way down Boy Scout Lane, hoping to find a farm or phone so that he could call the police. About halfway down the lane, he found the bus. It was wrapped around a large tree. Smoke was pouring from under the hood as well as from the windows and doors, which were all shattered and caved in. The outside was more black than yellow. The troop master is reported as saying that it looked like someone had taken a flame thrower to it. After a brief and unsuccessful search of the interior and all around the area, he continued on. No bus driver. No scouts.

The Scoutmaster ran to the first home that he saw, a small farmhouse at the edge of the road. He briefly explained what was happening and within an hour, he, the family of the farm, and the police were all out combing the woods, looking for the missing troop. Investigators were on site, but found no evidence of foul play. Of course, the troop master was the lead suspect, but they couldn't come up with any reason to hold him. Their focus then shifted to the bus driver.

Everyone else's focus was on finding those lost boys. Winter was fast approaching and not just any winter. A Wisconsin Winter. Everyone knew that no matter how well trained these boys were, there was no chance of them surviving long in the brutal conditions of a northern forest winter. Not to mention, the troop left EVERYTHING back at camp. Bedrolls, backpacks, rations, knives, blankets… it almost seemed as if they simple vanished as they slept.

The search continued for weeks. Snow crowned the trees and blanketed the roads. The chances of finding the boys alive diminished day by day as the brutal grasp of winter seized the small town of Steven's Point. Little by little, the search parties dwindled. Soon enough it was only families and friends that still clung to hope... their hope, too, was eventually buried beneath the snow.

There are many questions that, to this day, remain unanswered: Why did the children leave the safety and warmth of the blankets, tents, and fire of their campsite in the middle of the night. Why all of them? Why, if they left of their own accord, did they leave everything behind? What happened to the bus driver? What happened to the bus!?! Was this a tragic accident or something far more nefarious? Was the troop master really innocent? These are just a few of the myriad questions still haunting Boy Scout Lane.

As I alluded to before, what exactly happened and even how they died depends on who's telling the story. Some say that the scout leader murdered these boys in their sleep. That he went from tent to tent and picked them off one-by-one. Others point to the bus driver, who remains missing to this day. Some take the previously mentioned tent-by-tent scenario and just replace the scoutmaster with the bus driver. Others claim that the bus driver woke the young men and told them that they were heading to some overnight hike. That he got them all on the bus and left, planning on taking them to some remote area and killing them there, but that the boys became aware of this and fought back, causing the bus to careen into the tree and explode. Though, if this were the case, where did all the bodies go?

Where *did* all the bodies go anyway? I mean, no blood, no bodies, no foul play… that's just too weird.

I agree!

Here's what really happened:

It was a freak accident. The troop never actually made it to the campsite, but instead died in a horrible bus crash on the way there. The troop leader was the only survivor and he completely snapped after taking in the death and carnage all around him. He spent the entire day, all that night and the early parts of the next morning, transporting the burned and broken bodies of each boy and the bus driver to the campsite, burying them under each tent. He set up the entire campsite like nothing had happened and to this day, the bodies are still buried in shallow graves right there at the campsite.

The troop master disappeared after the search died down and many believe that he killed himself, not because of the guilt and shame that he felt for what he had done, but because he truly *had* snapped and out of some form of survivor's guilt could not bear to be alive any longer.

There is an old elm tree that reaches over Boy Scout Lane. Many have claimed to see the shadow of a man hanging from its branches. It is the troop master.

Despite who you talk to or what story you wish to believe, one thing is certain: Both the road and campsite are haunted.

Encounters

Though this land is now private property, many still risk the ire of the authorities and landowners to get a glimpse of this infamous area of River Run Woods. Most are simply seeking a scare, worked up by their own tellings and retellings of the events that played out here so many years ago. Some go to investigate. Regardless of why they go, they all leave (sometimes hastily, running for their lives) with the same account. There are ghosts in those woods.

Many report hearing children running through the woods and down Boy Scout Lane, laughing and shouting. Others claim that at night the whispers of boys can be heard and in the chill of winter even *seen* as unexplainable wisps of breath appear in unison with the murmuring. Others report seeing bobbing lights, swaying in the darkness, moving from tree to tree. This is thought to be lanterns or flashlights of the lost boys as they search for their way home.

It is said that if you call out by name any of the missing boys, that you will be answered. This is due to the scoutmaster having called out each individual boy by name during his frenzied search.

Everyone who comes away from Boy Scout Lane would agree and attest to the fact that something is off there. Twigs snapping in the distance, the foreboding sense of being watched. Shadows and lights appearing and disappearing…

This story from EarthBoundAngel was found on yourghoststories.com and it is her personal encounter with Boy Scout Lane:

> It was a warm July night in 2005. My friend Erin was visiting our mutual friend Michelle and I up in Stevens Point. Michelle and I had worked at a Boy Scout Camp (ironic, huh?) that summer, and Erin was to bring me back home to Minnesota when the weekend was over. We were bored, so Michelle suggested we go to Boy Scout Lane and do a little investigation. We had gone to a bookstore the day before and found the story in there. It intrigued us, so soon we were on our way with me in the backseat, video camera in hand.
>
> Right when we turned onto the road, we felt uneasy. You know, that dreaded feeling of being watched. Being the young adults we are, we

made jokes and tried to shake off that feeling. We went down the road and turned around, nothing special happened. What we saw when we got home is a different story.

Michelle hooked the video camera up to the television and played the footage. At first, it looked like nothing interesting. Until there was a point when I coughed (I had just gotten over a bad cold) and right after that, a heavy whispering breath followed. It was not me. Michelle, Erin, and I looked at each other with wide eyes and we turned back to the television. The other two saw a bright ball of light flash by the screen for a split second, but I did not.

As I recorded us driving back to the main road, I faced the rolled up window (as everyone does, never thinking that spirits can go THROUGH things) towards the field that was supposed to turn into a camp. I had the infrared light on the camera, in case something moved in the field. Nothing moved in the field. Instead, we saw a face pressed up against the window. And no, it was not my face. The small screen of the video camera did not project enough light and I was not pressed up against the window. When the three of us saw this, we screamed and Michelle's mother started yelling at us. We ran into her room and told her what happened. She scorned us, yet refused to watch the footage.

Another little tidbit that we saw: In the rearview mirror there were two stationary lights in the upper corners. The area of Boy Scout Lane is away from the city limits and no car was behind us. The lights did not leave until we got deep into town again. We have not gone out there since, but we have shown the tape to others and they see the same things. I don't know if Boy Scouts really haunt the area, but *something* does. I live in Stevens Point now and this town has a lot of history to it. Anything is possible and it just makes me more of a believer.

It is interesting that she ended her story with the idea that she doesn't know if boy scouts haunt the area, but something definitely does…

I did some digging into the area and it seems that Steven's Point is a hotspot for this kind of activity.

For instance, there is a bar in that area called Club Forest Bar. It used to be a brothel and was frequented by the likes of Al Copne and John Dillinger. Though the gangster and brothel days of the 30s and 40s are over, the remnants of that violent era linger here. It is said that a man named Melvin, a caretaker of the establishment, was murdered in cold blood in Club Forest by a two-bit criminal who was harassing a local patron. Apparently Small-Time was pestering a woman. He was getting a bit rowdy and handsy. Melvin stepped in to defend the woman and the gangster shot him. It is said that Melvin still haunts the bar and can still be felt there to this day. He will often play his favorite tune on the jukebox, turn up the TV or even tip over drinks and barstools anytime there is an unruly or loud man getting a bit too out of hand. The bar is grateful for what Melvin did that day all those years ago, so much so that they have named items on their menu after him.

HAUNTED BRIDGES

There are numerous haunted bridges in the Stevens Point Area. There is actually a hybrid Woman in White/Crying Bridge case here (both of which are covered in this mystical tome that you hold in your hands now) where a woman, a bride, on her wedding day, discovered that her husband had been unfaithful. She ran from the chapel and across Red Bridge on Casimir Road, where she was struck and killed. The first incident and evidence that her spirit remains in the area was that of a police officer. He was driving across "Bloody Bride Bridge" on Highway 66 near Jordan Park when he slammed his brakes halfway across the bridge, thinking that he had just struck a woman. He got out to investigate, but found nothing. No woman, no damage to his vehicle... nothing. So, he thought. He got back into his vehicle and out of habit looked into the review mirror where he met the gaze of a woman in a wedding dress, black hair, wet and matted around her face sitting in the back seat. The bride is said to haunt these 2 bridges and has even been associated with a third, called the Black Bridge.

All 3 of these bridges are well known fishing spots, so fishermen are often reported as having encounters with the "lady in white" as she roams and haunts.

There is also the small cafe known as The Cottage Cafe. The owners are sister who are also paranormal investigators. Hauntings here date back to the 1800s and show no signs of stopping. The sisters rarely open the cafe up for daily patronage, but do host a number of ghost and haunt-related events and even host a Halloween night paranormal group!

These are just a few of the stories that I found while boots to the ground in Steven's Point.

Needless to say, the area surrounding Steven's Point, Wisconsin is ripe with supernatural activity. We may never know what truly happened that night on Boy Scout Lane, and maybe it's better that way. But I think it's safe to say at this point that this road and the entire area surrounding it is haunted by that lost troop of young Boy Scouts, the bus driver, and the troop master.

CHAPTER 16

Pyramid Lake

A bloody and brutal battle. A heritage and legacy. A vengeful Mermaid. A Giant Flesh-Eating Serpent. Demonic Water-Babies.

Welcome to Pyramid Lake!

Set deep within Washoe County's Truckee River Basin is Pyramid Lake. Four cardinal sentinels keep watch over this historic and legendary lake. Pah-Rum Peak to the North, Tohakum Peak in the East, Virginia Peak to the South, and Tule Peak to the West. The mountains surround this majestic body of water, keeping it well guarded and well hidden. The lake is beautiful, no doubt. Its waters - crystal clear - shimmer and sparkle in radiant splendor. Its surface - smooth and calm - reflects the sun in a multicolored spectrum, a diamond-encrusted sheet of glass with nary but a ripple to disturb it. It is home to some fascinating and endangered fowl and fish. It is the ONLY habitat in the entire world that can sustain the ancient Cui-ui fish. It is also home to the rare Lahontan Cutthroat trout.

Pyramid Lake is all that remains of Lake Lahontan, a primordial monstrosity that blanketed the majority of what is now known as Nevada in the Pleistocene age. Lake Lahontan was a titan. An inland Sea covering over 110,000 square miles. Pyramid Lake is ancient and holds within its depths the histories and mysteries of ages. Yet, as beautiful and grandiose as this lake is, it is nothing compared to the horrors that lie beneath its opalescent surface.

The Legend

In 1860 a meeting of 3 native tribes was held. The Paiutes, the Bannocks, and the Shoshones assembled at Pyramid Lake to discuss the encroachment of settlers on their land. Settlers had made their way west and north in search of silver and expansion. In doing so they had leveled forests and disrupted not only the way of life of these native peoples but also the entire biosystem and ecosystem. One particularly sore point was the myriad pinyon trees that were cut down to be used as fuel for ore-processing. This *obliterated* an essential food and eco-economy for the Paiute people. The discussion was one of war vs peace and most were leaning towards war, not out of a desire for it but out of necessity, out of preservation of their way of life.

The decision was made for them as word arrived that a Bannock warrior and his war party had killed 5 settlers at Williams Station Pony Express. The warrior had heard that settlers had kidnapped 2 Paiute women and were keeping them there. The party went to William's station and demanded the women be released. One version of the story claims that the subsequent attack and "murders" were unprovoked, while another claims that the warriors were met with open hostility and had no choice but to fight in order to rescue their women.

I think we all know which version to believe.

Upon hearing of this attack and the killings, Chief Numaga, one of the staunch supporters of peace up to this point is recorded as saying, "There is no longer any use for counsel; we must prepare for war, for the soldiers will now come here to fight us." Thus, the first Battle at Pyramid Lake was begun.

The battle began as the army assembled to hunt down and eradicate the natives spotted a pair of Paiute scouts and gave chase. The chase was on in full and all seemed to be lost for the scouts until a much larger group of Paiute appeared from behind the bluffs and opened fire on the army. The battle was waged in earnest as the army advanced, but they were blinded by the sun as they marched west and uphill. The army was ill-prepared for not only the tactics of the native tribes but also the weaponry that they possessed. The Soldiers were expecting to face bow and arrow and maybe some pistol fire, but were met with long-range, powerful, and accurate rifles. It was a rout. Chief Numaga tried to call for a ceasefire and allow the settler army to surrender, but at this point, the warriors were in a blood-frenzy and would not stop. It was a wholesale slaughter. Only 29 settlers survived.

Can we take a moment here to admire the tactical prowess of the Paiute leaders? Awesome.

Chief Numaga and the Paiute warriors knew that this victory would be short-lived. They returned home and escorted their women and children to Black Rock Desert where they would be safe and then made their way back to Pyramid Lake, prepared for war.

The settlers had not been sitting idly by. They had underestimated the Paiute warriors to their own end, but would not do so again. A much larger army was amassed and marched out to Pyramid Lake. The battle raged for hours with neither side taking a distinct advantage. The casualties piled up, including 2 captains from the army. Chief Numaga, seeing that this had become a battle of attrition at this point, ordered a retreat. He and his warriors met up with the rest of their tribe at Black Rock Desert.

There was no clear winner of this battle, though in war there rarely is.

Nevada Historical Marker 148 reads:

On May 12, 1860, Northern Paiute warriors, fighting to retain their way of life, decisively defeated a volunteer army from Virginia City and nearby settlements. The battle and consequent white retreat began with a skillful ambush north of Nixon and continued along the plateau on the opposite side of the Truckee River almost to the present site of Wadsworth.

On June 2, 1860, a strong force of volunteers and regular U.S. Army troops engaged the Indians in battle along the tableland and mountainside. Several hundred braves, attempting a delaying action to allow their women, children, and elders to escape, fought with such courage and strategy that the superior Caucasian forces were held back during the day until the Indians withdrew.

Paiute war leader Numaga (Young Winnemucca), described as a "superior man of any race," desired only peace for his people.

What a story.

Mermaids, Demon Babies and Serpents. Oh My!

Pyramid lake is beautiful. It is serene. It captivates visitors and locals alike with its crystal-clear waters and wildlife. Even its rocks are mesmerizing. Tufa rock formations speckle the landscape in and around the lake. The most famous being the giant, pyramid-shaped rock that the lake is named after. Others include, the Stone Mother (which resembles a mother and child), Indian Head Rock, and Popcorn Rock.

People are often met with a sense of wonder and amazement when visiting Pyramid Lake, but they are also often met with a sense of dread. A dark and foreboding essence, a sinister veil covers the lake, especially after the sun goes down.

The memories of the tragic battles that took place here would be enough to cause pause, but there is something more…

It is said that a beautiful mermaid once lived in the ancient waters of Pyramid Lake. Long ago, a proud Paiute warrior caught the mermaid by accident while fishing off of Pyramid Rock. So taken by her was he, that he brought her back to his village and announced that they were to be married. His tribe would not have it, and so they were forced to wed in secret. They were madly in love and truly happy, that is until one day a Paiute woman saw them together on the shores of the lake in a loving embrace. She immediately ran back to the village to tell of what she had seen. The village stole the young warrior away from his bride and bore him back to the village. They then banished the mermaid from the shores!

Heartbroken and lost without her love, the mermaid became so bitter, so angry that she cursed the lake and the people. Some even say that she is the reason for the Battles at Pyramid Lake and for any bad luck that the Paiute people endured. To this day she haunts the shores of the Lake, eager to grab hold of any that wander too near and pull them down into the cold depths.

And as if watching out for a spiteful mermaid wasn't enough, Pyramid Lake is also reported as being haunted by demon-water babies. As the sun goes down, its last rays of light being split and cast about by the mountainous western peaks, the wails of abandoned and discarded children begin to ascend. It is said that culling was often necessary for the preservation of a people and that when babies were born that were weak or sickly or disfigured, they would be discarded into the lake and forgotten. These dismissed babies would undergo a sort of transformation in their death - perhaps as a direct result of the mermaid's curse upon the lake - and become something other. They would retain their infant-like forms, or at least have the ability to appear infant-like, but they were no longer human.

These demonic water babies will lure their victims by their sorrowful cries, lure them into the lake and then attack in droves. Angry, vile, and piranha-like they will feed and consume, until there is nothing left.

A variation of this tale is that a giant serpent, left over from a more ancient and magical time, preyed on the local people of Pyramid Lake for 7 years until a warrior brave enough to face the beast asked it what it wanted, what they could do to appease his hunger so that he would leave them alone. The great serpent responded that he would leave them in peace if they agreed to deliver him any child that was malformed or unwanted. The people agreed and sacrificed their unwanted children to the mighty beast in order to stay his hunger.

This giant serpent kind of reminds me of Jörmungandr, the Norse world serpent. Obviously, Jörmungandr was much larger, I mean big enough to wrap itself around the whole of Midgard, but I still pictured this story as I was researching Pyramid Lake.

A giant serpent, just beneath the surface. Demanding servitude and sacrifice from its people… I don't know… just kinda cool.

Conclusion

Every year visitors come to Pyramid Lake and every year someone goes missing. Never to be found. Often it is a fisherman that was out on calm waters when suddenly the waters begin to churn and thrash about widely tossing him overboard.

The bodies that go missing in Pyramid Lake often end up resurfacing in Lake Tahoe… 60 Miles away from Pyramid Lake. Not only that, but Pyramid Lake has NO outlets and does not feed Lake Tahoe or any other body of water.

'Splain that one...

Now normally, right about now I'd go into a "How to Kill It" segment, but kill what?!? A vengeful Mermaid? No thanks! A legion of Demon Babies? Uh-uh. A giant world serpent? Not happening. I am just gonna leave this one alone.

I was lucky enough to interview someone with a personal story about Pyramid Lake. He asked not to be identified, so for the sake of anonymity I will change his name to *Dude*.

> Hello my name is *Dude*. I have spent a lot of time at Pyramid Lake in NV. My dad moved to Pyramid Lake at a very young age, probably about 15 years old - basically ran away from home and started his life there. He is not native but he made close friends who were Paiute and they accepted him and they all became very close. Fast forward to the mid-80s and my dad left the lake, moved back to California and met my mom. As a kid my dad would always tell me stories about the lake water babies, the serpent on the lake and about a witch/demon that would chase down cars and then would never be seen again. I first visited Pyramid Lake for myself in 85 and we continued to visit 2 to 3 times a year until I

became an adult. There are so many legends about this place it almost seems evil but it's not. It's a very spiritual place and I believe in all the legends myself. There is not much on the reservation. Just a couple stores, some lodging and a bar. The bar is about 400 feet from the lake and that's about as close as you will ever see any one get after sun down because legend has it that the babies that were drowned there by the Paiute because of birth defects are now angry spirits and a lot of people go missing on the water every year and never found. All of the lake problems are said to stem from the curse of the lake. The mermaid's curse. Some of the tribe still blames the war with the American Cavalry on her and her curse.

Fun fact you can still walk through and see the reinforced caves that the US Calvary stored the weapons and ammo in during the battles.

The water on the lake can go from smooth as glass to extremely choppy in seconds. I have seen this many times. According to legends it is either the water babies or the serpent, depending on who you ask. There are natural geyser hot springs at the lake also but you have to know a local to find them.

Thanks, *Dude*!

Chapter 17

Leprechaun

I.
Little Cowboy, what have you heard,
Up on the lonely rath's green mound?
Only the plaintive yellow bird
Sighing in sultry fields around,
Chary, chary, chary, chee-ee!--
Only the grasshopper and the bee?--
"Tip-tap, rip-rap,
Tick-a-tack-too!
Scarlet leather, sewn together,
This will make a shoe.
Left, right, pull it tight;
Summer days are warm;
Underground in winter,
Laughing at the storm!
Lay your ear close to the hill.
Do you not catch the tiny clamour,
Busy click of an elfin hammer,
Voice of the Lepracaun singing shrill
As he merrily plies his trade?
He's a span

And a quarter in height.
Get him in sight, hold him tight,
And you're a made
Man!
II.
You watch your cattle the summer day,
Sup on potatoes, sleep in the hay;
How would you like to roll in your carriage.
Look for a duchess's daughter in marriage?
Seize the Shoemaker--then you may!
"Big boots a-hunting,
Sandals in the hall,
White for a wedding-feast,
Pink for a ball.
This way, that way,
So we make a shoe;
Getting rich every stitch,
Tick-tack-too!"
Nine-and-ninety treasure-crocks
This keen miser-fairy hath,
Hid in mountains, woods, and rocks,
Ruin and round-tow'r, cave and rath,
And where the cormorants build;
From times of old
Guarded by him;
Each of them fill'd
Full to the brim
With gold!
III.
I caught him at work one day, myself,
In the castle-ditch, where foxglove grows,--

A wrinkled, wizen'd and bearded Elf,
Spectacles stuck on his pointed nose,
Silver buckles to his hose,
Leather apron-shot in his lap--
"Rip-rap, tip-tap,
Tick-tack-too!
(A grasshopper on my cap!
Away the moth flew!)
Buskins for a fairy prince,
Brogues for his son,--
Pay me well, pay me well,
When the job is done! "
The rogue was mine, beyond a doubt.
I stared at him; he stared at me;
"Servant, Sir!" "Humph!" says he,
And pull'd a snuff-box out.
He took a long pinch, look'd better pleased,
The queer little Lepracaun;
Offer'd the box with a whimsical grace,-
Pouf! he flung the dust in my face,
And, while I sneezed,
Was gone!

The Leprechaun by William Allingham

The Legend

The Anglo-Irish word Leprechaun comes from the Old Irish luchorpán or lupracán, though the current spelling for this solitary fairy used throughout Ireland is leipreachán. Although, depending on what region you find yourself in, you could use any one of over 15 variants or names for this Tinker-Fairy.

John O'Donovan describes the Leprechaun as "a sprite, a pigmy; a fairy of a diminutive size, who always carries a purse containing a shilling" and although this gives us a cursory glance, it is far from the whole picture.

It seems as though the term has morphed over time, but - according to folk etymology - comes from the combined Leith (meaning half) and Brog (meaning brogue) LeighBrog - Though other translations tell us it means One Shoemaker (LeithBragan).

The earliest mention of the leprechaun is in the *Echtra Fergus mac Léti* or the (Adventure of Fergus son of Léti) written in the 7th or 8th century. In this ancient tome, Fergus Mac Leti, King of Ulster, is woken from a nap on the beach to find himself being dragged away by 3 lúchorpáin. He is able to capture the 3 fairies and is granted 3 wishes in exchange for their release.

The Leprechaun is a solitary fairy with a penchant for shoe-making and practical jokes. This definition was given by Irish folklorist John O'Hanlon. Later, author of *Irish Wonders*, D. R. McAnally, and writer and folklorist William Butler Yeats affirmed this description. According to Yeats, the Leprechaun is "not wholly good nor wholly evil, but rather sits comfortably somewhere in the middle, as he is the son of an 'evil spirit' and a degenerate fairy".

It is important to make and know this distinction because, though the leprechaun is known throughout Ireland as a mythical, magical being, he is NEVER to be associated with the Aos Sí (the People of the Mounds).

The Sidhe are a supernatural elf or fairy race in Gaelic folklore. They are believed to be of the Tuatha Dé Danann - the old gods of Irish mythology. The Sidhe are involved in the affairs of mortals. They are sinister or they are kind. They are malevolent or they are merciful... They are pleased or displeased depending on the behavior and offering of the people. The Leprechaun, on the other hand, is a lone fairy, content to hone and master his craft of shoe-making and get a few pranks or jokes in here and there where he can.

He may not have been quite so easily recognizable to us prior to the 20th century, as the leprechaun wore reds instead of greens. Samuel Lover, known as Ben Trovato, an Irish songwriter, wrote this of the Leprechaun: "... quite a beau in his dress, notwithstanding, for he wears a red square-cut coat, richly laced with gold, and inexpressible of the same, cocked hat, shoes and buckles"

And According to McAnally: "He is about three feet high, and is dressed in a little red jacket or roundabout, with red breeches buckled at the knee, gray or black stockings, and a hat, cocked in the style of a century ago, over a little, old, withered face. 'Round his neck is an Elizabethan ruff, and frills of lace are at his wrists. On the wild west coast, where the Atlantic winds bring almost constant rains, he dispenses with ruff and frills and wears a frieze overcoat over his pretty red suit, so that, unless on the lookout for the cocked hat, ye might pass a Leprechaun on the road and never know it's himself that's in it at all."

The modern visage of the leprechaun that we are all familiar with most likely came from folk etymology (which is a change in a word or phrase or even a description resulting from the replacement of an unfamiliar form by a more familiar one). This is how legends and lore (even urban legends) thrive, isn't it? The coat most likely shifted from red to green as the stories rippled further and further from the source. Green is the traditional color of Ireland, is it not? And as far as the hat and shoes and style of coat… it is believed that as more and more Irish made the treacherous pilgrimage to the United States and set foot on her shores, they were dressed in 19th century Elizabethan attire, as was still popular at that time in Ireland. So, the leprechaun made his way to the new world with his brave Irish families of the first immigration and from there garnered modern attention and appeal.

Leprechauns are tiny fairies that take the form of old men, never women (According to Carolyn White's *A History of Irish Fairies*) in green or red attire. They are solitary and mischievous creatures that like to make, mend and shine shoes and hoard gold in pots at the end of rainbows. They will also grant their captors 3 wishes in exchange for release if caught. Leprechauns are also known as The Clurican, a sprite with an insatiable thirst for liquor and getting drunk, and the Far Darrig (or Red Man), a red-clad prankster with a bit of a sour side.

The Leprechaun is a rogue trickster. He finds gold that has been long forgotten and collects it obsessively, not to use it, not to spend it, but simply as a way to trick humans into searching for it. He keeps his pot of gold at the end of the rainbow, because a rainbow has no specific beginning or end. The ultimate trick upon us mere mortals is the fact that there is a pot of gold… ultimate riches just over that next hill, or just beyond that last turn… and we will never… ever find it.

Tales tell of an ancient people, the Fir Bolg, who were from Ireland before the dawn of modern man. These Fir Bolg left Ireland for a time and traveled to Greece. Upon returning they established the Emerald Isle, divided it into provinces, and ruled over it… this rule was short-lived, however, as the Tuatha De Danann invaded and overthrew them.

The *Lebor Gabála Érenn* (or The Book of Invasions) tells this story in full. Ancient Ireland was settled 6 different times by 6 different peoples. Of these six peoples, only the Fir Bolg and the Tuatha De Danann survived. As we learned earlier, the leprechaun is NOT of the Tuatha De Danann…

I'm not necessarily saying that the leprechaun is Fir Bolg.

I'm saying that the leprechaun is as much part of the very fabric, the very essence, the very spirit and foundation of Ireland as the deities of the Tuatha De Danann and the mythical Fir Bolg, but we know that they are NOT Tuatha de Danann. I'm saying that perhaps the leprechaun is the very juxtaposition, the anchor, the fulcrum… the very force that bridges the gap between History and Legend… between reality and myth. Between Tuatha De Danann and Fir Bolg.

I know that these days we see the leprechaun on the cover of cereal boxes and as college football mascots… and we've already discussed the more modern idea of the leprechaun and even some of his history, but what about that other side… the darker, more menacing side?

Well, that comes from the rise of the Roman Catholic Church (doesn't it always?). As this form of

Christendom took over, the more pagan and mystical beliefs waned. The church began to paint sprites and fairies with a much darker pallet. The leprechaun was made out to be a baby snatcher. He would replace human babies with changelings and kill potential gold thieves instead of just trick them...

This type of character assassination continued even into the 19th and 20th centuries as prejudice toward Irish immigrants grew. The Irish immigrants were met on the shores of the United States with atrocious treatment and hatred. These Irish-Americans and their Celtic lore and pride were reduced to nothing. The once proud leprechaun, a symbol of the history and legend of the Irish became a stereotypical representation of drunkenness, irresponsibility, ignorance and greed. Many of these anti-Irish prejudices continue to this day and are even endorsed by the misrepresentation of the leprechaun.

Saint Patrick's Day

Saint Patrick's Day was first celebrated in the United States on March 17th, 1772 when Irish soldiers serving British forces were so homesick that they marched down the street of New York to honor Saint Patrick and their homeland. According to Britannica:

> "St. Patrick's Day, feast day (March 17) of St. Patrick, patron saint of Ireland. Born in Roman Britain in the late 4th century, he was kidnapped

at the age of 16 and taken to Ireland as a slave. He escaped but returned about 432 CE to convert the Irish to Christianity. By the time of his death on March 17, 461, he had established monasteries, churches, and schools. Many legends grew up around him—for example, that he drove the snakes out of Ireland and used the shamrock to explain the Trinity. Ireland came to celebrate his day with religious services and feasts."

Neither the saint nor his day have anything to do with the Leprechaun, but so popular was that first parade back in 1772, that as the years went by a symbol was needed for… you guessed it… marketing. Money. Enter the fat little drunk green man that dances about with his rainbows and 4-leaf clovers and gold coins!

CHAPTER 18

The Fouke Monster

A small town in Miller County, Arkansas. A young family excited and ready for the beginning of a new life together in a quaint little farmhouse in Texarkana that they had just purchased. The week had been filled with packing and unpacking, moving boxes and furniture, meeting the neighbors, and making new friends. Invitations for dinners and housewarmings were given and taken as liberally as the town gossip. Bobby and Elizabeth Ford were eating up every second of it, though this was just a sample, just a taste of the celebrity that they would soon be experiencing, albeit for circumstances akin to a much more exotic ilk.

In May of 1971 the Ford's started a new chapter of their lives as they moved into a rustic old farmhouse in Fouke, Arkansas. The setting was the perfect paragon of picturesque pastures and pulchritudinous plattelands. Rolling emerald fields, neighboring cows grazing and gossiping, forests full of bark-armored sentinels pridefully presenting their brand-new deep greens. The dull browns and yellows of winter were nothing but a memory. The old farmhouse may not have had a new coat of paint or a fancy paved driveway, but what it lacked in contemporary amenities it more than made up for in character. Mrs. Ford was often quoted as saying, "She may not have class, but she got stories for days" when describing her new home.

The young couple was happy. Everything was hunky-dory, except that on multiple occasions throughout that first week Mr. Ford swore that he had seen a large, dark shape lurking around his tree line. It never stayed long and it never approached them, at least not at first, but over the course of the next few days, Bobby began to grow concerned, and apparently, he was not the only one. There are multiple other eyewitnesses, including Bobby's brother and hunting-mates that had reported seeing a large bi-pedal creature prowling about.

Mr. Ford's first encounter with the creature was a colossal comedy of errors. It is reported that he was doing some yard work around the house when suddenly he was grabbed from behind. He reported that the creature was large. It was 7-8 feet tall and very, very strong. It was grunting and breathing heavily, had red glowing eyes and moved very quickly. Ford says that the creature's chest was enormous and it had dark, black hair all over its body. The creature had wrapped Ford up in some type of large, mammal-like hug and was squeezing him tight, too tight! Ford was getting light headed as his breathing became more and more labored, his lungs unable to function properly due to the constricting force of the creatures embrace. Fearing that he would soon succumb to his waning oxygen intake and pass out, Bobby flailed about wildly.

Through sheer determination and will to live, Ford was able to break free from the bear's... er, I mean the creature's grasp. He hit the ground hard and ran full-tilt toward the safety of his new home. So harrowed was he, so gripped by fear - though I suppose that's better than being gripped by a bear... er.... monster - that he wasn't even able to open his door! Instead, he burst through, the front door exploding into splinters. Sharp, jagged shards of serrated shrapnel careened through the entryway and through his skin. There, on the welcome mat of his new home, peppered with splinters from his front door, barely breathing, having narrowly escaped the clutches of the now famous Boggy Creek Monster, Bobby Ford passed out.

The Legend

Bobby Ford woke up the next day at a local hospital where he was being treated for minor scratches and shock.

- So, he basically knocked himself the heck out on his front door and got a bunch of splinters!

He gave his report of what happened to the Fouke constable, though his initial telling conveniently omitted the busted-down door. The story didn't gain much traction at that point and Bobby was back home and in the loving arms of Elizabeth before supper that evening. But that evening is when things really started to unravel. Bobby's brother and hunting buddies had come over to wish him well and to give him some much-deserved ribbing over the whole thing, when all of a sudden, one of his friends shouted that he had just seen the monster through a window!

It wasn't long before this motley crew of backwoods warriors were armed with rifles and flashlights and were making their way around to the back of the house in what I can only imagine was the most precise and perfect Hillbilly Flying V ever seen… not a Gibson Flying V, mind you… a Bombay Flying V. A D1 Flying V!

- Yes, I'm referencing The Mighty Ducks in a spooky urban legend book. Believe me, you'll understand why in just a little bit.

- And I'm not talking about the sissy-pants private school varsity D3 Ducks… I'm talking about the mean, lean street ducks…. D1 Ducks.

You see, the Flying V is impenetrable, except of course if your opponent chooses to use the super-secret yet highly-effective reverse V, but we're assuming that the Fouke Monster is unaware of such tactics... and there is, of course, just one of them... and it is of course just a bear...

No! No, it's not a bear! It's a monster! A cryptid! There were like 5 movies made about this creature! It is a monster!

So, this band of hunters form up and march out. Their mission: murder. Their motivation: revenge. Revenge for making dude look like a fool! Ain't nobody humiliate Bobby Ford and get away with it!

They turned the corner just in time to see this large, black-haired, red-eyed creature lumbering around the opposite side of the house. It was dark and the soft beams of flashlights bouncing and swaying in excitement offered little by way of any real help in seeing the beast, but they saw enough! They opened fire on the creature and saw it drop! It let out a pained and angry cry as it fell, obviously having taken at least one hit, if not more. The men marched toward their prize, but when they got there, it was gone!

Just then, as the search began anew, they heard a scream from within the home! Bobby ran back the way he had come, entering the home - which was easier than it should have been since he had destroyed the front door the night before - to find Elizabeth, visibly shaken, but otherwise unharmed. She fell into his arms, clearly distraught, and told him that moments after she had heard the gunfire, a giant arm covered in black fur or hair had reached in the window above the couch where she was sitting. She stated that it didn't reach specifically for her, but that its enormous claws were mere inches from her face.

A fruitless search went on well into the night. The constable arrived along with concerned or curious neighbors and ne'er-do-wells and they all did their best to comfort the traumatized couple. The constable inspected the location where the beast was downed, but could find neither beast nor blood. As a matter of fact, he found nothing but a strange set of tracks and some unfamiliar scratch marks of the Ford's patio.

A reporter for the Texarkana Gazette made his way out to the Ford residence the very next day to get the first-hand account of the encounter. He was met by a frantic and exhausted Mr. and Mrs. Ford. They were packing up their belongings and loading up their vehicles. Ford told the reporter that they had lived here exactly 1 week today and that was enough. They were moving out and getting as far away from there as possible. He did recount his tail… his and Elizabeth's both and it was published the next day in both the Texarkana Gazette and Texarkana Daily. The story was then wired to The Associated Press and The United Press International and ran in newspapers nationwide!

Fouke, Texarkana and Miller County have all had their fair share of sightings over the years, but none so notorious as the one in May of '71 at the old Ford home in Boggy Creek. There's not much more to report on Elizabeth Ford, but upon further investigation I found that Bobby Ford had quite an illustrious career as an outlaw! Apparently, he rode with the James/Younger gang and was one of Jesse James' most trusted allies, that is until he shot him in the back of the head…

- Ok, you may say that I'm all OVER the place on this one! That Bobby Ford was not The Coward Robert Ford who assassinated Jesse James!
- But then I would say to you, "Who freakin' cares! So, what if that was like 100 years apart!?? And yes, I have taken all my medications!

This story pissed me off to no end! 5 movies! 5 movies were made about this "Boggy Creek Fouke Monster" and it was obviously a bear! I wasn't even going to include this one, as it has clearly upset me and lessens the otherwise stellar quality of my storytelling, but I had to. I had to include it so that you would not be duped into thinking that the Fouke Monster was anything more than a farce!

Conclusion

While it's true that the Fords' celebrity was short lived, their story did make it onto the silver screen! The Legend of Boggy Creek released in theaters in 1972 and earned 20 million dollars!

20 MILLIOION DOLLARS

- I'm sorry… It's just this dang bear made some jabroni in Hollywood 20,000,000 dollars and I can't even get… You know what… Never mind.

The film spawned several sequels - both official and unofficial - including: Return to Boggy Creek, Boggy Creek II: And the Legend Continues, and Boggy Creek: The Legend is True. Though none of these films saw the same commercial success as the original, they all enjoyed some time in the spotlight. The original film, The Legend of Boggy Creek was recently remastered and screened nationwide.

There was even a book written about the Fouke Monster by someone we have seen here before. It seems that Lyle Blackburn, author of *Lizard Man: The True Story of the Bishopville Monster* also took a compelling look at the beast. He wrote *The Beast of Boggy Creek: The True Story of the Fouke Monster* and it is currently available on Amazon sitting at 214 ratings with a 4.5-star score!

- Lyle, could you share your secret. Please? I need to get paid, man!

I would be remiss if I did not do my due diligence here after introducing you to such a harrowing monster if I didn't tell you how to kill it. Well, luckily for you, while I have never killed a Fouke Monster before, I have seen a ton of movies that have bear fights in them and since we all know this Fouke Monster was just a hungry black bear, I think I can reference a few of those more popular films and be on my way.

Kill the Fouker!

#1 Punch it in the nose. This works every time and it is an automatic one-shot kill.

#2 If you simply want to escape the bear or "Fouke Monster" and you have a little time on your hands, you may first hollow out a large tree, place a cute window in it and make it look very inviting to the beast. Then once the creature has taken up residence within the tree, you may feed it honey. Lots of HONEY. This will fatten that silly old bear right up and it will get stuck trying to go out the window!

#3 If you ever find yourself stranded in the wilderness with a bitter rival AND a bear, simply carve a spear out of a tree branch and wait for the bear to fall on it whilst trying to eat you. The bear will then use its own weight to impale itself on said spear and then you and your rival can survive on bear meat. Or Fouke meat... whatever.

#4 Last but not least, simply lie down where you are... Bears/Foukes are innately afraid of delicious and helpless meals if said delicious and helpless meals happen to be laying down in a fetal position.

If you follow these 4 steps, these Micah Campbell approved instructions, you will be murdering Fouke Monsters in no time!

Now give me my 20 million and make me sammich!

Conclusion

Ya, I know... I was about 20 minutes into researching this monster I realized it was a bear and then everything else just went out the window!

We can talk about the actual encounter. How sad/funny it is that the Fords were in and out of that house in 7 days... We can talk about him knocking himself out busting through the front door... etc. - all that was probably real. But I am a supernatural and paranormal **expert**. I am a **top** cryptozoologist. I can tell you with 100% certainty that while the rest of the legends in this compendium are 100% true, this one... this "Fouke Monster" was complete bull.

Disclaimer: We do not really recommend or approve of anyone trying ANY of those steps listed in our "how to kill it" segment. Don't mess with bears… or Fouke Monsters, for that matter.

CHAPTER 19

The Lady in White

Misty wisps of New York fog roll and whip across the Durand Eastman Park in Rochester, New York. Eastman Lake and Durand Lake offer their own attempts at obscuring the grounds in and around the area but are minor players in this mysterious vapor that so easily obfuscates the senses on this dark and lonely night. Things that are, appear not to be and things that are not, suddenly become very, very real. The major player in this nightly subterfuge is often considered to be Great Lake Ontario that shores upon the northern expanse of the park, and surely with its choppy waters, icy depths and fell northern winds its contributions are adequate, but even this mighty inland sea is not enough to cause the dense, menacing bank of fog that stalks about, almost alive, almost as if it is subject to the will of someone… or something.

Hounds are heard from somewhere within the mire. Their lugubrious baying ever enough to keep away even the most stalwart of adventurers. Often reported as howling or snarling, these animalistic roars are full of recondite warning. But warning of what and to whom?

Within the rolling haze are caught brief glimpses of ivy-lined stone. Enormous groups of vines cling to and crawl up and over giant walls en masse. Centuries-old steps that are carved into the hills ascend a multi-tiered walkway. A jagged and broken parapet tops a multi-level bulwark that is integrated into the very foundation of the earth. The remains of a castle appear here. A castle long ago forgotten. But the sins and tragedies that fell upon the proprietor of the castle are very much remembered to this day. This was the Lady in White's castle. Those beasts that can be heard when the mist thickens are hers. And this mist itself is hers, doing her bidding as she stalks the night.

But why does she roam? Why does she linger? What is she seeking?

The Legend

The Lady in White or the White Lady is a well-known and oft-told tale of a woman who has usually either been slighted by a lover or has lost a child to murder or some other tragedy. She is a ghost or spectre often found in rural areas and is associated with or tied to local legends of tragedy or betrayal. She is known around the world and can be found in the forests of Buskett, Malta in the Verdala Palace or high on the cliffs of Montmorency Falls, near Quebec City. The White Lady of Rochester, New York - who we were looking at in the intro - is also known as The Lady of the Lake, as she is often seen floating across the 2 small lakes that surround her once majestic castle in Durand Eastman Park. It is said that the Lady lost her only daughter one night many years ago, when the mists of the lakes were especially dense and mischievous.

The daughter's boyfriend had lured her outside of the watchful eyes of the castle and had murdered her, discarding her body in the bogs of the lake. The Lady in White searched and searched for her daughter, often being out for days without rest. She even had 2 large wolfhounds brought over from Ireland to assist in the search. The hounds took immediately to their lady and assisted her in her never-ending quarry.

Day after day, year after year the Lady in White searched, until one day she fell. She was exhausted and malnourished and far from the glow of the castle's flaming torches. She fell asleep there in the forest, alone, except for her 2 mighty wolfhounds. She did not wake and the hounds did not leave her side. They, too, perished. Loyal and somber they watched over their their Lady until they could keep watch no longer.

Now, centuries later, the lady and her hounds roam the areas around Durand Eastman Park, where her castle once stood. Where she and her daughter one laughed and sang and danced… where her daughter had died at the hands of her lover and where she, too, eventually died looking for her. The castle has been toppled by time and progress. Only a sliver, just a piece of its once majestic visage, remains and so, too, does a sliver remain of this woesome lady. Even in death she has not given up the search for her daughter. Her dogs, ever loyal, remain by her side even after death. They search as they did in life; diligently and with purpose.

It is said that The Lady and her hounds haunt the patrons of Durand Eastman Park in the overnight hours. She is especially attentive to those who would visit the park for more carnal reasons, as she is convinced that her daughter was murdered by her boyfriend who was frustrated and resentful with her vow of chastity.

Many young lovers have been chased off after seeing the White Lady. Some stay, perhaps indignant, perhaps curious, but those too are found quickly running for their lives as the ghostly spectres of the Lady's hounds appear and let out a howl that is half mournful lament, half viscous warning.

The Lady in White is rarely violent, and her hounds are honor-bound to stay by her side always. She stays her hand and they remain docile per her command, but woe to those who would be found being violent or aggressive toward a woman on these nights. There have been reports of unexplained deaths and animal attacks within and around Durand Eastman Park. These deaths remain unsolved, as the guilty party is a vengeful spirit ever seeking her lost child.

A Different Angle

The most recent inhabitants of Blenkinsopp Castle in Northumberland in England reported a woman in white that had begun haunting their young boy at night. The parents were awakened by the sounds of the child screaming "The White Lady! The White Lady!", but by the time they got to his room, the lady was gone. The boy told his parents that she had gotten angry with him after he refused to accompany her to the cellars far below the castle. She told him there was a box of gold there and that he could have it if only he would remove it from the castle - for the gold was cursed and she could not rest until it was gone.

For 3 nights in a row the boy was visited by the woman, but she would only show herself to him. On the 4th night, the boy decided that he would follow the White Lady. And so, she led him down, down, down, to the depths of the castle and there in a hollowed-out portion of the cellar walls was a small tinderbox heavy with gold. The inscription on the box read: B. Rose.

Beatrice Rose had been a maid in the castle centuries before and had disappeared one night after having stolen a bag of gold coins from the master of the house. She had stolen the money in order to pay off a flesh debt that her brother owed, as he was sick and no longer able to perform manual labor. She had every intention of paying her master back. Her body was found days later hanging in the very cellars that she had hidden the money in, though the gold was never found. It is said that her body was littered with burns and cuts and it is believed that the master of the house had her tortured and killed. The money was never retrieved by her brother either, because the master had him killed as well.

A Feel-Good Story

One well circulated story is that of your A-typical jock type jerk. He is ultra-popular, ultra-alpha and an ultra-loser. He starts dating this girl. Grade A student type, pretty, quiet, loves her family and Jesus and Elvis… remind anyone else of a song? Tom Petty? No? No one? Anyway, soon after they start dating, this guy starts laying hands on her, belittling her, and pushing her around. Her grades start to suffer as well as her social life and her home life. Everyone knows what's going on, but she never admits it. He's not HITTING her or anything. He just gets mad sometimes… r-i-i-i-ght.

So, one night he drives her out to the park to make out. She says no and that gets him going… then she does something, spills her soda or whatever and he flies off the hinges. He starts screaming at her and threatening to hit her. Then all of a sudden there is a bright light, an explosion, but without the bang. They are blinded momentarily, but that doesn't stop ultra-jock from jumping out of the car and puffing out his chest. He slams the door shut and steps away from the vehicle. She can't see anything yet, but the car starts shaking violently and the bright light is back. She hears him screaming… she also hears what sounds like howls and snarls.

Suddenly the door opens and he gets in. Doesn't say a word… his face and hands are all scratched up and bleeding and the whole way home he just mumbles, "The White Lady. The White Lady".

Of course, they break up after this and she gets things back in order, but he… he loses everything. He never speaks again. He just mumbles, over and over again he mumbles… "The White Lady"

Ultra-jock got off easy if you ask me. The Lady in White should have ended that dude.

Rochester, New York is not the only area that the Lady in White haunts or searches. In fact, she is one of the most prevalent legends out there. Here in the states alone, she is seen in dozens of different locations including Madisonville, Louisiana. Hattiesburg, Mississippi. Yermo and Freemont, California. The list goes on. And not just here, but around the world. She shows up in the Celtic mythology of Wales, Portchester Castle in Hampshire, Thailand, the Philippines, Russia. She is everywhere.

A Woman Scorned

Some of the most prominent accounts of her presence are those that involve a bride on her wedding day succumbing to some sort of tragedy, often involving unfaithful or violent spouses. She is known as the White Lady because she was wearing her wedding gown at the time of her death and as we've learned previously, ghosts or spectres are often caught in a loop, replaying over and over again their last calamitous moments - this is called residual haunting, and is where most spirits that "miss the train" start and where most of them stay. Though there are those that break free of this cycle, either by going mad or losing all connection with their former lives and whatever it is that anchors them or both. They become angry and chaotic. Violent. They lose all semblance of what they once were and now simply *are*. And what they are is vengeful.

The White Lady is *not* a vengeful spirit. You have those spirits whose sphere of influence simply expands. Picture a stone tossed into the water… except that every ripple expands instead of shrinks. Every rhythmic pulse sends the circle out just a bit further and some stones simply produce a wider ripple. The White Lady would fall into this category.

That's not to say she *can't* be violent or seek revenge. I think that is only natural, especially in the cases where she or a loved one was murdered - especially as ghosts rarely have the conscience to govern retributive or acrimonious desires the way that we do. But she is always aware of her actions. She has not lost who she is or once was.

In one Maltese tale, the White Lady is a woman of some renown in Mdina (known as the Silent City). This picturesque city was the capital of Malta for centuries and sits high on a hilltop overlooking all of Malta. Stepping through the gates of Mdina is like stepping through a time warp. You'll see no automobiles here and it is very, very quiet, as Mdina adheres to a strict noise restriction. Mdina was established by the Phoenician people sometime around 1000-700 BC and remains much the same.

It is said that a woman was deeply and happily in love and had plans to marry, but that her father had promised her to another. She was well-liked in the community and spent much of her time in orphanages and elderly homes. Young boys and old men alike were taken by her beauty and her charm and she loved them all. She was kind and generous and very giving of both her time and her wealth. Her lover was a jealous man and would often become irate at the attention that she received from these young boys and older men. It is said that when he discovered that she had been promised to another, he became so enraged that even the promise of them running away together was not enough to assuage his fury.

He killed her on the steps of the orphanage. She was wearing a plain white silk gown. She is often seen gliding up and down the old, stone street of Mdina after midnight. Over the centuries she has appeared to young boys, heart-broken teens, and old men alike. She comforts and consoles them. She tells the children to go home and go to sleep. To the heart-broken teens she advises to "find another", and to those teenage boys who cannot find another and to the old men she bids them follow her. Join her in her "shadow". She lures them away with promises of comfort and they are never seen again.

A rather haunting tale is one from Haapsalu Castle in Estonia, where a woman caught the eye of a canon, or priest. He fell in love with her and they carried on an illicit and forbidden affair within the castle. She hid in plain sight as an altar boy and was quite content to remain so, as the priest showered her with affection and wealth. She was discovered when the bishop of Ösel-Wiek visited Haapsalu. She had hidden within a wall in the chapel but was found out. The bishop was so angry, that he had the woman immured within the wall.

Now for those of you that don't know, immurement is the act of imprisoning someone in a very small, tight, confined space with no exit. This form of capital punishment is especially grotesque because unlike, say, burying someone alive where one would die painfully and full of fear, but relatively quickly, immurement ensures that the victim dies slowly over the course of days, not minutes, by starvation or dehydration. Often the victims can still hear the goings on of "normal life" from just beyond their prison. They hear laughing and singing and all forms of merriment just inches away, as their bodies and their minds wither away slowly and agonizingly.

Immurement was often used as a ritual. A form of human sacrifice to bless or curse a new construction or building. Skeletal remains have been found inside walls of archaic structures for centuries. Such was the fate of our Lady in White. Even today she can be seen looking out of the baptistery window and can be heard calling for her love from within the walls. On clear nights of a full-moon, she can be seen roaming the halls of the castle and its grounds.

Interestingly enough, this is not the only known tale about a Lady in White and immurement. In Westphalia, Germany a prince went away to battle in the Thirty Years War. He was gone for many years and his bride took a traveling minstrel as a lover. When the prince returned, he found his lover and the minstrel in intimate embrace. So pure was his anger that he dragged the minstrel out to the moat surrounding his castle and drowned him right then and there. He returned to his wife, his anger unabated, and encased her behind a wall in their bedroom. He gave her food and drink, as his goal was not to kill her, but to keep her from cheating on him again as he returned to war.

The prince was killed in battle and his wife, trapped behind the wall, perished from starvation and dehydration. She haunts the castle to this day. When the castle was renovated some years later, the builders were ordered to tear down the interior walls. The unlucky craftsman that found the woman's remains fell off the roof and broke his neck the very next day. The White Lady can still be seen wandering about the castle grounds near the moat, searching for the drowned minstrel.

The stories go on and on. The Lady in White or the White Lady is a legend that transcends time and place. Her story is ever-changing. A kaleidoscope of tragedy and betrayal. She is as constant and consistent as life itself, yet as fleeting and fickle as the wind.

CHAPTER 20

The Dogman

The film is grainy. It flickers and flashes. The camera is unstable throughout the entirety of the home video. It is blurry and there is no sound. There are glimpses of a father cutting wood and taking a much-deserved respite for a sip of water. That man is Aaron Gable and this 3-minute film seems to be some sort of found-footage montage of a family vacation or simply a family's home movie. 2 boys are seen riding snowmobiles. These are Aaron's sons. The film often cuts to the wide expanse of a snow-covered Michigan wilderness and sprinkles in clips of the boys and the family dog here and there. There is a scene where we see Aaron Gable working under the hood of a beat-up old Ford pickup and then speaking to the camera holder. We assume that in this case, he was speaking to one of his sons because we quickly catch a glimpse of the boy in the passenger-side mirror as he films the family driving down a winding backwoods road.

The camera strafes from right to left and back again, as the young Gable boy captures the dead and fallen trees of the Michigan winter woods. All seems in order until the 2-minute and 45-second mark, at which point we see, just for the briefest of moments, what appears to be some sort of quad-pedal creature in the woods. The film then cuts to - who we can assume to be - Mr. Gable, carrying the camera through the woods, obviously intent on seeking out this creature that his son had caught in the last frame. There are some intense moments here of walking and then running through the trees. It is very eerie, almost disturbing, as again, there is no sound and the camera-work seems to become more and more frantic as it continues to capture what is happening. We catch glimpses here and there of what might be the creature but are never really sure. We are left wondering through the next 15-20 seconds, then... at the 3-minute and 9-second mark, we are given our first solid look at the beast.

Though the condition of the recording leaves much to be desired, one thing stands out in crystal-clear quality: it is massive. The size and shape of the creature is jarring. It looks like - and if this wasn't in the middle of Michigan, I'd swear it was - a silver-back gorilla. Try to imagine a great silverback gorilla with a body more akin to a grizzly and the head of a wolf. Even through all the grain and fuzz of the home video you can see its muscles stretch under the boulder-like form of its body. We're only given a few seconds to take this all in, as it almost immediately begins to charge Mr. Gable. Its speed and ferocity are nothing short of awe-inspiring - in an incredibly frightening sort of way. There is a blur of ground, then sky, then trees as Mr. Gable runs for his life. The last frame of the film is a giant, hungry maw opened wide and ravenous, spittle flying everywhere, as it clamps down on the camera and we are left staring at a blank black screen.

The Legend

In the late 1800s, Michigan was the leader in white pine production. So, it is only fitting that our Michigan Dogman was discovered by a group of lumberjacks. It is said that these men were high in the mountains and deep in the Michigan forests when they came across a strange-looking dog. It was still quite a ways away, but it caught their attention, and they honestly probably needed the distraction, as the area that they were in was quite remote and there was really nothing to occupy their time but sleep and work… and so a chase ensued.

They described the dog initially as being large but oddly proportioned, having an extended and very muscular body, much like a track athlete. The men reported that it seemed very, very frightened… which is why they gave chase.

You know, cause a bunch of huge lumberjacks chasing you with axes or saws or whatever is really going to calm you down, right?

Right?

So anyway, they cornered the dog in a small copse of fallen trees. It had nowhere to go, so it hid inside a large hollowed-out log...

Now, being the mature upstanding men I'm sure these guys were, they decided to leave well enough alone and head back to work, right? They'd had their fun, blown off some steam... Now it's time to head home?

Well, you'd think, but no. They proceeded to poke at it with their axes trying to coax it out.

Obviously, I'm rooting for the dog here. But really, was I ever not?

So, the dog was yelping and crying and even this did not deter the lumberjacks from their game... but the yelps and cries became less and less a frightened, pained thing and more an angry and ferocious thing. Before the men could reconsider their course of action or abandon it altogether, they were blown back by a force so powerful that it lifted them from the ground.

Shards and splinters flew as a giant 7-foot tall bi-pedal beast burst forth. Its teeth were like spears. Its roar was the thing of nightmares. Its eyes were icy and cold... crystal blue and piercing. It reached out and grabbed one of the woodsman's axes and snapped it in two. The head of the ax dropped to the ground with a muffled thud, the handle - fractured and fragmented - still in its clawed, fur-covered hand - a vice grip of fury and rage.

The men fled for their lives, abandoning their posts and their possessions as their flight took them down the mountain and as far away from the creature as they could get. They reported their experience to the authorities and soon enough, an investigation was in full swing. Lumberjacks, the authorities, and curious civilians all combed through the wooded mountain area looking for the beast, or at least signs that would point to such a monster.

They found the small copse. They found the exploded log and the splintered axe. They found large canine-like prints, some in groups of 4 and some in groups of 2, but they did not find the creature. The creature would not be seen for another 10 years, but the rumors and gossip and stories of the legend of the Michigan Dogman would surely trumpet its return.

Now that is intense! Though the part that I find crazy about all of this is NOT the fact that there was apparently a giant half-dog/half-man beast in Michigan, but that said beast didn't eat the loggers!

I mean it's crazy that the dogman didn't straight up chow down on those fools! Like, who just chases a forest animal around with axes and then pokes on it when they have it trapped!

Look, all I'm saying is that they are lucky that I wasn't the dogman, cause if I was, I'd have eaten them, spit out their bones, and then gone and peed on their sleeping bags or mattresses or whatever, just for kicks!

Ok, so it is said that the dogman only appears every 10 years and this seems to be backed up by witness accounts that, more often than not, seem to be reported within that cycle. 1887 was the first reported sighting, but certainly not the first sighting ever. It seems that every 10 years there are multiple sightings of the Dogman, or should I say Dogmen, from all across the US.

Encounters

There are hundreds of recorded encounters alluding to or outright claiming to have seen or had some kind of exchange with the beast. One of the most chilling was that of a fisherman by the name of Reynolds. Reynolds was fly fishing in the Manistee River, also known as Big Manistee in Northern Michigan. In the report, he stated that he had been there all day and was getting frustrated because he had usually caught all that he could carry by then, but for some reason, the fish just weren't biting. He knew it probably had something to do with Homer, his young black lab that he had brought with him for the first time. He had thought better of it and had almost left him at home, but the look in his big brown, dumb, puppy dog eyes got the better of him.

Yes, Homer was running around barking and darting in and out of the trees and chasing squirrels, but he wasn't getting near the water. Reynolds made a mental note that this was something that he would have to train out of him eventually, but today was not the day. Homer was leaving the river and the fish alone… but that wasn't it. He couldn't put his finger on it, but it was abnormally silent. Strangely still. It had been all day. Outside of the random squirrel or rabbit that Homer stirred up, there was nothing. No movement. No sound… Just Homer. And then even that stopped… no more barking. No more running… No more Homer.

Reynolds tried not to let his imagination run wild. He set his rod down as calmly as he could and started scanning the tree line. "Homer", he called. "Come here, boy!"

Nothing…

Then, there in the shadows of the tree line stood a dark dog or wolf-like creature… it was massive. The report states that it was standing on 2 legs, approximately 7-8 feet tall, and staring directly at Reynolds. Reynolds sucked in an audible gasp but could do little else. He was frozen in fear. From head to toe, the creature was covered in dark grey, almost sable fur. Its ears were sharp, pointing straight up. Little tufts of lighter colored hair or fur glistened in the setting sun from the points. Reynolds stated that its mountainous shoulders rose and fell slowly with each deep synchronous draw of breath. Its muscular frame promised defeat and Reynolds knew he would not be able to beat it or outrun it. He just had to wait.

Waiting was difficult, because in the creature's right hand was the small, broken body of Homer. His black fur was slick with blood. This was almost enough to make Reynolds move, but then the creature did something that haunted Reynolds to the day he died. It smiled at him. Reynolds is quoted as saying, "I know you won't believe me. I still don't know if I believe me… but that damned thing was trying to smile. It locked eyes with me and wouldn't let me look away. Its eyes were the bluest, coldest eyes I have ever seen. And it smiled… It just smiled and walked away."

Apparently, the Dogman just let Reynolds go. It took poor Homer with it and just walked away, disappearing into the forest. Reynolds never saw it again.

What a story!

Ok, this one is strange, but one of the more interesting facets of the Michigan Dogman has to do with a radio DJ in the late 80's.

In 1987 a disc jockey named Steve Cook thought it would be fun to put a few of these stories together in a song and play it on the air. So, he - accompanied by a keyboard played by his producer, Bob Farley - released this 5-minute, super minimalistic tune retelling some of the earlier tales of the dogman. They expected that to be that. They'd play it once as kind of a joke/homage and be done, but that was not the case. The radio's phone line lit up with people from all over not only requesting to hear the song again and asking where they could purchase it, but with people wanting to tell their own stories, their own personal encounters with the dogman.

They became overnight sensations and the song was requested over and over again. Cook and Farley rushed to make copies - on cassette tapes that they had purchased themselves - and ended up selling them for 3 dollars apiece. They did this multiple times and never seemed to have enough in stock.

It goes like this:

> "A cool summer morning in early June is when the legend began... at a nameless logging camp in Wexford County where the Manistee River ran...
>
> 11 lumberjacks near the Garland Swamp found an animal they thought was a dog... in a playful mood, they chased it round, til it ran inside a log.

A logger named Johnson grabbed him a stick and poked around inside… then the thing let out an unearthly scream and came out… and stood upright

None of those men ever said very much about whatever happened then… they just packed up their belongings and left that night and were never heard from again…

It was 10 years later in '97 when a farmer near Buckley was found… slumped over his plow, his heart had stopped, there were dog tracks all around.

7 years past the turn of the century they say a crazy old widow had a dream… of dogs that circled her house at night. They walked like men and screamed.

    In 1917 a sheriff who was out walkin… found a driverless wagon and tracks in the dust like wolves had been a stalkin…

Near the roadside, a four-horse team lay dead with their eyes open wide… when the vet finished up his investigation he said it looked like they died of fright

In '57 a man of the cloth found claw marks on an old church door… the newspaper said they'd been made by a dog… but he'd had to of stood 7' 4…

In '67 a vanload of hippies told a park ranger named Quinlan… They'd been awakened in the night by a scratch at the window… there was a dog-man lookin' in and grinnin…

Then in the summer of '87 near Luther it happened again…at a cabin in the woods, it looked like maybe someone had tried to break in… there were cuts around the doors that could only have been made by very sharp teeth and claws… he didn't have shoes cause he didn't have feet - he walked on just 2 paws…

And somewhere in the North wood's darkness, a creature walks upright… and the best advice you may ever get, is don't go out at night

I cannot recommend enough that you all go out and listen to this song. It is a really cool piece of history and it's pretty eerie. There is a newer re-mastered version that has a few more instruments kind of filling things out that you can find on Youtube if you look hard enough.

Conclusion

We now know the story of the Michigan Dogman and its legacy, but where did it come from? Sadly, we may never know. We know that it is out there. We know from the multitude of eyewitnesses that it is very large and intimidating. That it is athletic and strong. There are numerous reports of the dogman jumping over and across 2 and even 4 lanes of traffic in a single leap. There are eyewitness accounts of the beast killing livestock and family pets, but never, not once killing a human… at least on purpose. There are those reports of people found dead from apparent heart attacks or simply dying of fear, but never killed.

What we don't know is: what is it? Where did it come from? Why every 10 years?

I wasn't able to answer these questions during the time that I had to research them, but maybe that's for the best. Maybe this creature, the dogman, is a legit true cryptid. I personally believe that it is. It's in cases like that of the Fouke Monster where the legitimacy of these wonderful creatures of lore and legend are disproven and the relevance and authenticity of true cryptids are called into question. I don't think that is the case here. I believe in cases like this, and that of Bigfoot or Nessy or any one of the myriad *true* cryptids, there are some things that we'll never know… because we aren't meant to.

CHAPTER 21

Friday the 13th

Some people loathe this day... some celebrate it... and some - approximately 8% of the population - fear it. Fear of this day is known as Paraskevidekatriaphobia, based on the Greek words "Paraskevi", meaning Friday, "dekatria" meaning thirteen, and of course "phobia" - a suffix indicating fear or fear of. This fear has led to an estimated 800-million-dollar financial loss annually, as many of the population avoid such things as weddings, funerals, and traveling on this day.

I think the first thing we need to do is address the day itself - Friday the 13th. Why is this day synonymous with bad luck, catastrophe, and even death? Is it simply the number 13? Is it because of the 80's and 90's films of the same name? Did the serial killer that donned a hockey mask and machete start this fear and fascination? Or is there more at work here than Jason and his killing spree?

I mean we all know that 13 is an unlucky number… right? But is it just the number? And if so, then why isn't Monday the 13th or Wednesday the 13th just as ominous, just as infamous? Does that mean that Voorhees, his decades-long rampage, and the subsequent documentaries chronicling them are truly the genesis of this most feared calendar day that repeats a mere once or twice a year (maybe 3 times, if you're "lucky")?

No. The curse of Friday the 13th has a much more storied and sinister past than that of Jason Voorhees. I think we need to take a look at what came before to understand what is happening now.

The Legend

Let's look at the number 13… Why 13?

I think we can trace this back… *far* back to approximately 1750 BC, when Hammurabi, the 6th Babylonian king, proclaimed a collection of rules and laws known as the *Code of Hammurabi*. This codex related the laws, punishments, rules, and regulations of the Babylonian empire and was etched into a giant black stone pillar. It also famously omitted a 13th law. This was most likely just a clerical error, as the edict does not include any numerical structure at all, but a line of text is, indeed, missing… the 13th line.

In Norse mythology, the Pantheon of Norse gods was invited to a dinner party... all save one. Odin, unwilling to put up with the trickster god Loki's antics this night, simply did not invite him. This did not stop Loki, however, and not only did Loki crash Odin's dinner party, but he arranged for Hoder (the blind god of darkness) to loose an arrow and kill Balder (the god of joy). Odin's love for Balder was known by all and also his decree that nothing, living or dead, would ever be able to harm him. This infuriated Loki and so he tricked Hoder to shoot Balder. This arrow, even the arrow of a god, would not have harmed Balder, per Odin's decree, except that Odin had forgotten mistletoe when he named off all things alive and dead that could not harm him. Loki had covered the arrow that he gave to Hoder in mistletoe and when the arrow struck true, as Loki knew it would, Balder fell. The entire world grieved with Odin that day.

Ok, I'm sure you love hearing about Norse Mythology and Odin and Loki and all, but what does this have to do with Friday the 13th?

I'm glad you asked, as I must have forgotten to mention that Odin's invitation list had 12 names on it. The gatecrasher - Loki - was the 13th and uninvited guest!

That could very well play a part in why 13 is considered an unlucky number. That and the *Code of Hammurabi*...

One of the more recently recorded legends of the number 13 is that of a Captain in the US Army in the late 1800s by the name of William Fowler. Capt. Fowler found that his life had somewhat been inexplicably tied to the number 13. He attended public school district #13 and fought in 13 battles during the Civil War, for example. Capt. Fowler was well connected to high society and in open defiance against any power or sway that this number held over him, he started a society called The Thirteen Club. The first meeting was held on Sept. 13th 1881. Fowler and guests would walk under crossed ladders and dine at tables littered with spilled salt. Mirrors were broken and umbrellas were left open. This story doesn't end tragically... but it actually did quite a bit to bring to light the idea that the number 13 was an unlucky number.

In certain pagan beliefs and religions, 13 is seen as the last stage of life. The first 12 lives are lived out here... in this mortal coil. The last, the 13th, is the afterlife.

There is also the story of Freya, goddess of love and fertility. Freya was ostracized and exiled to the mountaintops and labeled a witch (Side notes: we get the symbolism of a witch's black cats from Freya, as she was gifted 2 black cats by Thor, the god of thunder. You get that one for free!). She was spiteful after this ousting and hated humanity. Out of her spite, she created a gathering of 11 other witches and the devil himself... 12

plus 1, the gathering of 13.

A most cursed number, indeed.

But why Friday?

Well, and this is 100% conjecture: Unfounded and unproven biblically - is the idea that Friday is the day that Adam and Eve were kicked out of the Garden of Eden *and* is the day that the Great Flood began. Again, I was not able to confirm that biblically, so we'll count that as speculative at best... Though it is worth noting that Mariners avoid launching on Fridays because of this.

I think the number and the day actually came together on Friday, October 13th, 1307 when King Philip the IV of France had his officers arrest hundreds of the Knights Templar. The Knights Templar or simply, the Templars were (or some believe, still are) a military order established in 1119 at Temple Mount in Jerusalem. They were also known as The Poor Fellow-Soldiers of Christ and of the Temple of Solomon or the Order of Solomon's Temple. They were among the most skillful fighters and heavily associated with the Crusades. That and certain rumored initiation practices along with many, many secrets made them a feared and often mistrusted organization.

King Phillip the IV was in great debt and leaped upon the opportunity to play upon the public's growing mistrust of the Templars while at the same time ridding himself of the nuisance. He had them arrested, tortured until they gave false testimony and then burned at the stake. He did all this under the guise of eliminating a criminal organization, but really it was to eliminate his debt… and his enemies. This is why many cite the route of the Templars as the origin of Friday the 13th.

A few more modern tragedies and disasters that would cement Friday the 13th as a day of foreboding are:

1. The bombing of Buckingham Palace in 1940 by German Forces

2. The murder of Kitty Genovese in Kew Gardens, where 38 people witness the stabbing of 28-year-old Genovese and not one called the Police or tried to intervene, thus giving name to the bystander effect known as "Genovese Syndrome" where bystanders are paralyzed with fear and are unable or unwilling to act

3. A cyclone in Bangladesh that killed over 300,000 people

4. The disappearance of an entire airplane over the Andes

5. The death of hip hop artist Tupac Shakur

6. The crash of a cruise ship off the coast of Italy that

killed 30 people

All of these events took place on a Friday the 13th

But perhaps most telling of all, even more so than any of these previously listed - on Friday, March 13th 2020, the United States braced for a lock-down spurred by fears concerning the COVID-19 pandemic that we still haven't emerged from.

Friday the 13th sucks. Right?

Big Time!

Hellmouth in the Heartlands
Stull, Kansas

The witching hour on the morn of the spring equinox, 5 best friends in a borrowed minivan gaze down the grim and eerily quiet road leading to Stull, Ks. Even in the dead of night, they expected maybe a late-night/or early morning 9–5'er or the blue and green flicker of television light bouncing off eggshell-white living room walls, creeping out of drawn plastic blinds… but there was nothing.

On the south side of the aptly named Stull Road are 3 occupied homes, quaint and inviting, followed by the Stull United Methodist Church, the Stull post office, and the church pantry. There is a dirt road that splits the small town here and winds its way deeper into the rolling fields of central Kansas. After that, there are 2 more "turn-of-the-century" type homes, complete with old wooden and rotting wrap-around porches and decorative columns chipping and peeling yellow-stained white paint.

That's it. That is the entire town of Stull, Kansas.

To the right, occupying exactly half of this unincorporated community, surrounded by a 6ft chain link fence and patrolled by county deputies and a K-9 unit, is the Stull Cemetery.

Ghostly wisps of dense fog blanket the road, making it seem an almost pulsing, living thing. Sentient and eager for visitors, it slithers in anticipation. The hazy brume, wafting from right to left, wraps itself protectively around the homes and buildings while at the same time drawing attention to the cemetery gates and the ruins of the Evangelical Emmanuel Church; the crumbled nidus of this rumored gateway to hell.

Fancying themselves amateur Ghost Hunters — at least for this, their latest attempt to quell the post-college, pre-adult continuum that they had found themselves loathing and yet thriving in — they sit at the zenith of Stull Road plotting their infiltration.

Minutes pass as they get their timing down on the patrol and work up the nerve to scale the fence. It is agreed that there will be no vandalism or tomfoolery here, this was a serious and somber quest to uncover the mysteries of a local legend that had garnered worldwide interest and fame.

With deep breaths, dirty jokes, and excuses out of the way and nothing else to stall them, the quintet poured out the sliding side door, having covered the dome light with an old handkerchief (yes, they had thought of everything), and stealthily made their way along the eastern fence approx. 200 yards behind the guard as he made rounds.

Dead trees and decorative stone works lined the approach.

Cobwebs, overgrown vines and hedge-works, and an owl's cryptic questions of "hoo…hooo" greeted them as they neared. This had once been a lovely place of solitude, rest, and remembrance, but that was a long time ago.

Now it is a haunted and broken place that even the pope dares not tread.

The Legend

Tales say that there are 7 gateways to the netherworld:

1. The Cape Matapan Caves in Greece — Home of Hades, god of the dead.
2. The Hekla Volcano in Iceland where covens gather to commune with their underlord.
3. The bottomless and insatiable chasm known as Lacus Curtius in Rome.
4. The Ploutonion at Hierapolis in Greece where to this day birds still drop dead if their flight takes them too near to the noxious vapors that permeate from the portal there.
5. The Fengdu City of Ghosts in Chongqing, China where 2 imperial officials Yin and Wang wandered in their quest to become immortal — Their names together "yinwang" actually means

"King of Hell".

    6.   St Patrick's Purgatory in Lough Derg, Ireland where sojourners would find the end, or rather the beginning of their eternal pilgrimage.

    7.   Stull Cemetery in Stull, Ks where a wayward priest killed his forbidden lover and their unborn child.

It's said that twice a year, on Halloween and again on the Spring Equinox, a seal is lifted from a stairway in a well somewhere in Stull Cemetery and from 3 am to 4 am, the fabric separating our world from the netherworld is so thin that if one would dare descend the steps, they would be drawn into the land of the dead.

The stairway is not long, only a few hundred feet, but once at the bottom, it would take someone 2 weeks or more to return to the top — If they were able - though to them it would only seem like a few minutes.

There *have* been those brave enough (or foolish enough) to descend the steps in the past, only to disappear and be considered missing — and often reported as such — returning weeks later wondering why all the commotion and worry; because to them no time had passed.

The well is said to be nearly impossible to find and even if found would be so nondescript that it would easily be disregarded as just another broken bit of stonework littering the cemetery.

First-hand accounts of this well and stairway even being found are nearly impossible to track down, but I believe — I truly and honestly believe — that I did just that.

You see, the fearless 5 mentioned at the beginning of this tale were me and my 4 best friends!

But let's not get back to that just yet...

As one might suspect, you wouldn't have this kind of portal on the mortal plane without some level of residual effect.

Much of the flora and fauna surrounding the area is in a year-round withered state. Dead trees and bare shrubbery evidence the poison that seems to seep out of the gateway. At the vertex of the cemetery lies the crumbled ruins of the Evangelical Emmanuel Church. The epicenter of all evil can be traced back to this church, or really the practices of a priest who presided there.

Priestly Duties

It is said that long ago a priest had a verboten tryst with a parishioner.

Theirs was a taboo affair, not only because of the sacred vows taken by the priest to remain celibate but also because the woman was rumored to be a witch. Though no one had come right out and accused her of such things, it was a well-circulating whisper that drifted in and out of the societies and cliques of the congregation.

The priest and his mistress attempted to keep their illicit sins secret, but as such things of a forbidden and carnal nature as this often do, what was to be kept unseen soon became all too visible as the woman discovered that she was with child.

Weeks went by as the priest tried to find some way out of this most damning predicament (some way to avoid the inevitable) but he was running out of time as his lover had begun to show visible signs of carrying a child… his child.

The church began to distance themselves not only from her but from him as well, as the small community started to put things together.

Seeing no other choice, the priest bade his followers gather behind the church after Sunday service and confessed his sins… he confessed that he had been seduced by a witch and that this witch was with them even now!

With hatred in his eyes, he pointed a crooked and skeletal finger toward his lover and condemned her to death.

It didn't take long for the congregation to devolve into a mob. Cursing and shouting, they dragged the poor woman off to the west side of the church to a towering pine to be hanged.

Long and slender shadows danced about like

maddened, macabre marionettes across the cemetery grounds as the sun, just starting to set, cast them about. This only heightened the frenzy and chaos of the fanatical multitude. Accusations and damnations were flung at the helpless woman as she was manhandled and bound with rope.

Before nightfall of that very same day, the woman was hanged.

Her body was left lifeless and swinging as the men dug a shallow grave next to an old well. The women and children went about preparing themselves and their homes for a peaceful night's sleep, secure, confident, and at ease as if nothing at all peculiar had happened.

Just before 3 in the morning, it was done.

The woman was buried. The child still in her womb, having been robbed of life by the lies of its father, buried with her.

A stone was placed on the grave that simply read: WITTCH.

2 weeks later, on the spring equinox, some nefarious, necromantic power seeped into that shallow grave and called to the child. The child was born in the dark and dirt of that shallow grave and clawed its way down, down, down… far below, leaving behind it a cursed stairway formed of its pain.

Today the stone that reads WITTCH can still be found if you look hard enough, but it is now split in two, having been sundered the night that the child was born unto death. *WIT-TCH*.

Celebrity and Seance

This is a pretty dark story and one that has caught the attention of more than a few noted celebrities.

Kurt Cobain made it a mission to visit Stull Cemetery whenever Nirvana played in Lawrence, Ks.

Ariana Grande claims to have visited… and left in a rush, frightened by her experiences, with the smell of sulfur still burning in her nostrils.

Slash (Guns n' Roses) has a production company that produced a film called "Nothing Left to Fear" based on Stull.

Also, one of my favorite shows, Supernatural, ended season 5 with a battle between the Archangel Michael and Lucifer in Stull Cemetery… although I hear it was actually filmed in Vancouver, so that kind of ruins it a little…

Is a story itself enough to garner the kind of worldwide notoriety that Stull Cemetery has…

Maybe, but I think there's a little more to it and I can personally attest that there are at least some weird and unexplainable phenomena that occur there.

Take for example the persistent story that says if you hold 2 glass bottles perpendicular to each other and throw them against where the northwest side of the church would have been (because remember, there are just ruins there now) that no matter how hard you throw them and no matter what you throw them against, they will not break.

I can attest to this one. I'm not proud to say it — no, I guess I *am* proud to say it because we *did* pick them up — but the night that we went, we did indeed hold up 2 bottles in the shape of a cross, and then we threw them hard and multiple times against the old fallen stones of the church.

Every single time, we were met with a dull thud instead of a shrill, shattering crash.

We could not get those bottles to break.

I believe this is supposed to be because of the disturbance caused by the two worlds colliding, causing unnatural results from natural actions.

How about back when the four walls of the church were still standing (no roof, though)?

The stories say that one could stand within the walls on a rainy night and not feel the rain.

This was said to have been because of a curse placed on the grounds by the coven that the woman who was hanged had belonged to.

While I can't actually confirm that one, I can say that when we visited, the walls were still there (although not really standing per se) and when we went "inside" we could no longer feel the breeze that was kicking around right "outside".

Within the area of the church, there was no wind. Yikes!

Let's talk about the tree. A tall and imposing pine that, until 1998 stood healthy and strong, all except for a single outstretched limb that seemed never to grow at all over the years. This limb was the very limb that the woman and countless other witches had been hanged on.

It still had the indentation of a rope around it until it, along with the rest of the tree, was cut down in '98 to dissuade ghost-hunters and thrill seekers from climbing it and hurting themselves.

And let's not forget the prerequisite "strange or unexplained death" stories that seem to go hand-in-hand with any legend worth its weight in blood:

1. The young boy that was accidentally burned alive by his father on a road aptly named "Devil's Road", which can be found on old city maps in the Stull archives, though doesn't appear to be there any longer.
2. The old man who hanged himself on the very same pine that hundreds of years ago was used to hang witches…

Needless to say, Stull is steeped in the dark lore of death and evil. But still, does that really mean that it is an extraplanar portal to the Underworld… a Hellmouth in the Heartland?

The Pope certainly thinks so.

It is rumored that when the pope or the "*Cittadino Vaticanos*" (Vatican citizens) travel within the states, they will ensure that the planes' flight paths avoid flying over that area. They will not even fly over this hellish portal.

My Personal Experience

Right, ok… so we crept our way up to the church ruins. This was no easy thing. It was creepy out there! And the guard had a dog, a Doberman Pincher!

The muted cast of the moon's glow filtered everything in a strange silvery dreamscape. We couldn't help but stifle a laugh at every twig snapped or leaf crunched underfoot, not to mention the subtle, too quiet noises some were making in a faux-attempt to "alert" the guard. We knew good and well that he'd never hear, but that "what if" sensation just added to the adrenaline and "fear factor".

We had opted for no flashlights, as that would have, no doubt, alerted the patrol to our location, so the moonlight was really it as far as being able to see.

There were no lights inside the cemetery and those on the outside seemed to hold little sway within.

So, giggling like children, with visibility low, a guard about 200 yards in front of us, and adrenaline pumping so hard that we are either on the verge of a laughing fit or a panic attack, we inched forward.

We began investigating the area up on the hill, where the old church used to sit. We were immediately drawn to it as it was the largest structure and easily the most foreboding.

Much to our disappointment, most of the cemetery was in decent shape. Headstones were intact and the lawn and walkways were well-manicured, but the area on the hill was a different story.

Most of the grass and shrubbery here was dead and what wasn't dead was overgrown and choking in its conquest of dominance — vines and moss, mostly.

I've already told you about our experiment with the bottles, how we could not get them to break.

That freaked us out.

So much so that it almost sent us running back to the van right then and there!

But our mission was not to break glass. Our mission was to locate the well.

It was not an uncomfortable morning and under any other circumstances would have been fine, bordering on pleasant, but the moisture from the fog seemed to seep into our clothing just a little too much, and the constant vigilance that it took to keep tabs on barney fife made things just a bit cumbrous.

It took us a little over an hour to find it.

Not the well, but the stone... split directly in two it

read: WIT on one half and TCH on the other.

This was it!

This was the stone of the woman who had been hanged all those centuries before… and if it was here, the well had to be, too.

Frantically, we all began looking.

Bolstered by our find, and adrenaline somewhat abated at this point, we must have let our guard down because before long we heard a bark. Not the random bark of a domesticated dog gossiping to other domesticated dogs across fences. This was a baying. The trained baying of a dog that had caught a scent… Our scent… we knew it…

Torn between scrambling for the van, knowing that we had little to no familiarity with the landscape or any hidden rabbit holes, stumps, or stones that might have been hiding in wait to trip us up, or staying to search for just a few more minutes, we chose to stay.

We *had* to.

Desperately we searched, whispering excited shouts of "here it is" and "over there".

Finally, one of our friends (we'll call him Rob for anonymity) shouted that he had actually found it!

Apparently deciding that the time for stealth was over and that the patrol guard knew at least something was up over here, Rob had decided to go with a shout to ensure that everyone heard him.

We all convened by a large tree stump expectantly and trepidatiously, wide eyes asking questions that our throats could not as we gasped for breath. And there buried beneath centuries of overgrowth, low to the ground, stones broken and fallen all around, barely visible, like the eyes of a crocodile, just breaching the surface of still waters…

Small and unassuming, but with the promise of a disastrous and violent end… was a stone seal.

It looked like a man-hole cover but was made entirely of stone.

It was besieged by stacks of stone that had been precisely measured and cut. There were no distinct markings on it decrying what it was, yet it *couldn't* have been anything else.

We heard a fence slam shut behind us and knew that our time was up.

We darted north and then east around the other side of the ruins in an attempt to create as much distance and as many obstacles between us and the guard… or really between us and the dog.

We ran for all we were worth.

Low hanging limbs and cobwebs decorated our faces with angry red scratches and sticky silks.

We were young and relatively confident that we

could outrun the rent-a-cop, but we *knew* the dog was gaining on us.

None of us were really all that athletic, and I don't know if you've ever been in a full-on sprint for your life, but let me tell you, your legs stop working the way you want them to REALLY quickly. Each of us took our fair share of tumbles and one of us lost our ball cap.

We kept going.

The fence was in sight and just like that — 1, 2, 3, 4, and all 5 of us were over.

Rob hopped in the driver's seat as the rest of us dove headfirst through the side door.

Most of us made it through.

One of our buds - he was our group's "Chunk" (from Goonies) - brought up the rear. He was last to the van. His approach was too fast, too erratic! He leaped more *up* than forward and slammed his head on the top of the van.

I mean, he just creamed it.

It rocked the whole vehicle!

I hope someone saw it because it had to have looked *hilarious*! Not one of us were laughing.

The dude was out cold. Laid out flat on the street right there in the middle of Stull, Ks.

A few of us leaned down and pulled hard as Rob

turned the engine over. We got him in just as Rob punched the gas. I had never had any respect for minivans before that night, but I swear that van peeled out, burning all kinds of rubber, leaving Fido and Barny in a cloud of smoke!

We never got caught or got into any kind of trouble (on that occasion), but we all left Stull, Kansas changed young men.

Is Stull, Kansas really a gateway to hell?

Who knows... but it makes for one heck of a story!

CHAPTER 23

The White Thang

If I were to say "Bigfoot" or "Sasquatch" it wouldn't take too much for you to conjure up an image of a giant bi-pedal beast lumbering through dense forests, maybe clinging to and hiding behind each massive oak as it passes. Large, intelligent eyes, so human-like, beckoning you to engage in some form of communication as it hides its face from you. Course almost hair-like fur covering mammoth hands that wrap around rough bark, so large and dangerous and strong, yet so human, so full of warmth and possibility. Then it's gone, giving you just the briefest of glimpses before it shuffles off deeper and deeper into the trees, leaving you with more questions than answers.

Maybe you'd recall your favorite scene from William Dear's 1987 cult classic Harry and the Hendersons... or if you're like me, the saddest scene... which of course is at the end when George - played by the always-compelling John Lithgow - reluctant and heartbroken as family Henderson looks on, resorts to striking and yelling at the titular cryptid in order to save his life. The scene is crushing and one that ran over and over again in my mind as I researched chapter.

To be honest I actually looked it up and watched that scene on YouTube and totally teared up…

I'm not crying. You're crying!

When I say "Bigfoot" or "Sasquatch" something akin to what I've just described must materialize in your consciousness.

So, what would your mind's eye call forth upon the mention of the Alabama White Thang?

Nothing?

For me, the only thing that popped up (and to be honest even now is still spinning around in my head) is The Troggs 1966 classic "Wild Thing" - not Tone Loc's '89 track of the same title. Although to be honest, now that one's spinning around up there, too.

But that's it! Nothing seemingly innately ingrained in my consciousness, no scenes from modern media or film… Nothing at all.

What the heck is White Thang?

And do I mean White Thing?

The 2nd question is easy to answer: No, I don't mean White Thing. I mean White Thang... with an "ang".

It's the first question that is going to take a little more time to unpack...

The Legend

The northern forests of Alabama are home to many creatures worthy of conversation: The Northern Long-Eared Myotis, The Mexican Free-Tailed Bat... The American Black Bear, Coyote, The Gray and Red Fox, Cougars, and Bobcats etc. But what distinguishes the deep forests of northern Alabama and their species of native mammals from the myriad other forests in the US is that these woods are home to the fabled and elusive White Thang.

The Alabama White Thang is a beast of local legend and fame. According to The American Bestiary's, *CashNetUSA's US Creature Compilation*, "The Alabama White Thang is a giant ape-man relative of bigfoot. Similar in height and stature - somewhere around 8-9' tall - this gargantuan is incredibly athletic with unmatched speed and strength."

Though descriptions of its physical appearance differ ever so slightly, there a few fundamental elements that endure throughout... most critical is that it is white.

Not necessarily that its *skin* is white, but that it is covered from head to toe in coarse shaggy white fur. The other being its "scream" or howl. It is said to sound like a woman screaming for her life. It is unnerving and probably the most unsettling and disturbing feature of the beast.

This shriek is said to be so terrifying that it will turn your blood cold, literally sending shivers up your spine. Often a point of contention among White Thang enthusiasts is whether or not this scream, or howl, or shriek is supernatural. Apparently, the terror that it evokes is unnatural and can cause the hearer to react severely, often falling to the ground disoriented. Though accounts never give us much detail as to how or why they end up there.

White Thang's notoriety began in the early 1900's, maybe as late as the 1940's when, according to Peter J. Gossett of freestateofwinston.org, his aunt, Feneda Martin Smith gave what seems to be the first recorded report of White Thang stating, "Old man George Norris seen it over there in Enon graveyard, and he said it looked like a lion…you know, bushy, betwixt a dog and a lion. It was white and slick with long hair. It had a slick tail, down on the end of the tail a big ol' bush of hair. He lent up against a tree and fell asleep. When he woke up the sun was just rising, and the 'white thang' was laying right beside him, and it was looking at him. He said it didn't offer to hurt him or nothing."

Indeed, old Man Norris was not hurt, and as I searched and searched for some report, some story, some personal encounter with White Thang that ended in violence or death, I was left wanting. It seems that this elusive cryptid is something of a pacifist, if not an altogether benignant philanthropist... but we'll get into that later.

White Thang - or at least the most prevalent iteration of White Thang - seems to limit its roaming to a relatively small area and doesn't much stray outside of it. Its neck of the woods consists almost exclusively of Etowah, Jefferson, and Morgan counties, though other more fringe iterations of the creature have been reported outside of this triangular stomping ground.

We aren't going to spend too much time on those other more fringe iterations because they seem to be the exceptions, not the rule, but they warrant mentioning all the same. Whereas most encounters and reports of White Thang describe it as a large bi-pedal ape or sasquatch-like creature, some have described it as being more of a shaggy dog or a fluffy wolf-shaped creature that can seamlessly switch between walking upright to all fours. Some have even called it a spectre or ghost, likening its screams or howls to that of a banshee or a siren or a wight. But I think the one that takes the cake is the idea that The Alabama White Thang has - are you ready for this? - the body of a kangaroo and the head of a cat!

Go look it up. It'll be worth your time. It. Is. Hilarious.

Residents of Huntsville report White Thang as a bipedal, humanoid creature that lives in caves and is so white that it glows in the dark. It has no eyes or ears and its shriek is actually a mournful wail lamenting its sightless, soundless existence.

Well, that's just sad… and while I don't buy this particular explanation, I am confident that its wail is much more than just an animalistic screech.

Skeptics dismiss claims of White Thang and explain it as either an albino bear or a large white wolf. But, with so many stories and local encounters, there has to be some truth to this, right? Of course, there is! And that's where I come in! If Bigfoot, Yeti, and the Wendigo exist, then dargarnit (real word, look it up), so does White Thang!

Encounters

I reached out to the Facebook group *Alabama White Thang* asking if anyone had a personal encounter that they could share. Oscar Goodwin of the Mystery Junkie Channel on YouTube said,

"Well, this is my grandfather's experience. It would've been in the 1950s in the Hanceville/Garden City area on Mount Doom."

Ok, what??? Mount Doom...? Are you serious? Did we just stumble upon Amon Amarth in Mordor!?!?! Are we about to embark on a grand adventure in the 3rd age to destroy the one ring!?!? Are we chosen to usher in the age of men? Am... am I Aragorn son of Arathorn, and am called Elessar??? Are you... Samwise Gamgee, portly and loyal sidekick to Frodo Baggins and true hero of the Lord of the...

Ok, whoa. Sorry... I malfunctioned for a moment there. But Mount Doom?!!? That is AMAZING! Oscar, you made my week, dude. Thank you!

Ok, where was I?

Oh ya,

"It would've been in the 1950s in the Hanceville/Garden City area on Mount Doom.

He was walking down the mountain one night heading home after visiting family members.... He heard something following him and when he turned to look up the road, he saw something big and white. He thought it was a ghost at first with how white it was but hearing the footsteps decided it was someone who was going to rob him. He went off the trail got behind a bush and fired a warning shot with the pistol he had. It then got on all 4s and sprint off extremely fast so he knew it wasn't a human and he believed until the day he died he had seen the legendary White Thang."

That's amazing!

It would have been amazinger if the warning shot would have been from the Bow of the Galadhrim, but whatever... still cool. Thanks, Oscar!

Another well-circulated story among White Thang's fandom is that of a young couple out on an evening stroll. Summer had ceded its dominance to autumn and accepting this surrender, she made quick work of her canvass. The temperatures were cooling, leaves the colors of fire and sunset that once canopied the forest ceiling blanketed the ground and crunched underfoot. The young lovers huddled together against the northern breeze as it stirred this picturesque kaleidoscope before them. Then, out of the corners of their eyes, they saw a large, hulking, man-like creature staring silently at them from within the carapace of the trees.

Upon being found out, it quickly leaped away on all fours and climbed high into the branches of a tree where it resumed its study of the couple. It was not aggressive and not threatening. If anything, it was curious and almost forlorn and lonely. This story captures not only the athletic prowess of White Thang but also its... humanity, if I could call it that... its curiosity and its desire for connection and relationship.

I was also told that a couple young ladies were sneaking out of their house late at night to meet up with some boys. As they made their way down the driveway, they witnessed a large bipedal figure resembling a giant black bear, but of course it was white. It was high upon a hill overlooking the house and the girls, its hulking form, a ghostly silhouette against the star-filled Alabama night. The girls quickly reversed course and went back inside! As the father of 2 girls all I can say here is, good on you, White Thang! Watching out for those girls! And while you're at it, you should go give those boys a good whoopin!

There are many tales and stories that have been passed down from generation to generation:

> Two men - sometimes father and son, sometimes brothers - hunting with their dogs at dusk when the dogs suddenly turned tail and ran for home. The men, upon seeing the "giant White Thang" that spooked the dogs take off at a full sprint and didn't slow until returning home.

You know, those kinds of stories.

Often these encounters involve White Thang simply being there, watching as the victims go about normal everyday activities like mowing the lawn, hanging clothes out to dry, playing in the backyard. White Thang is always watching, but he is never violent or menacing in any way.

A story published on gadsdenmessenger.com gives the account of Eddy Arnold Smith, he says:

"My sister and I saw it when we were kids off Green Valley Road. It had to be around 1958-59. It was late afternoon in the fall and the leaves were almost all fallen. We were in the woods behind Green Valley Church about 1/4 mile from Pine Grove Cemetery. The description is very good. We were about 50 yards away. The creature was pale white… made the high-pitched sound of a crying woman. We were scared out of our skin. It made no attempt to approach us or seem threatening in any way. It actually turned its head away from us. My children and now my grandchildren have heard this story many times. Yes, they think we were hallucinating, but they still love the story!"

Harbinger of Death

One of the more interesting and persistent facets of this creature is its propensity to death. Not that it causes it or is in some way responsible for it, but that it always seems to be there when death is involved. For over 100 years there have been accounts of White Thang being present during wakes and funerals, even during hunts and predator kills.

One unexplained encounter was that of a farmer who woke to the frightening sounds of squeals and snarls as his pigs were being attacked and killed by a pack of coyotes. The farmer ran out and chased the predators away with angry shouts and the roar of his shotgun. Upon surveying the damage, the farmer saw White Thang up on the hill. It was watching him, then it let out its infamous cry that had the farmer running back into the house. Later that morning the farmer and a few of his fellows went out to hunt down the pack of coyotes. He warned his party to be careful and watchful, as White Thang was out there, too.

The farmers came across a gruesome scene some way into the forest. The entire pack of coyotes were laying in a copse of trees, their bodies broken and twisted. The farmer had no explanation for this until he saw what he swore until his death was White Thang making his way through the trees beyond the thicket.

Was White Thing exacting some sort of vengeance on the coyotes for harming the pigs? Was it empathetic to the farmers emotions, carrying out the farmers intentions? Was it an offering of friendship? An attempt to win the farmer's affections?

There is a theory that has only grown in popularity over the years that White Thang is a Harbinger of Death. Though not in the more widely known sense, such as Omens, Screaming Banshees or the Black Shuck that would portend a gruesome and violent death, but more in line with the Mothman. More of a benevolent cryptid, intensely invested in the lives of the people in its area.

Often watching and warning. An overseer. A protector.

White Thang is often seen lurking near graveyards and churches during times of mourning and remembrance. Even today there are stories, eye witness accounts, of White Thang looking on during times of grieving. Is White Thang drawn to death by some morbid curiosity or obsession or is it drawn by the undeniable pull of such strong emotions as sorrow, grief, loss and fear that we emit in times of heartache.

Conclusion

I am convinced that this Alabama White Thang is a misunderstood gentle giant. It is compassionate and empathetic. It is forced to live on the fringes of a society that doesn't understand it and therefor fears it. It has more in common with man than not - we have always rejected things that we fear and don't understand. So, it watches, alone and crestfallen. A mighty and majestic beast reduced to taking comfort in the shadows. Its wail is not one of warning or aggression. It is not supernatural or mystic… it is simply a cry. A wretched lament of a lonely and downcast being.

CHAPTER 24

Krampus

Hear the bells, Christmas bells, ringing in the distance,
Past the moon, across the sky, we knew him in an instant
A small lad from the town, in the valley far below
Shouts "look up!" to all, "I can see Rudolph's bright red nose"
way up there, the small reindeer, pointing out the way
the gangs all here, as twelve more appear, to guide old Santa's sleigh
Santa brings a special glee, a sparkle to the eye
But brats take haste, the Krampus comes, to darken up the sky
A jolly old soul with a heart of gold, Santa Claus is coming
With cloven hoofs and goatish horns, the Krampus sends em' running
As good Saint Nick will fill with toys, his magical red sack

The Krampus has a birch club, strapped across his back
Much larger than his counterpart, with fur from head to toe
Two horns as large as antlers, and claws where hands should go
All the naughty children, in rusty chains, are bound
They'll smell the stench of brimstone, as it rises through the ground
The earth will start to rumble, there's fire all around
The pits of hell will open wide, and he'll throw the children down
So sinister a creature, this frigid hungry beast
Will eat their burning bodies, for a crispy Christmas treat
as Santa leaves our snowy town
the remaining kids will gather 'round
for their friends they'll shed a final tear
and know that the Krampus will be back in a year

- Kenneth Widman

This fearsome poem crafted by Kenneth Widman is only 4 short stanzas, yet it so expertly promulgates the horrendous nature of this holiday antagonist. Let's explore the terrifying and true story of Krampus, the depraved contradiction to Saint Nicholas.

The Legend

Emerging from Austrian Alpine folklore is a half-goat, half-man demon. He carries a wicker basket or burlap sack and can be heard lurking in the shadows by the tell-tale jingle of copper chains and shackles that adorn his waist and arms. His long, thick, black and brown fur - cascading down from his head to his ankles - limns his muscles, corded and taught from years and years of hard labor in the depths of hades. Giant, spiraling horns breach his skull and careen upward, a fiendish stretch toward the heavens. He walks on great, cloven hooves that click and clack as he stalks his victims, striking fear in the hearts of all who hear. Claws born of fire and sharpened by hate - made for rending flesh - clasp leather whip and birch rod. These are for penance and pain. A serpent's tongue, long and pointed, flicks about tasting the panic and dread of his prey. And eyes so black, the black of his soul, peer to and fro, ever searching… ever seeking those that he might punish.

Krampus

According to legend, Krampus is the son of Hel (not HELL as in the lake of fire). Hel is the daughter of the trickster god, Loki. She is the Norse goddess of Niflheim - the underworld. These Norse gods were revered and worshiped in pagan Norse religions for centuries. Krampus was not known as he is today during that time. Instead, he would often manifest as a Yule Goat, a pagan Norse figure traditionally associated with the Winter

Solstice. It wasn't until somewhere in the 15th or 16th century when Christianity began to gain popularity in Europe and beyond - post Inquisition, the Crusades and Criticism of Corruption - that Germany and Austria's Yuletide celebrations started to become less and less about Yuletide and the Yule Goat and became more focused on Christmas and a much cheerier Yuletide character, Saint Nicholas.

Saint Nicholas of Myra, yes a real-life person, was sainted in 800 *AD* and is known as Nicholas the Wonderworker due to his generosity and legendary habit of secretly giving gifts.

The Yule Goat would often demand sacrifices and offerings during Yuletide and would frighten children into paying homage to him and the other Norse gods and into properly honoring them and the Winter Solstice. As attention and dedication to the gods began to wane, so too did the offerings and gifts. This angered the gods and so, because of his hideous and grotesque visage and that being akin to a goat, Krampus ascended Niflheim and assumed the duties of the Yule Goat, though he was cruel and malevolent and remains so to this day. He whips and beats children who are naughty and have lost their way. He will even bind them and drag them back to the depths of the Underworld as punishment until they learn their lesson.

The Feast of Saint Nicholas is observed on December 6th. On the eve before, Saint Nick would travel far and wide dispensing gifts and merriment. It is said that Krampus confronted Saint Nick on the night of December 5th many years ago and demanded that he be allowed to accompany Saint Nicholas and dole out punishments to all the naughty girls and boys. He would most often leave bundles of birch wood and coal for the bad children, but for the especially naughty, he would maim and beat and even kidnap them for a year... dragging them down, down to the 6th layer of hell, the layer reserved for heretics. There they would spend their year, imprisoned in a flaming tomb.

Rise in Popularity

Krampus worked low to the ground, flying under the radar for hundreds of years. Saint Nicholas was satisfied to let him have the wayward children, and more often than not, saw quite the return when he came around the next year and found those once-bad-apples behaving well, full of gratitude and kindness. Krampus was quite alright with this: lurking in the shadows... remaining a relatively unknown counterpart to the brighter and much more wholesome Saint Nick, but nothing good lasts forever.

In the 1890's Germany and Austria's postcard industry exploded. In fact, Germany is the second largest producer of postcards even today. With the low cost of printing and the low wages there, Germany was at one time producing 2/3rds of the world's postcards. If you were anyone or anything of any renown, chances are your face was going to be plastered onto thousands of small rectangles of cardstock and shipped all over the world. Krampus was no exception here.

Unlike most other postcards which portrayed beautiful landscapes, vacations spots, families and industries, the cards showing Krampus were just as dark and disturbing as you'd expect. Depictions of children being whipped and beaten, oftentimes in the presence of their families, by a devilish goatman were all the rage. Illustrations of Krampus stuffing unruly girls and boys into wicker baskets as they reached and screamed for help or chain gangs of children being led down to hell came with the caption "Gruss vom Krampus" or ("Greetings from Krampus").

After some time, the postcards and other printed works veered toward the more… adult in nature. Krampus harassing and proposing to women, female Krampus' whipping bound men, etc. These printings took on political, humorous and sexual tones, turning Krampus into a vehicle for any number of agendas and narratives.

As you can imagine, this led to quite a frenzy. Krampus was now a household name. Everyone knew about him now. Children were terrified and adults were elated by the prospects of an evil demi-god goat demon terrorizing naughty girls and boys. The Catholic church had been trying for years to distance the idea of Santa Claus and Christmas from Krampus. This completely upended all of their work. The cat was out of the bag. Krampus was real and he was among us.

His infamy remained by and large confined to European countries for years. It wasn't until recently that Krampus became well known to the US. His legend continued to grow, but he did not become a household name until art director Monte Beauchamp published a collection of these Krampus cards and arranged displays and art shows inspired by them.

From there Krampus-mania spread like the fires of hell. Now you can fill your Amazon cart with Krampus merchandise! Ugly Krampus Sweater? Sure! Krampus lunchbox? Absolutely! And how about those old 1890s Krampus postcards? Well, now you can get all kinds of Krampus cards! You can even find graphic novels, comic books and action figures of this demonic Yule Goat.

But what does Krampus think about all this?

Krampus is not to be taken lightly, nor is his work. It is a dark and gruesome thing. Krampus, the son of Hel - goddess of Niflheim - portrayed as a common boogeyman in low-budget B horror movies? Krampus, grandson of the trickster-god Loki reduced to a gimmick or a cartoonish imp hopping about slapping coal in children's stockings? Krampus, the son of a Norse goddess who ascended from the netherworld to punish those who had forsaken their gods is now adorning Christmas candles?

Krampus *does* seem to have a sense of humor though, or at least doesn't mind being amused by us mere mortals. This is evidenced by the Krampus Parade held every year in Austria where hundreds of adults fill the streets dressed as Krampus and Perchten elves. The parade culminates in the Krampuslauf or Krampus Run, where men in ornate Krampus costumes get drunk and run through the streets racing and frightening the children. It is a terrifying sight for sure, as the costumes are very well made and lifelike, and it is in the middle of the night. It is a dark and drunken homage in candlelight - a hellish version of the running of the bulls, if you will.

But this yearly tribute is a far stretch from the frivolous pop-culture treatment he receives in many parts of the world, including the US. There is not a ton of information as to how Krampus chooses to interact with us in this modern era. Where does a true demi-god of pagan religions-past fit in when Thor, the god of thunder is portrayed by a hunky sun-kissed Australian and Kratos, the Greek god of war is somehow transported to Norse realm of Midgard? Don't get me wrong, I love Marvel and Hemsworth's Thor and Santa Monica Studio's God of War, but I can't help but wonder how Krampus feels being so trivialized.

I'd wager he's a bit pissed.

And what kind of paranormal, supernatural, cryptozoologist, warlock-ninja author of a bestselling book about Urban Legends would I be if I didn't prepare you for the eventual inevitability of your chancing upon him!

This you can take to the bank: I wouldn't let you all go out there on this Christmas Night, knowing that Krampus stalks the streets and is most likely stalking you right now, without telling you how to kill him.

Death to All and to All a Good Night

It's true that Krampus is an immortal demi-god from the times before time, but that doesn't mean we can't kill him. The standard methods for slaying supernatural baddies may not work here to kill the yule goat, but will definitely slow him down. Impalement, silver or iron, and fire are all good options to create a little breathing room between you and Old Saint Nick's uglier half.

But I don't want to create space, Micah! I want to KILL IT!

Right! Of course, you do… so we really just need to add on a little to what we already know about killin' beasties. The trick here isn't necessarily your method, but more your weapon. If you want to take down the big bad Christmas demon, you're going to need an evergreen. A Christmas tree. Not the whole thing, but you need enough of it to do some real damage. A splinter won't cut it here, folks. You craft a yuletide spear and run him through. A Christmas-time cutlass and chop his head off. A holiday halberd and do a little of both. You need a weapon made out of a Christmas tree and you need to cause some major internal damage. Then, once that's done, just light it up like a Festivus Fire and you're golden.

That's how you kill Krampus... and it's really not all that difficult, right? I mean, outside of having super-fast reflexes, a heart of steel and enough strength to push a Christmas tree through a god. But, if you've got all that, and the Christmas tree itself, you're all set!

CHAPTER 25

The Ozark Howler

It is said to absorb the souls of the dying so that it may *never* die.

Is it a harbinger of death... a death omen?

Yes, and yes.

It is known by many names across many county lines: The Nightshade Bear. The Devil Cat. The Hoo-Hoo.

But there is one name that immediately strikes fear into every man, woman, and child that calls the Ozarks home...

The Ozark Howler.

It could be mistaken for a monstrous grizzly or some mutated mountain lion. Stalking the grounds of Missouri, Arkansas, Oklahoma, and Texas it has been erroneously thought of as just that, but there are 2 tell-tale signs that betray this falsity.

First is its cry. This is no roar or growl, it is a scream, a bawl... a howl. It is a fusion between a wolf's howl and an elk's bugle, but there is an undertone of lunacy, as well; cackling, maniacal, guttural laughter, like that of a hyena, but less sane.

And second, its horns. Not devilish and skyward like that of the Krampus or the devil, but just as menacing. They are akin to that of an antelope, though much thicker and much more wicked. Sharp and barbed they trace the natural contour of the skull, reaching more backward than upward.

The creature stalks about on all fours. It is enormous and muscled like a bear, but quick and agile like a cougar. Its course, black fur keeps it well hidden in the shadows, but its bright red eyes will always reveal its location. Though by that time it is too late.

Bearcat. Wampus Cat. Wowzer. The Black Howler... even more names ascribed to the one and only Ozark Howler.

Rest assured, whatever it is that you call it, it is not a cat. It is not a bear. It is not a large dog or a wolf.

It is a massive and soleus boulder of flesh and fur. Its stealth and athleticism belay its size, as it can quickly and quietly leap from the forest floors to mountainous heights without a sound. It noiselessly stalks its prey, creeping about the woodland giving nary a thought to the fallen branches, leaves, and needles that lay about, threatening to betray its position. It is said to have legs as thick as tree trunks and a neck the size of a small bull.

There have often been false reports filed, frantic phone calls declaring murder and mayhem in the mountains, as the Ozark Howler's cries are often mistaken for a woman's screams *and* the unhinged laughter of a madman all at once.

The Legend

It is believed that the first sighting of The Ozark Howler was by none other than Daniel Boone. Boone was a frontiersman whose adventures made him one of the first American folk heroes. He is known for his pioneering and the settlement that would one day become Kentucky. He lived most of his life there, helping the new settlements, but he spent the last 2 decades of his life in Missouri. Though history and fiction seem to meld together to form a hybrid truth of Boone's days and deeds, one thing that is *not,* nor cannot, be considered fantasy is his encounter with an Ozark Howler.

In 1810, just outside of what is now known as Cuba, Missouri, Boone had a run-in with a Howler. He would have been 75 years old at the time and was in the middle of a hunting trip on the Platt River. The most amazing thing about this encounter is that it is *not* second-hand. Boone, himself, wrote of his encounter while composing a letter to his sister-in-law:

> *"I leev you with a alarming storey of a black creecher I fownd and woonded on the Sooder Creek. Blak and swarthy*

with horns on its sculp. Ignerant of its naym I am tolled of the sownd it maykes with a terabul owling in the niyt. Warrnings of this for settlers shulled be past along. Your omble sarvent, Daniel Boone"

Hard to read, I know. But the misspelling and brokenness of this paragraph ads such a real, earthy authenticity, don't you think?

It bears noting here that Boone tells his sister-in-law that he wounded the beast… he did not kill it. Now, Daniel Boone was many things… some true, others fabricated, but one thing he was *not* was a bad shot.

Daniel Boone was an avid hunter and known for his marksmanship. If he hit this creature with the intent to kill, it would have been dead. Except for the fact that this was no ordinary beast. This was an Ozark Howler. Its strength and size, along with its speed and agility were more than enough to combat even the .44 caliber flintlock rifle that Boone was no doubt firing at it (this was Boone's weapon of choice for hunting and marksmanship).

Boone was well into his 80s when he would again face the beast. It is said that 10 years after this harrowing encounter, Daniel Boone came face to face with the Ozark Howler once again, though this time no shots were fired.

Boone was out walking his property lines when from within the tree line he saw a pair of eyes, blazing a fiery red. He froze for a moment, not from fear, but more just a wary curiosity. After a few moments, a large, dark-haired behemoth emerged from the trees, its great horns and immense shoulders easily parting the smaller trees and shrubs.

Boone was old and no longer had the strength to carry, let alone raise and fire, his famed rifle. The creature was wounded. It limped heavily on its right side. The side that Boone had struck those 10 years earlier on the Platt.

They stared hard at each other for a few moments. An understanding, a mutual respect between two American legends. Then, as if a deal had been struck, the Howler turned back and disappeared into the woods and Boone turned toward his home. He would be laid to rest soon thereafter, having seen death in the eyes of the Howler.

Now that's the first documented encounter, and it makes for one heck of a story, but where does it come from?

The Origin Abroad

The Ozark Howler is not native to America, at least not entirely. It, like most of us here, is a hybrid. America is known as the great melting pot. That term was coined to represent the immigration, the coming together, and the merging of many different cultures and peoples as if they were metals that were being melted down and combined into a stronger alloy. These cultures and peoples brought with them their heritage, their beliefs, their hopes and dreams, their stories, and their lore and legends.

The British Black Dogs of Death are death omens. They are large ghostly creatures that take on the form of massive black dogs. Surely you have heard of these harbingers of death. Sherlock Holmes speaks to these fearsome beasts in "The Hounds of Baskerville".

They often go by a number of names, including Black Shuck, Barghest, Hairy Jack, Church Grim, Gytrash, and Bogey Beast.

These are found in other great stories such as Jane Eyre and Harry Potter, as well!

Immigrants from England began to settle in the Midwest in the late 1800s but had been arriving on the shores of America since the late 1600s. Many stories of the British Black Dogs made their way here to the States during that time.

But as I said… this is a melting pot. It is not just English lore that we pull from here.

Along with The British Black Dogs of Death, we have mythologies and ancestral tales of the Welsh, the Irish, and the Scottish.

Here we find the legends of Cù Sìth, Bean Sidhe, and Cŵn Annwn respectively.

This is another death hound, but instead of being an omen of death, this creature is death itself. Much akin to the Grim Reaper, Cù Sìth takes the soul of the departing and ushers it away to the afterlife. It is said to be the size of a young bull and has the form of a wolf. Its paws are the size of a fully grown man's hand and its tail is either coiled or braided.

Cù Sìth are known to hunt in complete silence. It is only when they let out their horrifying cries does one know that it is near. The Cù Sìth will let out its cry in 3's and legends say that you must find shelter and be well inside by the time it reaches its third, or you will be dragged away, your life forfeit.

That is unless you are a nursing mother. In this case, you would not be harmed, but you would be taken. Taken deep into the Fae Wilds to forever provide milk for their young.

The Ozark Howler, The Black Dogs of Death, and Cù Sìth — all large dog-like creatures that portend death.

But our Howler has been mistaken for a large cat at times… it seems to have some type of hybrid wolf/panther form. How is that?

Well, like I said… melting pot. I said the Ozark Howler wasn't *entirely* native to America.

A Closer Connection

The Ojibwa and Cree tribes tell of a fearsome beast with the body of a mountain lion.

Mishipeshu.

Mishipeshu is a giant cat with great copper horns. It is also known as the underwater panther. It would swim from bank to bank and often choose to bless people with copper from its horns or grant safe passage across the waters, but oftentimes brought
only death and misfortune. It is believed that the Ozark Howler was created by the merging of Mishipeshu and these other legends.

But there are a couple more *ancient* legends that we must take into consideration.

Of Myths and Mysticism

Cerberus.

Cerberus is the Great Hound of Hades. He is often depicted as a large three-headed dog and is a known harbinger of death.

He was Hercules' 12th labor, as imposed by Eurystheus — not out of any desire *for* Cerberus, but simply because Eurystheus believed it an impossible task.

Cerberus is known to be incredibly strong and quick, often preferring to take the form of a Hellhound.

And while I do not believe the Ozark Howler to *be* Cerberus, I do not think it out of the realm of possibility that it be a *descendent* of the great Hound.

The other is Fenrir, Loki's son.

Fenrir, the great wolf, is fated to devour the sun and to kill Odin at Ragnarök.

Fenrir is the father Skoll, and brother to Hel. He bit off the arm of Tyr, the god of the formalities of war, and has great foreknowing.

Again, The Ozark Howler is not Fenrir — we should only BE so lucky! But a long-lost descendant of the fearsome god-creature? One can hope, right?

Traits such as Cerberus' link to death and Fenrir's viciousness and foreknowing come into play as were look at the Howler's own attributes.

The Occult

There are more recent theories in the lore and legend of this beast that portray the Howler as a shapeshifting witch.

Some tales will tell of a power passed on from generation to generation by blood. A shapeshifting power believed to have been brought to the Ozarks by Gerald Gardner, an anthropologist, archeologist, and Wiccan.

Gardner is credited as the father of modern Wicca and even established the tradition of Gardnerian Wicca.

His faith was developed by borrowing from Freemasonry, ceremonial magic, and the writings of Aleister Crowley — Remember that name, we'll get back to it in a moment.

He spent decades abroad practicing and honing his craft and in the early 1900s, he even found his way to America. More specifically, the Midwest.

It is believed that Gardner established a coven of witches in the Ozarks and that they remain there to this day. This coven acts as a scale. A weight and counterbalance. In the form of large quad-pedal beasts, they roam the Ozark Mountains bringing balance and harmony. They are the Coven of Howlers.

A slightly different narrative tells of a woman whose husband and children died during one exceptionally bad winter. She alone survived, but she had to kill and eat the only livestock that she owned to do so.

When the thaw came, weary and malnourished, she made the trek across the mountain pass to the nearest neighbor's home. She begged for help in burying the remains of her family and perhaps some rations to see her through until she was able to get back on her feet.

The gentlemen of whom she implored this was dealing with his own tragedy, as his wife, too had passed during the winter. So filled with despair was he, that he sent her away empty-handed, having not the time nor the heart to hear her pleas.

Dejected and weak she tottered away.

She knew that she would not make it back home and she didn't care. What did she have to go back to?

Deep in the Ozark woods, she stumbled. She crawled in the melting snow for a while, but then stopped. She laid her head upon the snow and closed her eyes, eager to be reunited with her husband and children.

It is said that she was visited by a large wolf and that it spoke to her. It told her that her life was now forfeit, but not finished.

He told her that he had seen the tragedy and the treatment that she had endured and that he had a plan for her. A deal was struck then. The wolf granted the woman a new form and powers beyond that of any other creature.

She was to be a reaper. A collector of souls.

She turned then and made her way back to the farmer who had rejected her. The last thing that he saw were giant, helical horns and flaming red eyes… and the last thing he heard was the horrendous cry of a broken woman… of the Ozark Howler.

And then there was Crowley

More modern adaptations connect the Ozark Howler to the occult by way of Aleister Crowley.

Crowley was once known as the "Wickedest Man in the world". We've touched on him before.

He was a British occultist, a practitioner of the dark arts, and founder of his own order and religion.

He was also the main antagonist in the exceptional CW series Supernatural and the subject of an incredible 1980 Ozzy song. (Nerd Alert!)

Crowley did not spend much time in the states, but in the early 1900s, while in New York acting as a double agent for Britain, he traveled to the west coast. En route, he visited the Ozark Mountains, as it was and still is known for its deep magic and lay lines.

Legend says that Crowley opened a multidimensional portal here and released the Keymaster and the Gatekeeper — yes, the very same Keymaster and Gatekeeper from the Ghostbusters Movie — and that through some combination of ritual magic, a bear or cougar, and some hanky-panky he left behind the Ozark Howler.

These more modern, occult-based theories are fringe at best but have gained considerable momentum.

The comic book series *Tale of an Ozark Howler*, the folk tales *The Goat and the Howler,* and *Jack the Howler* all lend credence to these more outlandish concepts.

Putting a bow on it

In the early 1900s Cumberland Presbyterian Church in Russellville, Arkansas was burned to the ground. Just days before this happened, the new preacher to the church had a stained-glass image of the Ozark Howler removed as he said that it was "diabolical" and did not belong in a house of worship.

The fire, causing total destruction of the Cumberland Presbyterian Church, is still to this day credited to The Ozark Howler.

This event is eerily reminiscent of the church fires in Blythburg and Bungay Bungee, England.

It is believed in both of these cases that the churches were burned to the ground by a Church Grim. This grim most often takes the form of a large black shaggy dog. In both of these cases, the grim was offended by the congregation and, while it is there to protect the church and the graveyard, will not abide wrongdoing.

The Ozark Howler and the Black Dogs of Death are both described as "shaggy". They are both death omens. Both are known for their distinct and terrifying howls.

The Cù Sìth is a silent hunter known for its freakish cry. Mishipeshu had great coper horns in the same vein as the Howler.

Cerberus' death-dealing and Fenrir's foreknowing. Wiccan shape-shifters and a god-like wolf. Crowley and all of his Dr. Moreau-esqu magic.

The most logical explanation here is that the Ozark Howler is a descendant or variant of The British Black Dogs of Death with a bit of myth from many different places and peoples sprinkled in. There are too many similarities to ignore. Not to mention how easy it would have been for these hellhounds to travel to the states during the immigration boom. Just like so many things, this story, this legend, crossed the Atlantic and found its way into the heart of American folklore.

Werewolves

The *Epic of Gilgamesh* is a legendary poem from 2100-1200 BCE. It is the 2nd oldest known religious text in existence and is noted as the earliest form of literature ever. It is an epic poem from ancient Mesopotamia and is said to have had a heavy influence on Homer and his *Iliad* and *Odyssey*. It is also considered to be the first mention of lycanthropy

The werewolf is ancient.

Werewolves also appear in early Greek mythology, such as in the *Legend of Lycaon*. Here, Lycaon, son of Pelasgus, is turned into a wolf by an angry Zeus. And, of course there is early Nordic mention as well, as in the *Saga of the Volsungs*, where a father and son come across a pair of wolf hides and, after donning them, turn into ravenous wolf-men that go on a killing rampage.

The Legend

A werewolf or lycanthrope (or lycan for short) is a

human with the ability - or curse - to shape-shift into a wolf or human-wolf hybrid either by intent or under the power of a curse or infection (usually transferred via bite or scratch from another cursed or infected were). Classically, this shift comes by the draw or power of a full moon.

The word or term, "werewolf" comes from the Old English combination of "wer" meaning man and "wulf", obviously meaning wolf - Werwulf. Before this term was used, the Ancient Greek term, Lycanthrope, was used to define the act of changing into a wolf *and* one who possessed such an ability. It is a combination of the word "Lukos" meaning wolf and "Anthropos" meaning human.

Our modern ideology of the werewolf comes from Proto-Indo-European mythology, where the act of turning "men to wolves" was used in an initiation during warrior training *and* by the role the wolf plays in Germanic paganism. Both are heavily immersed in violence and even devilry.

Herodotus, whom we have heard from before, spoke of men turning into wolves off of the coast of Scythia as mentioned not only in his histories but also by Pomponius Mela.

In the *Satyricon* (written by Gaius Petronius Arbiter) one of the characters, Niceros, says this about a friend who turned into a wolf at a banquet:

> "When I look for my buddy, I see he'd stripped and piled his clothes by the roadside... He pees in a circle round his clothes and then, just like that, turns into a wolf!... after he turned into a wolf he started howling and then ran off into the woods."

This was circa 60 A.D.

Augustine of Hippo speaks to lycanthropy in *The City of God* when he says:

> "It is very generally believed that by certain witches spells men may be turned into wolves..."

King Cnut warned, in his *Ecclesiastical Ordinances,* of "...the madly audacious werewolf" and gave specific edicts to follow so that they "do not too widely devastate, nor bite too many of the spiritual flock".

In Gerald of Wales's *Werewolves of Ossory* and Gervase's of Tilbury's *Otia Imperiala,* we are told of the existence of werewolves in no uncertain terms, Gervase even stating that "...in England we have often seen men change into wolves."

The Lore

Throughout the Middle Ages the legend of the werewolf grew, and along with the legend came the lore. All across Europe, the idea of werewolves among us began to take shape. Werewolves began to be blamed for the deaths of cattle and livestock… even disappearances and murders.

This led to numerous serial killers being accused of lycanthropy and to massive "Wolf-Hunts", where accused werewolves would be hung or drowned or burned alive, much in the same vein as the witch hunts. This shift from truth and tales of ancient times to folklore and fear occurred between 1450 and 1750 when hundreds of innocent men, women and even children were killed because they were believed to be werewolves.

This is believed to stem from the works of Richard Verstegan, primarily from his 1628 piece entitled, *Restitution of Decayed Intelligence,* where he states that werewolves:

> "are certain sorcerers, who having anointed their bodies with an ointment which they make by the instinct of the devil, and putting on a certain enchanted girdle, does not only unto the view of others seem as wolves, but to their own thinking have both the shape and nature of wolves, so long as they wear the said girdle. And they do dispose themselves as very wolves, in worrying and killing, and most human creatures."

Lycanthropy was also considered a curse by God, mostly due to the tragic end of Lycaon when Zeus turned him into a wolf and exiled him. The Roman

Catholic Church would later state that those excommunicated from the church would themselves become werewolves.

A noteworthy exception here is that of an 80-year-old man named Thiess. Thiess went before a tribunal in Jürgensburg, Livonia in 1692 and swore under oath that he and his pack of werewolves were under *divine* command and were known as the Hounds of God. He testified that they went down to hell, protected by God, to do battle with witches and demons and to ensure that the devil would not succeed in carrying away the grain from the local harvest. He was unwavering in his testimony and insisted that when werewolves died, they were welcomed into heaven with open arms. He was ultimately sentenced to lashing and sent to prison for idolatry.

Serbia, Greece, Germany, Bulgaria, France... All across Eastern Europe there was a belief that persisted well into the 20th century that werewolves, if not destroyed upon death, would return as revenants and feast upon dying soldiers.

And speaking about evil, demonic curses - the Nazis used the Old English phrasing WerWulf as a codename for one of their hidden headquarters! Now that's evil!

Fast forward to the 20th and 21st century and you'll not find much belief in the werewolf. At least not the impassioned almost religious and reverent belief that we've previously discussed, but that doesn't mean that the werewolf is any less prevalent, feared or celebrated.

Modern Media and Pop Culture

I found over 300 books, 180 movies, 90 television shows, 75 songs, 55 video games and 15 comics dedicated to werewolves. To say that werewolves are popular in modern culture would be an injustice and egregious understatement.

But why are we so enamored with the shape-shifting beasts?

Professor Charlotte Otten attributes this modern appeal to "our continuing interest in metamorphosis." She goes on to say that "uncertainty about the nature of a human being and his/her relationship to the animal kingdom..." and that "...ultimately, we find ambiguities and mysteries." within these werewolves.

I'll buy that!

I think the mystery has a lot to do with it. I also think that there is something very sensual and very powerful about the possibility of turning into a wolf. To be turned over to a more basic primal state with the speed and strength and prowess of a highly developed hunter... an absolute Alpha. The werewolf represents a primordial return to base instincts... elemental and innate urges that must be and *are* suppressed by societal norms. It is the embrace of darkness, of a violence, but not evil. Not necessarily... At least for most.

Evil Urges and Just Desserts

Two Frenchmen by the names of Pierre Burgot and Michel Verdun confessed to swearing allegiance to the devil in exchange for a serum that turned them into wolves. They confessed to savagely and brutally murdering numerous men, women *and* children and were both burned alive.

The Werewolf of Dole, Giles Garnier, confessed to changing into a wolf and killing and eating multiple children. He too, was burned alive.

Perhaps the most notable person in history to have given into the evil side of lycanthropy was Peter Stubbe, a wealthy farmer in Bedburg, Germany. He had control over his lycanthropy and would shift at will to devour the citizens of Bedburg for months! He confessed to practicing witchcraft from the age of 12 years old and to making a deal with the devil for his powers. His murderous and cannibalistic endeavors are far too brutal to discuss in detail here.

It is said that he received one of the most gruesome executions ever recorded. He was "put to the wheel", along with his daughter *and* mistress who had both joined him in many of his crimes. They were flayed alive and *then* had their bones broken by a blunt axe (this was to ensure that they did not return from the grave once dead and buried… um, ya… they weren't dead yet). After they were skinned and their arms and legs shattered, they were strangled to death, beheaded and burned upon a pyre. The torture wheel was then erected on a pole over his grave and a wolf was carved into it as a warning to other werewolves. Stubbs' head, which was not burned, was placed at the very top of the pole and left there for all to see.

One of the most recent and most bizarre cases ever recorded was one between August of 2008 and July of 2009 at Calvary Mater Newcastle Hospital in Australia. Here, 91 patients succumbed to their innate and base desires and became acutely violent, attacking staff and other patients alike. This behavior happened during every full moon of that year. It is reported that every month the full moon would bring out the "Beast" in certain patients and all hell would break loose.

I leave you with this: Are werewolves real? Yes. You bet they are. We have proved that.

Are they evil? No. Not always. I think that has to do more with the person afflicted with lycanthropy than the curse or ability itself.

CHAPTER 27

Hell's Gate Bridge

In its most simple form, a crybaby bridge is a bridge that has been cursed by the death of a child (or children) and their lingering cries draw new victims into succumbing to whatever nefarious designs said curse entails. That legend has grown and taken many different shapes over the years, but certainly, the meat and potatoes - the root details - always linger no matter who's telling the story, when it happened or where.

It goes like this: There is a tragedy on a bridge and if you stop your vehicle on that bridge, you will be subjected to whatever haunting or curse that has left its mark there - a baby crying, handprints or footprints across your windshield, a visit from a spectre or spirit, whatever the case may be.

These types of legends are strewn all about the United States - Virginia, Kentucky, Ohio, Maryland, Texas, Utah... etcetera. Almost every single state seems to have one or more of its own crybaby bridges. This legend seems to thrive within the states, some of the most famous being Rogue's Hollow, The Screaming Bridge of Maud Hughes Road, and Port Neches. But the one we're focusing on today is special in that it not only falls within the category of a crybaby bridge, but it also provides unlucky passersby with a glimpse into the roaring inferno of the Underworld.

The Legend

Hell's Gate Bridge in Oxford, Alabama has been condemned and deemed "unusable" since November of 2005. Having once bridged the banks of the Choccolocco Creek on Boiling Springs Road it is now almost completely hidden away by overgrown grass and trees. Concrete barriers and chain-link fences prevent vehicles from crossing this old truss bridge and are even quite the obstacle for those on foot who are trying to access it, but then again, why would you want to... it is, after all, a cursed and haunted bridge. A new and less haunted road called Leon Smith Parkway was built to connect Friendship Road to The Oxford Exchange, leaving the old twisted bridge and road forgotten and wasting away, blocked off and abandoned.

It is said that if you were to stop your vehicle exactly in the middle of the bridge and turn off the engine, along with all the lights, you will be visited by the spirits of a lovelorn couple who perished there decades before. They will not haunt you or try to frighten you. They will most likely not even try to communicate with you. You probably wouldn't even notice that they were there... until later when you notice a wet spot in the seat next to you, as if someone had walked right out of the creek and - still dripping wet - sat down beside you.

They seem to simply want to sit. Maybe catch a ride off the bridge. Maybe they *can't* communicate but desperately want to. Perhaps there is something keeping them there... something tethering them to this place. But why? What would keep a young couple in love bound here in limbo... in stasis? Why haven't they moved on?

Well, that question brings us to the 2nd part of this curse, though it may simply provide more questions than answers. Rumor has it that the veil between this world and the Netherworld is so thin here, that if one were to travel across the bridge and turn back to look behind them at exactly the midpoint of the bridge, they would - for the briefest of moments - be witness to the very flames of hell through a shimmering, secret window at the entrance of the bridge.

Now these 2 stories seem to share nothing in common and there doesn't seem to be anything to connect the two at a first cursory glance, but here at my super-secret lair/headquarters/closet-office that just won't do. I pride myself in not only my top-notch, for-the-people writing, reporting and editing that I do here, but I don't want to forget or take for granted the little guys, those in the trenches battling forces both natural and supernatural all day every day, just to bring this content to you, the people... I'm talking about my investigative team. My street reporters. My lifeline to the real world. Yes, without them, I would have given up here. I would have laid out the 2 stories as they are and then would have filled the rest of the chapter with nonsense. But, no! Not me. Not Micah Campbell. You want answers... you deserve answers... and you are going to get answers!

And I'm serious when I say that I am SO proud of my investigative team for putting this one together. For finding the hidden puzzle pieces and making sense of it all. Honestly, outside of right here in this book, you **will not** find this. This is what I believe to be the true origin of The Hell's Gate Bridge!

Now I'm about to lay some stuff on you and you gon have to keep up. Take notes and hold on tight, babe, cause I only got one speed and that's forward... fastly!

You'll recall that in Stull Cemetery lies one of the legendary 7 gateways to hell, caused by a child born of sin and into darkness. Children are innocent and therefore the death or abuse of a child is especially heinous and oftentimes a catalyst to a shift in the natural order, a harbinger of the otherworldly.

This is not just the case in Stull. This is evidenced everywhere in every culture. Take the Myling, the Utburd, or the Ihtiriekko: All legends of spectral incarnations of lost children haunting the living until they receive a proper burial on sacred ground. The Norwegian word "utburd" actually means "that which is taken outside" and is a term for abandoning an unwanted child. In the Scottish version of Changeling lore, it is said that fairies will take newborn children and replace them with faerie children. The newborn human children would then be used as a tiend (or tithe) to the underworld for another 7 years reign on the mortal plane as found in *The Ballad of Thomas the Rhymer,* as well as in the story of *Tam Lin*.

The bones of a child, known forevermore as the Crystal Maiden, were found in the "Cave of the Crystal Sepulchre" in modern-day Belize. It is said that this child was sacrificed to keep a portal to the Underworld closed and that when the bones were found they had been calcified and were sparkling and crystalline in appearance.

I say all this to reinforce the idea that unearthly occurrences and the wrongdoings of children go hand in hand. I could write a whole chapter on just this premise, but that would be entirely too long and too dark for what we're here to do, which is simply to bring to light an urban legend and see what everyone thinks about it.

What comes next was **NOT** easy info to come by!

Honestly, even if you do some pretty intense digging and research on the bridge, all you're going to find is the same couple of paragraphs repeated over and over again…on every website or blog that you come across: "The lovelorn couple and the window to hell" There was NOTHING else.

But I KNEW there was something else here… there had to be! This couldn't just be a made-up story that shifted and mutated and grew into an urban legend out of nowhere. This was looking like it might get the better of me. Our investigators were at a dead end, they were tired, they were hungry… they wanted to go home. So, I did what any good red-blooded American boss of an International Paranormal Investigative Conglomerate would do. I sent them home to their mommies, I put on some pants (which I hadn't done since March, because of the whole shutdown thing), and I went digging!

Side note here - there is no team. It's me… it's all me. **That** is how awesome I am.

The Real Real

Audrey Marie Hilley was born in 1933 in Anniston County, Alabama. Can you guess what city is in Anniston, Alabama? Right! Oxford. Audrey Marie Hilley was also the subject of a telefilm called *Wife, Mother, Murderer*, as she was charged with the murder of her husband and attempted murder of her daughter by poisoning *and* is suspected of killing Sonya Marcelle Gibson, an 11-year-old friend of Hilley's daughter along with poisoning numerous other children in the neighborhood - a neighborhood in Oxford, Alabama where the Hell's Gate Bridge is located. Hilley was apprehended and then escaped numerous times until she was finally caught by Anniston Police after a 4-day manhunt, soaking wet and suffering from hyperthermia. She died of a heart attack while being treated.

In 1975 Hilley's husband, Frank, visited his physician complaining of tenderness in his abdomen as well as nausea. At first, he was diagnosed with viral stomach aches, but as conditions worsened, he was diagnosed with liver failure and infectious hepatitis. Frank died in a hospital bed on May, 25th, loving wife and children at his side. With Mrs. Hilley's permission, an autopsy was performed revealing inflammation of the lungs, kidneys and stomach, as well as hepatitis and pneumonia. Further testing was deemed unnecessary and the cause of death was listed as hepatitis.

The grieving widow promptly cashed in on Mr. Hilley's life insurance policy and was awarded 31,000-dollars. About 3 years later, Hilley took out a 25,000-dollar accidental death policy on her daughter, Carol. The policy went into effect in August of 1978. Shortly thereafter, young Carol began exhibiting signs of nausea and stomach pains. She was taken to the ER multiple times but no cause could be determined. Symptoms worsened and she eventually began to lose feeling in her extremities. Carol was eventually admitted and subjected to a battery of tests and procedures, none producing any answers or diagnosis. The doctor eventually brought in a psychiatrist, as he was concerned that these symptoms could be more psychosomatic in nature.

While undergoing psychiatric analysis and with ever worsening symptoms - such as foot-drop due to the numbness in her extremities and the loss of deep tendon reflexes, including nerve palsy - Mrs. Hilley discharged her daughter and took her home. Admitting her to a different hospital days later. Audrey Hilley was ruthless and cold-hearted and may very easily have gotten away with the murder of her husband *and* the murder of her daughter, if it had not been for some bad checks that she had written - ironically enough - to cover the life insurance policy she had taken out on her daughter.

Hilley was picked up for bad checks as the doctor currently seeing her daughter began to suspect heavy metal poisoning. During one of their routine visits, Carol mentioned that her mother was administering daily shots to her and had been for some time, even while she was in the hospital. She stated that her mother told her it was a special medicine to help alleviate the aches and pains. Eventually doctors discovered Aldrich-Mees' lines in Carols fingernails and toenails, a sign of arsenic poisoning. It was then discovered that Carol had about 50 times the normal arsenic levels and that she had been being given larger and larger amounts of arsenic over about an 8-month period. Frank Hilley's body was exhumed and it was discovered that he had high amounts of arsenic as well, and had been poisoned for months before his death.

Audrey, still incarcerated for the bad checks, was promptly charged with murder and attempted murder. She was released on bail and checked into a local hotel under the name Emily Stephens. She changed her identity multiple times and became a fugitive from the law for years until she was finally captured wet, frozen and dying from hyperthermia.

Carol recovered and lived a long and relatively normal and quiet life, but the investigation uncovered a startling discovery: Frank was not the only murder Audrey was guilty of, nor was Carol the only attempted murder. Apparently, Mrs. Hilley had "practiced" her craft on local neighborhood children and seemingly perfected it when a young 11-year-old girl named Sonya mysteriously died in 1978.

I found that the legend of the bridge, itself, originated in the late '70s and it started as commuters began to report strange occurrences on the bridge. Now there is no evidence of a couple ever crashing or perishing on this road or near this bridge, so when looking into what the possible genesis of this haunting could be I was again met with a big old pile of nothing… zilch… but not to worry! I still had my digging pants on!

In 1978 a man by the name of Robert E. Hendrick, Jr. - a volunteer firefighter - died tragically whilst en route to a reported fire in the Coldwater Community in

Oxford. He was in a car wreck caused by excessive speed as he rushed to help. The call ended up being a false alarm, claiming Robert's life in a calamitous series of unfortunate events. Robert was recognized by the state of Alabama for his service and his name can be found among the heroes remembered in the Fallen Firefighters Memorial in Tuscaloosa. Fire station #2 is named in his honor. Fire Station #2 is located on Friendship Road.

Putting it Together

So let me see if I can put it all together for you: We have a haunted bridge that carries with it the weight of not 1 but 2 curses. The first being the unseen spectre who will sit with you in your vehicle when you are parked in the middle of the bridge and have all your lights off, and the second being the window into the fiery abyss as seen when you are in the *same* location and looking backwards. Everyone immediately assumes that this is a gateway to hell, but after my extensive investigation I am leaning more toward perhaps a portend of things to come or a harbinger of fate. I think the window is there, it's just waiting for something… or someone.

We have the crybaby bridge, but no one has ever reported hearing the cries of a child… well, that's because our child was 11 years old and slowly poisoned. She doesn't know that she was killed. And we have a firefighter - a modern-day, dragon-slaying knight - who died doing what he was called to do - to protect.

Put on a hair-net, people. You're gonna have to catch your brain, cause I'm about to 'splode it!

I believe that in 1978 our knight met his end as he was startled by the spectre of the little girl as she was out on the bridge, scared and alone looking for her way home. The "couple" that haunts the bridge is not some lovelorn teen duo, but instead are Gallant Sir Richard and 11-year-old Sonya Gibson. Sonya cannot find her way home and Richard will not leave her side until she does. They cling desperately to any possibility of rescue or transport out of this purgatory but cannot actually interact with anyone or anything, so they do the only thing they can do. Sit near to the living and plead for them to hear. Of course, no one ever does and all that is left behind is a wet spot from where they were seated.

Ghosts cannot move forward until they are at rest with this mortal world. They can only move backward, and unfortunately, there is no going backward for these two, because behind them is a gateway to the Netherworld. It is not opened for them and it is not there to entice or accept the innocent. It was opened when Audrey Marie Hilley murdered poor, little Sonya Gibson. That unnatural and heinous act was enough to infuriate and disturb the natural order to the point of spawning this Hell Gate and it will remain open and starving - poised to devour - until the spirit of Audrey Marie Hilley is trapped forevermore within its hungry and waiting maw.

She was well within its grasp that day long ago when she was lost and dying of hyperthermia, but the portal was robbed of its prize when she was found and taken to a local hospital. Dying there on a surgery table instead of in the cold, unforgiving arms of fate.

So, unable to move from the bridge as it is bookended by the fiery torment of the abyss, our fireman and his adopted little girl wait. Our brave knight is unable to move on to the afterlife because he refuses to leave the beautiful child, and poor Sonya can't find her way home because she doesn't know that she was killed. They are forever trapped in this infinite cycle of woe, though they are not alone. They have each other. He, her eternal guardian and she, his forever child.

He is bound by an oath that he took all those years before:

> "I will always be at my station, alert and attending to my duties. I shall sell my life dearly to my enemy fire but give it freely to rescue those in peril. With God's help, I shall endeavor to be one of His noblest Works."

A special thank you to those brave men and women battling true hellfire day in and day out, putting their very lives on the line for us. We salute you. We love you and we pray for you.

CHAPTER 28

El Chupacabra

It is one of the most well-known cryptids in the modern world. Though they may not have the knowledge or context to fabricate an accurate reference, almost everyone has heard the name Chupacabra. But what is it? Where did it come from? Theories and hypotheses abound as to the nature and origin of this blood-sucking beast. A bi-pedal humanoid? A dog-like, saber-tooth dinosaur complete with jagged, spiked spines? A perverse military experiment gone wrong? A vampire? An Alien?

Some even speculate that El Chupacabra is the devil himself, though others postulate that it is a revolutionary, artificial intelligence machine - a robot that has learned and grown to think and behave on its own… ah la Skynet

A cybernetic organism. Living tissue over a metal endoskeleton

There are many ideas and thoughts as to what El Chupacabra is and those ideas have evolved and developed over time - such is the nature of stories that are hushed in daylight and spread through whispers. I am here to uncover the reality of this menacing monster. I am prepared to find the truth behind this desert demon, no matter what the cost. I am... Micah Campbell.

The Legend

Chupacabra literally translates to "Goat-Sucker", and while that sounds like a crude childhood taunt (and I guess maybe it should, as the name was originally coined by a Puerto Rican comedian by the name of Silverio Pérez), it is actually one of the most well-known and most notorious cryptids in the Americas. It is legendary among the southern states and especially in Puerto Rico, a Caribbean Island which is actually considered an unincorporated US territory. One of the most interesting facts about El Chupacabra and one that I want to get out of the way right here in the beginning, is that although it is one of the most well-known and easily recognizable cryptids ever (at least by name, if not by appearance) El Chupacabra is certainly one of - if not THE youngest of legendary cryptids.

Get this, El Chupacabra was not discovered until 1995! That is crazy! Bigfoot, Nessy, Wendigo, even the Jersey Devil and the Mothman... have all been around for 50+ years, with origins going back millennia! El Chupacabra was discovered when I was... well, I won't say how old I was, but suffice it to say, I was alive. That is just so exciting to me! That we are still discovering new cryptids even today!

Something else I want to touch on - but not dwell on - is the political aspect of El Chupacabra. El Chupacabra is somewhat of a symbol of pride or an anti-hero to the people of Puerto Rico. You see, Puerto Rico is considered a commonwealth of the United States. So, Puerto Rico is governed by the laws and legislation of the United States even though the people of Puerto Rico have no say in those laws or legislations. They can't vote in US elections. This is also true for American Samoa, Guam, Northern Mariana Islands and the US Virgin Islands. The people of Puerto Rico hold fast to El Chupacabra as an emblem or token of otherness. They are a people set apart. They are outsiders in their own country. Because of the obscurity and mystery surrounding the El Chupacabra, along with its celebrity, the people of Puerto Rico have a kinship with the *idea* of it, if not the beast itself.

In March of 1995 in a small village outside of the Puerto Rican town of Orocovis, a farmer made a gruesome and unexplainable discovery. He found 8 sheep from his flock dead. They were completely drained of blood and each had small, circular incisions around its chest area. Just a few months later, in August, a woman by the name of Madelyne Tolentino reported over 150 farm animals and pets killed in this very same way in the Puerto Rican town of Canóvanas. She is considered to be the first eyewitness of the Chupacabra.

Similar reports came in from Moca, a small town in the Northwest. Soon, reports from all over Puerto Rico and beyond were coming in. Farm animals and pets were turning up dead all over the island and all in the same manner: bled dry by small, circular incisions. This was initially blamed on a satanic cult or ritual, but that was never able to be proved.

Madelyne Tolentino described the creature as a scaly or leathery… definitely hairless… reptilian, with spines or spikes along its back. She stated that it was the size of a large dog, though it moved (ran, hopped, walked) more like a kangaroo. It would switch between standing on all fours and standing upright. It had pronounced claws and fangs, which would explain the ease in which it is able to capture and bleed its victims. She also said that its eyes were bulging, protruding inches from its skull and were bright red, like lasers.

One of the most frightening aspects of these earlier attacks was the fact that every animal reported dead was left completely intact. Except, of course, for the missing blood.

Over the course of the next year, more than 2,000 animals were reported dead and drained around the Puerto Rico area.

By August of 1996, word of El Chupacabra had spread. First, from the island into Latin America and from there into the southern states. The US media got wind of these strange animal killings and the eyewitness accounts. Stories started running. There was a new cryptid in town. One thing this beast had going for it as far as getting its name out there was the Internet. Yes, this cryptid was discovered in the age of the Internet, and there is where it thrived. UFO and paranormal enthusiasts from all around the world quickly latched onto these stories. Encounters and stories began to pile in. Merchandise was made and sold everywhere and there were even mainstream bands such as Chixdiggit, a Canadian pop punk band, that got in on the action with their hit song about the beast.

Chupacabra-mania was all the rage! And why wouldn't it be? We have a cryptid that has been verified by multiple eyewitnesses and countless local sources, and it doesn't try to kill us! What's not to love!?! By the early 2000's El Chupacabra's notoriety had extended all the way to Maine, US. It was being featured in everything from the Looney Tunes cartoons to Hollywood Studio productions. It quickly rose in fame to the same grand echelon of world renown cryptids as Sasquatch and the Loch Ness Monster and was at that point a household name.

I just still can't wrap my head around the fact that the Chupacabra, a cryptid I've known about almost all my life - at least all my adult life - is actually YOUNGER than I am! That just blows my mind... doesn't that mess you up?

I mean when I see Guns N' Roses' *Appetite for Destruction* is 33 years old or Metallica's *Black* album is 30 years old... *Lord of the Rings* is 20 years old...

That's our childhood!

Nessy was brought to world-wide fame in 1933 but is suspected to be *much* older than that. Bigfoot gained popularity in the 50's but is thought to have first been discovered in the early 1800's!

I'm fine with that. That feels right. But for El Chupacabra to have been discovered when I was turning 15?!? I'm done... I'm too old... I'm hanging it up. Gimmie a walker and some fake teeth and sit me down in front of Wheel-of-Fortune with some sugarless hard candies, cause I give up!

I guess it's pretty great. It means El Chupacabra is part of our generation, right?

But, wow. Just too wild!

The Hunt is on!

José Ramón Soto Rivera or "Chemo Soto", was - and as far as I could tell still is - the mayor of Canóvanas, Puerto Rico. He holds the longest consecutive running tenure on the island and is a staunch believer in El Chupacabra. So much so, that he has organized and led 5 quests to capture it. He sees the bigger picture here. He believes that beyond the legends and the stories is a grave danger that threatens his people and all peoples of Puerto Rico and that is the extinction of the entire animal population at the hands of a blood-hungry creature.

Chemo is a champion for the people and they love him for it. They re-elect him time and time again. His crusades have thus far rendered little by way of actual proof of the existence of El Chupacabra, let alone capturing the creature, but this does not deter him or his people. It does, however, cause other government agencies to turn a deaf ear to his pleas for support.

Chemo, along with a group of experts and a crack-team of anti-Chupacabra muscle has developed a "cone-trap" that is said to be state-of-the-art technology, and with this he has guaranteed the capture of El Chupacabra this year (2020). Chemo is said to have endured the strictest of schedules as far as his training and studying this time around. He has watched all of the Indiana Jones movies multiple times and was seen buying a leather jacket, a fedora and a bull whip at a local Sears (this is **not** made up). On top of his team of experts and sell-swords, Chemo has also enlisted the aid of a spiritual adviser and a journalist from *El Vocero*, a newspaper known for their honesty and "integrity".

His plan is simple: He, along with 200 trusted warriors, will caravan throughout the island. Chemo will, of course, be front and center in an armored wagon. With him will be men armed with automatic weapons. He will, meanwhile, be armed with a 12' silver crucifix, as he cannot be sure that El Chupacabra is *not* a vampire. He is doubling down on his precautions here, having consumed garlic so that his breath is a weapon lethal to vampires and he will also be armed with a water gun filled with holy water (again, **not** made up).

Behind the wagon will be the cone trap. As far as I can tell from the pictures online, this is a live goat caged within a canvas covered "cone" wherein there are fake goats and fake blood. The Chupacabra will be drawn to the trap via the bleating and aroma of the live goat and then once there, it will be coaxed into the cone, which is lined with heavy netting. He has also asked Raulito Carbonell a Puerto Rican film and comedy actor, salsa singer and lawyer to accompany him on his expedition as "Papo Swing", one of his television characters. Chemo believes that El Chupacabra will be frightened of Papo Swing's face and therefore avoid attacking them.

Have I mentioned yet that I am not making **any** of this up?

And I'm glad I haven't!

This guy, this Chemo Soto sounds absolutely amazing and I would vote for him 5 times too! Oh, and he has also stated that once El Chupacabra *is* captured that he will turn his attention to uncovering other cryptic Puerto Rican legends, such as Zuleika, the mystery woman of the Internet. (*shrugs shoulders)

The Other Legends

We can kind of put together for ourselves how the stories of the Chupacabra being a vampire got started, but what about the alien theory or the robot theory?

Well, the alien theory is actually pretty funny. It is said that many of the original eyewitnesses (and being original would make them the authority) described El Chupacabra as a hairless, bi-pedal creature with extended canine legs, a barbed back and tail, and claws. This was 1995 and released in theaters at that very same time was the movie *Species* starring Natasha Henstridge.

This movie's alien is almost identical to some early descriptions of the beast. After a five-year investigation into the Chupacabra, Benjamin Radford documented and reported in his 2011 book *Tracking the Chupacabra* that this was the most likely reason behind the alien theories - that and the fact that if it can't be explained any other way… you guessed it, if you can't explain it then it must be aliens, right?

There is also a fringe theory that El Chupacabra is a government experiment gone terribly wrong. A secret project Code Name: Chupacabra was being conducted at Fort Buchanan just northwest of Canóvanas, right where the very first sighting took place. The creature is actually a robot disguised as a canine, created to infiltrate and spy on US citizens.

All in the name of national security, right?

Of course!

So, the story goes that the robot/animals learned too much too fast and eventually got too smart. They broke out of the military facilities and have been on the loose ever since. The reason that they kill and drain the blood, but don't consume the flesh of the animals is because it was programmed with certain animalistic attributes, one being a dog. It learned enough about a dog to know that dogs like to hunt and kill, but it has no need for nourishment, so that's all it does… it just hunts and kills.

El Chupacabra was one of the more interesting cryptids that I ran across during my research for this first volume of Urban Legends, Ghost-Stories, and Folklore. I absolutely loved Chemo! I am really looking forward to finding more of these lesser-known pieces to widely-known stories in the next volume.

URBAN LEGENDS

GHOST STORIES
AND
FOLKLORE

Thank you all so much for purchasing and reading my book. I hope you enjoyed it. I hope you learned something new, and I hope that you laughed all the way through!

This was a labor of love, and one that I would – actually one that I *will* – do again!

I hope that you will continue on with me as I journey down this path of exploration, realization and unknowns.

If you would like to follow along with everything that I am doing, please follow me on Instagram @micahcampbellwrites and at www.MicahCampbell.com

Until next time, I've been Micah… and you have been a beautiful audience.

Micah Campbell lives in Midwest, USA with his wife, 3 children, and a crap-ton of animals. He grew up playing in punk rock and metal bands and reading a stolen copy of The Hobbit over and over until the spine wore out (he didn't steal it... his drummer did).

He is already a world-renowned supernatural investigator, a decorated Cryptozoologist, and a monster slayer. He is now adding "famous author" to his litany of accolades.

Micah is currently working on the first book in his fantasy trilogy, *The Singing Blade*, and has plans to write a horror thriller, as well. Oh, and Volume 2 of *Urban Legends, Ghost Stories, and Folklore*, of course!

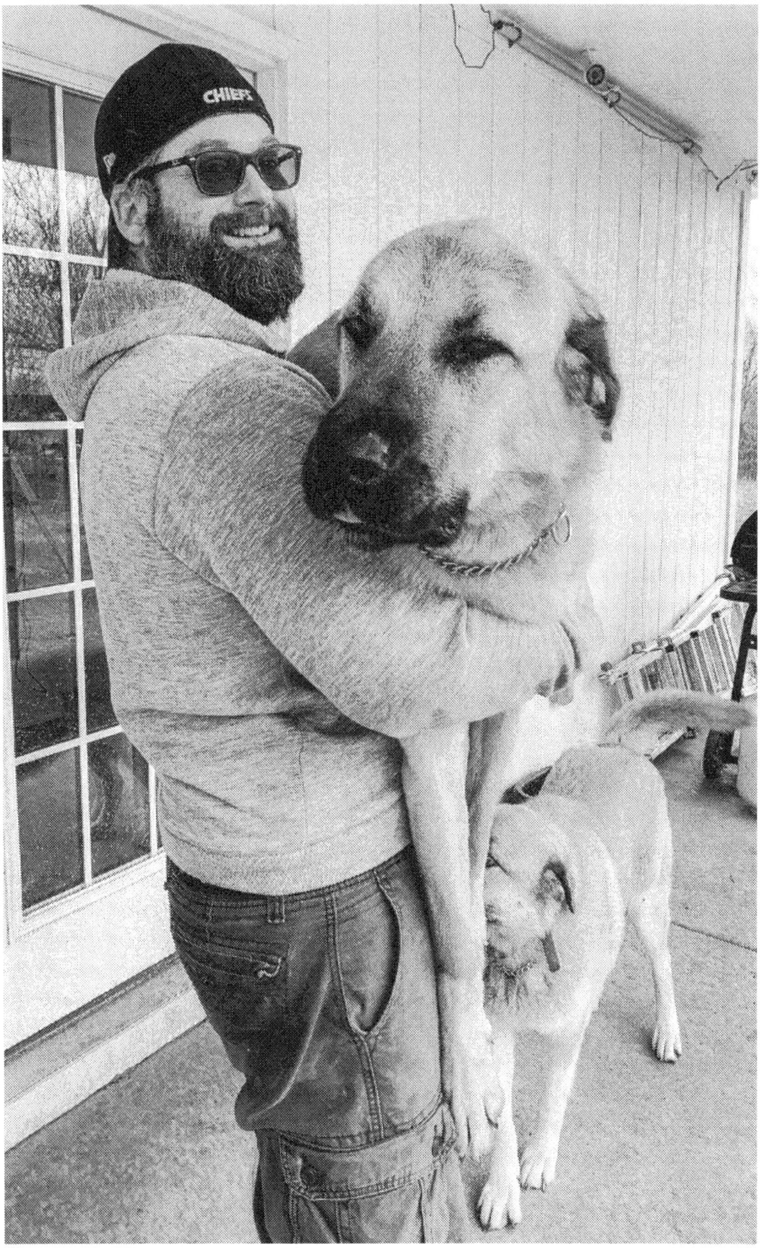
CHIEFS

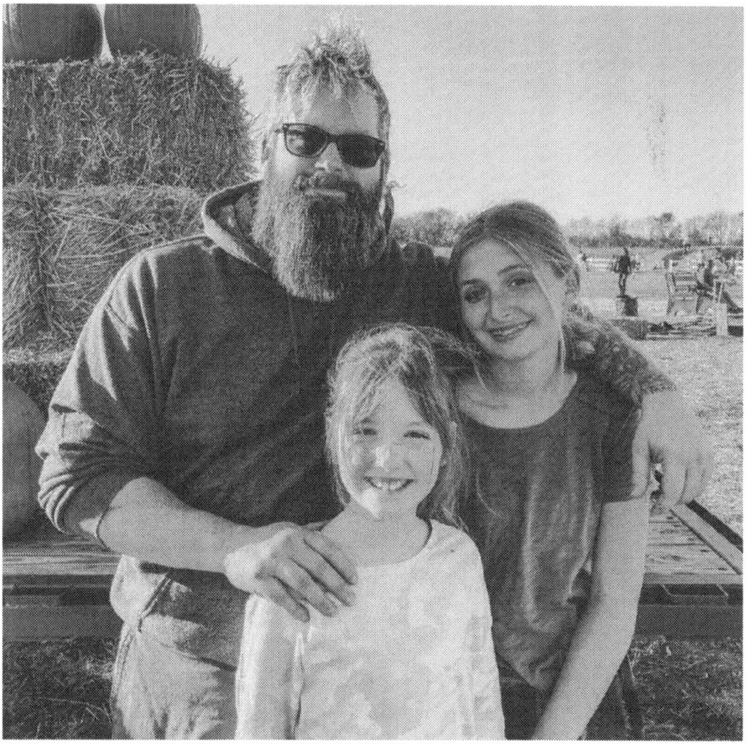

The End

Made in the USA
Coppell, TX
03 September 2022